The Secret
Circle

The Secret Circle: The Cozy Cat Bookstore Mysteries Book 1

To request permissions, contact the publisher at publisher@revelarebooks.com.

Paperback: 978-1-7373295-0-3
e-book: 978-1-7373295-1-0

Cover art copyright © 2021 Ivy Wooldridge

Revelare Books
Redwood City, CA

www.revelarebooks.com

THE COZY CAT
BOOKSTORE MYSTERIES
1

The Secret Circle

Lisa-Anne Wooldridge

Revelare
Books

To Andrew

You are my anchor and my float—you keep my head above
water and make sure I stay right where I want to be.

L ucy Patterson locked the door, flipped over the sign, and turned off the lights. She rested against the door for a moment and enjoyed the warm glow of the old-fashioned streetlight. It gave her such a homey feeling as it illuminated the little bookstore, the light falling on her grandfather's leather club chairs, on her grandmother's knitted throws, and on the moody cat she'd inherited along with the store.

She'd always loved her grandparents' shop, The Cozy Cat Bookstore. Dusty treasures and old books filled the packed shelves and small alcoves right alongside the new releases. Every kind of knickknack imaginable was squeezed into every available space. It had been just a house once upon a time, an old Victorian three-story complete with gingerbread trim and a grand tower. The round room on the ground floor was now a snug reading space with a semi-circular, velvet-cushioned window seat. There was a little kitchen in the back from which the most amazing smells were known to come, luring in customers and little children alike. No one could resist one of her grandmother's vanilla pudding cookies!

Lucy made her way through the store, picking up a book here and straightening a lampshade there, setting to rights a top-heavy stack of dusty old books left there by her grandfather on the day he and her grandmother had gone missing. She wanted to keep everything just as it was. Lucy had taken over the operation of the bookstore almost right away, even before the authorities were sure her grandparents were dead. After living and working summers there most of her life, the familiar, slow days of selling a few books to regular customers and tourists felt like a way to stay close to her grandparents.

Lucy put the kettle on and shook out a tablespoon of her favorite tea—it had notes of cinnamon and vanilla and something else Lucy could never quite figure out. Her grandmother made the blend herself, but the recipe was top secret. Lucy hoped she'd find it written down someday when she had time to look through her grandmother's staggering collection of cookbooks, notebooks, and journals. In the meantime, there was no sense in letting it go to waste.

The tea had a calming effect on her as soon as she poured the boiling water into the pot. *This is at least a two-cup night,* she thought. She loaded a tray with cookies and her tea things and made her way up the tight wooden staircase—the servants' stairs—to the room she'd moved into. She meant to only stay there temporarily, but weeks had turned to months, and now she felt more at home in the bookstore than she did in her tiny, modern apartment.

Her grandparents had lived in one of the smaller bedrooms, preferring it to the large suite Lucy currently occupied. It was easier to take care of, her grandmother said, and they were only ever in there to sleep. The smile in her eyes indicated that her grandmother might not be telling the whole truth. Married for just over fifty-one years, it was apparent that the romance had never faded between those two. Lucy had given up hope of ever having that kind of relationship in her own life. Men like her grandfather were rare indeed! These days, she was never sure if she was going on a date or just "hanging out."

And the men she'd met were in no hurry to commit themselves to one person. It was just as well, she thought, that she liked books and cats so much.

The antique bed was piled high with featherbeds and soft blankets and downy pillows. The sheets were that crisp, cool, soft cotton that could only come from quality and age. After so many washings, the fabric was as smooth as satin to her cheek, and she fell asleep almost immediately. Somewhere in her subconscious mind, though, she heard a muffled thump downstairs, which troubled her dreams.

The next morning brought a small rush of customers. A couple passing through on an anniversary road trip came in looking for something to read on the beach. A half dozen local children came in wanting cookies. Then an elderly woman spent lengthy periods in each of the alcoves, carefully examining books and knickknacks before putting them back precisely and carefully where they were before. When Lucy offered to help her find something, the lady stiffened and hurried from the store. Something about her seemed familiar, but nothing came to mind. Lucy chalked it up to the eccentricities of the elderly.

She took her lunch at her usual spot—the grand, oversized secretary her grandmother had loved. It was a beautiful, well-made piece of furniture with craftsmanship unheard of in contemporary furnishings. When she sat, something seemed off to Lucy. She realized that her chair—a modern office style with plush leather and adjustable positions—was all wrong. It was too high for her, and the back was straight up and down instead of leaning back an inch or two the way Lucy liked it.

How odd, someone's been sitting in my chair!

Laughing at her own Goldilocks joke, she readjusted the seat and put it out of her mind. The tuna salad on lettuce was delicious and had a garlic pesto dressing she'd purchased at a small cafe in town. Unfortunately, Victor Admetus Bombalurina thought so too. The cat, named after a ridiculous T.S. Eliot poem on naming cats, jumped from the floor to the top of the secretary and stared down at Lucy. Or rather, at Lucy's lunch.

"Oh, no you don't." Lucy waved her fork at the black-and-white tuxedo cat. "You may be a very distinguished cat, but you can't have my lunch!"

Tor, short for Victor, as her grandfather called him, wasn't impressed. He feigned indifference, but just when Lucy thought he'd gotten the message, he reached a sly paw toward her plate. This caused a series of events. First, Lucy stood up to remove the cute pest from the desk, but Tor's paw brushed a decorative enamel panel on the upper portion of the secretary, which, in turn, triggered a small, hidden drawer to swing out from the desk. The effect of all this movement startled Tor, who jumped to the floor just as Lucy's tuna salad, pushed by the opening drawer, tumbled down beside him. Purring, Tor tucked into the fish while Lucy stood glued in place, trying to figure out what just happened.

A hidden drawer! Where did that come from? She'd never seen any sign of it before, and she'd spent years there, coloring, playing, and doing her homework. Her grandparents certainly never mentioned it. In the drawer was a card-sized blue velvet bag pulled tight with a drawstring, a gold-colored pen, and a folded piece of paper on top of a leather-bound book. As she tried to take it all in, including the loss of her lunch, chimes jingled at the front door of the shop. Instinctively, she pushed the drawer closed and noticed that it disappeared seamlessly into the wood around it.

She turned to greet the customer, ready to apologize for the mess. It was the elderly lady who'd been in earlier, and something in her demeanor made Lucy wary.

Uh-oh, Lucy thought. The diminutive senior woman stood just inside the door, with a scowl on her face and her hands hovering just above her hips. A picture floated through Lucy's mind as she imagined herself and this woman on a dusty street in an old Western town, squared off for a duel at high noon. Lucy's imagination always made her laugh, and even with the flint-faced woman staring her down, she repressed a smile.

"It was you, wasn't it?" The woman spat venom at Lucy.

"Excuse me? I don't know what you're talking about."

"You did it. You did away with your grandparents so you could have the shop. There's no other explanation! I never knew you were such a greedy child, Lucy!"

Stunned, Lucy leaned back on the secretary behind her. How could this woman say such things to her? She'd adored her grandparents, loved them with her whole heart. Tears sprang to her eyes as she struggled to regain her voice.

"Do I know you? You can't speak to me that way!"

Then Lucy realized she *did* know the woman. She remembered her from childhood—a friend of her grandmother's who frequently used to stop in for tea and cookies and a chat at the dropleaf table squeezed into a corner of the old-fashioned kitchen. At some point, she stopped seeing the woman, but it never occurred to her to wonder why.

"I do know you," Lucy continued. "You used to come here to see my grandmother. Why on earth would you accuse me of something so horrible?"

The woman's face crumbled, and her shoulders slumped forward. She shook her head.

"I didn't think you'd remember me," she said.

Lucy, still shaken, said, "You're Mrs. Butterfly, aren't you?"

One corner of the woman's mouth twisted into a half-smile. "Yes, that's what you used to call me. It's Mrs. Butterfield. Fuchsia Butterfield. I was a friend of your grandmother's, yes. But then we had a falling out. I can't even remember what it was about anymore. Something silly and unimportant, I'm sure. But my stubborn pride kept me from coming back, and now it's too late!"

The sun poked an afternoon ray through the top of the shop window, highlighting the lines on the woman's powdered cheek. Lucy watched as an illuminated tear made a wet track down her weathered face. She observed how frail the woman was, especially now that the rush of adrenaline appeared to be over.

"Come over here and sit down, Mrs. Butterfield. Let me get you a cup of tea, and then you can tell me why you think I'd ever hurt my grandparents." She led the woman to one of the leather chairs and helped her sit.

Lucy turned to go, but the woman clutched her with a bony hand. The veins showed through her translucent skin as if they were painted on.

"You really don't know? You don't know what your grandparents were doing here?" She scanned Lucy's face.

"Again," Lucy said, "I don't know what you're talking about. I'll be right back with some tea."

Lucy gently pried the woman's hand from her arm and headed toward the kitchen. She collected her plate, now clean of any trace of tuna, and gathered up the bits of salad that littered the floor. Then she began putting together a tray for tea, but just as the kettle whistled, she heard the door chimes. Lucy sighed and turned off the stove. She knew without looking, the elderly woman was gone.

Chapter Two

I can do this," Lucy insisted. "Don't look at me like that!"
Tor, taking offense to her tone, flounced off to find the
sunny patch on his favorite chair. "Concentrate," she told herself. "If the cat can do it, I can do it." But after a solid hour
of trying to reopen the secret drawer—pushing decorative but-
tons, pulling handles, twisting knobs, and even climbing under
the old desk to see what she could discover—Lucy had to admit
defeat.

"Don't look so smug, Tor. I'm going out for dinner. When
I get back, I'm going to want your help." Tor yawned and rear-
ranged himself, blinking at Lucy with his green and gold-flecked
eyes. Lucy locked up the shop and set off on foot to the charming cafe downtown.

Like The Cozy Cat Bookstore, the Lace Curtain Cafe was
a well-preserved throwback to an earlier time. The cafe, a light
blue Victorian home built a couple of decades after the Civil
War, was nestled into a colorful garden with ornamental trees
and flowers that delighted customers all year round. The outdoor tables with colorful umbrellas were always in demand.
The century-old pepper tree rained down tiny white blossoms
in the spring and later in the year, peppercorns over the diners.
As a child, Lucy loved to dance under the tree until her long

strawberry blonde hair and fancy dress were full of the delicate, lacy flowers.

A broad veranda looked out over the gardens, which gave diners not only a beautiful view but also the benefit of hidden wall plugs and free Wi-Fi. On pleasant days, Lucy might find just about anyone working from their "home away from home" at the cafe. Today the veranda was mostly empty. The mayor sat on one side, chatting into his phone, so Lucy headed to the other end and settled into an antique wrought iron chair. She set her bag next to her in an old wooden chair with a newly rewoven rush seat. Everything in the cafe was mismatched, ancient, and whimsical, including its owner, Miss Hattie.

Miss Hattie's hair was the color of wheat just before the harvest, and her eyes the brightest cornflower blue Lucy had ever seen. Everyone knew Miss Hattie had a standing appointment at the town's only hair salon the first Monday of every month to make sure it remained harvest wheat and not "senior silver," as she called it. She was a thin woman, but no one would ever know it from the flowing, loose dresses she tended to wear. Miss Hattie told anyone who'd listen that she was an old hippie because she was already old when she became a hippie! For some reason, that always made her laugh, and her laugh was so musical and unique that no one ever seemed to tire of hearing it. She always had a flower tucked behind her ear plucked straight from the cafe gardens.

Lucy had grown up visiting the cafe with her grandmother and had many happy memories there. She'd always been fascinated by the intricate lace curtains that hung from every window. They were heirlooms inherited from Miss Hattie's great-grandmother, an Irish woman who immigrated to marry the handsome Irish boy who'd gone ahead of her. The cafe was the home he'd built for his bride, and the curtains were part of her dowry.

Miss Hattie, who always wanted to know who she was cooking for, popped her head out of the front door. When she spied the mayor, she pursed her mouth. When she spotted Lucy, however, her face lit up. Shooing the waitress away, Miss Hattie made a beeline for Lucy and pulled up a chair to sit next to her.

"Darlin', you are a sight for sore eyes!" Miss Hattie's bright eyes were full of light. Lucy thought she looked more vibrant than ever.

"Miss Hattie! I'm sorry I haven't been by in a while. I've been so busy trying to fill my grandparents' shoes and take care of everything," Lucy said.

A slight furrow briefly appeared between Miss Hattie's eyes, but she quickly smoothed it out.

"I worry about you," Miss Hattie replied, "staying there by yourself and nobody knowing whatever happened to your grandparents. I have a spare room upstairs. I'd love to have you here. Your grandmother and I go way back. I know she'd want me to look after you."

Lucy sighed and smiled. "Thank you, I appreciate the offer. I just have so much to do, and I wouldn't want to leave Tor there all alone. He gets into too much mischief to have the place all to himself. But I would like to talk to you sometime when you're not busy." Lucy nodded toward the group of people coming up the sidewalk with several small children. "Looks like you're in for making a lot of your famous Jammie Sammies! I'm tempted to order one myself!"

Lucy's mouth watered at the memory of the special sandwich. Miss Hattie made them herself, not trusting any cook to get it right. One layer was peanut butter mixed with honey, and the other layer consisted of bananas mashed with vanilla and cinnamon mixed in.

"I'll bring your usual. Let me go put your order in before I'm mobbed by the kindergarten crowd!" Miss Hattie ducked quickly back inside, the screen door creaking behind her.

Lucy looked out over the garden, drinking it all in. Roses bloomed next to hydrangeas in many colors, and azaleas flowered wildly at the base of the pepper tree. It was one of the most beautiful places Lucy had ever seen. It made her heart ache for her grandmother, and tears blurred her vision. "Looks like a Monet painting," she said to herself. Her grandmother loved Monet.

The first stars of the evening were shyly appearing in the sky as Lucy walked back to The Cozy Cat. It was a beautiful summer evening, mildly warm with a faint breeze carrying the scent of night-blooming jasmine. She could hear the Main Street Band warming up a few streets over in the village center, in the town's ancient and repeatedly repaired gazebo. Twice a month, they held concerts on the lawn between the courthouse and the library, where both the old and the young enjoyed sitting in camp chairs or dancing in front of the musicians. Any other evening, Lucy wouldn't have missed it for the world.

She cut through Artisan's Alley, where half a dozen cute shops lined the short street, and fairy lights hung from awning to awning. At the corner, a coffee shop was the only business still open, two bored teenagers scrolling on their phones behind the counter. One looked up as Lucy passed by and offered a half-interested nod, perhaps hoping she'd come in and buy something to break up the quiet evening shift. Lucy had a mission, though, and hurried past the shop and down the sidewalk toward home.

The Cozy Cat Bookstore sat on the edge of the small town, separated by the sizeable grounds original to the property. Long ago, her grandparents had walled off a section of it for use as a community garden. It wasn't unusual to see people working the individual plots of land any time of day or early evening, and often someone occupied the vintage tree bench or the cafe table and chairs that her grandfather had dragged down there one summer. The shadows had faded, and it was too dark to see the back of the garden, but Lucy had the odd sensation that someone was there watching her walk past.

Lucy quickened her steps and hurried up to the short, tree-lined lane that led to the front door of The Cozy Cat.

The streetlights flickered on, marking the boundary of the municipal street. The light streamed into the front window of the store. Lucy froze in place. Someone was inside the store, moving quickly, holding a cell phone to his ear. His back turned to her, he crossed through the room, passed the bookshelves and alcoves, and headed straight for the kitchen.

Lucy, holding her breath, wasn't sure if she should hide, call for help, or sneak around to the back of the house to peek in the windows. Just as she'd made up her mind to hide, she felt a hard thump on the back of her head and watched the grass rise to meet her.

Chapter Three

*L*ucy heard voices murmuring somewhere far off. She couldn't quite open her eyes, but she could hear anxious and angry voices. The voices came closer to her as she began to drift off again. Before she faded completely into the darkness, she heard someone say, "We'll have to take her with us. There's no other choice."

When Lucy woke, her mouth felt like cotton and the room rocked from side to side. She opened her eyes to an unfamiliar ceiling above her. It seemed oddly close to her face. The pain behind her eyes throbbed in rhythm with the rolling motion of the room, and her head felt tender where it rested on a pillow.

"Hello? Is anyone there?" She tried to raise her head, but that just caused the room to spin. She stretched her arms out to the side. She only had a few inches on either side of her body before she hit something solid. She was trapped in a small place. Too small!

Lucy started to panic as her memories flooded in. Someone was in the shop . . . and . . . nothing. She couldn't remember anything past that point but guessed it was daytime because of how the light filtered through the wooden slats on her left side. On her right was a wall of smooth, varnished wood that matched the ceiling. She felt a quilt wrapped around her, and a pillow supported her head, but the solid surface beneath her wasn't at all comfortable.

"Oh, God," she whispered, "where am I?"

Lucy hadn't prayed in a long time—like so much else in her life, God seemed like a childhood memory. She'd often gone with her grandmother to the old white church on a hill overlooking the bay. Lucy loved the gothic, carpenter-style building constructed by fishermen in the 1880s. The wooden wall next to her reminded her of the church—the varnished panels were almost identical.

Gingerly, she rolled onto her side, peering through the slats on her left. She couldn't see anyone, but much of the room was cut off from her view, so she couldn't be sure it was empty. She pushed against the wood and felt it give slightly. The wood was pine, fresh and thin. Lucy thought she could break through it with enough force.

Overhead, footsteps thumped, followed by a loud bang that reverberated through her. *What was that?* A moment later, the fast vibration of a motor, loud at first and quickly fading away, provided more clues. *I'm on a boat*, Lucy realized.

Pushing as hard as she could with her right hand, she strained against the boards, but they stayed firm. Lucy rolled onto her back and tried a sharp blow with her elbow and upper arm, but that effort failed as well. She took a deep breath, trying to quell the pain in her head and now her arm.

"I have to get out of here," Lucy said to herself. Mustering up all her strength, Lucy rolled first to the right and then as hard as she could to the left. The entire length and weight of her body hit the wooden slats, causing several to give way.

"Ooooft." The pain in Lucy's head was quite sharp now. Her nose had taken some of the impact, and Lucy could feel an abrasion on the tip of it. She managed to get an arm and a leg under the remaining slats and used them for leverage to push the rest out. The boards fell a few feet before landing, so Lucy cautiously leaned over the side.

She was in a sailor's berth built into the ship's wall, solid on three sides. She slowly slid her legs over the edge and held on to the bunk with her hands as gravity pulled her toward the floor. Lucy was just tall enough to reach the ground with balls of her feet, which kept her from falling.

It crossed Lucy's mind that someone might have heard her break out of confinement, so she leaned over and picked up a couple of pieces of the pine slats, holding them like a bat against her shoulder. She waited there for several minutes, but no one came rushing down the stairs from the deck above.

Cautiously, she crept across the floor to the bottom of the stairs. She had just put a foot on the bottom step when she heard a siren and a bullhorn.

"Mendocino Maiden, this is the Coast Guard. Prepare to be boarded." Lucy, weak with relief, sank to her knees on the second stair.

"I'm telling you, I don't know!" Lucy sighed. How many times was this man going to make her answer the same questions?

She shifted in her seat and leaned her head back against the dingy wall. Interview room number two, he'd called it, as he led her into the stuffy, bare room. *More like dungeon cell number two.*

"I need you to pay attention, Ms. Patterson. It's in your best interest." The haggard detective rubbed the skin under his nose and then offered Lucy a plate with a couple of doughnuts. Lucy shook her head vigorously, completely put off by the sorry-looking pastries and for what passed as hygiene in the local police department. Lucy wished the captain of the Coast Guard vessel had stayed with her. His questions she wouldn't mind answering over and over. He had seemed to believe her and even gave her an ice pack for the tender lump that remained on the back of her head.

"Listen to me, Officer—what was your name again? Mooney? I'm only going to say this one more time. Write it down so you don't have to ask me again." Lucy glared at him. She was tired, hungry, and in pain. Why didn't he believe her?

"I was walking home after having dinner. I saw someone in the shop. I was going to hide and call, well, you, and that's the *last* thing I remember. The next thing I know, I'm lying in a boarded-up bunk on a boat, and I had to break myself free. That's when the Coast Guard came. I don't know anything else, and I didn't *do* anything else."

"I called Dr. Wilson," he said. "He'll be here in a few minutes to look you over. If he says you're fit to go, you can leave, but don't go far. We're going to need to ask you some more questions. Stay here until I get back."

Officer Mooney left, taking his doughnuts with him. Lucy was glad because the combination of his aftershave and the sweet smell of the pastry made her queasy. She put her head down on her arms, resigned to wait.

Why are they treating me as if I did something wrong? I'm the victim here! She thought perhaps she should call someone, but she didn't know who to call. The only lawyer she knew, a friend of her grandfather's, had closed shop and retired to an island somewhere. Surely, she could get this whole mess sorted out without a lawyer. She sighed again.

"Lucy? Wake up, hon. How are you feeling?" A light shone in her eyes.

"Huh?" she asked, trying to remember where she was. For a moment, she thought she might be back on the ship, and she tried to stand up suddenly.

"Woah, hang on there a minute," the man in front of her

said. "You nearly fell clean over! Sit right back down and let me look at you."

Lucy recognized Dr. Wilson, who'd treated her for scraped knees and a fever or two when she was young. She remembered him as a kind man who always had peppermints in a jar on his desk. She liked that so much better than the standard lollipops other doctors usually handed out.

The doctor quickly checked her over and tested her reflexes. He winced when he touched the goose egg on her skull. There was quite a bit of debris and dried blood hiding in her hair. He startled Lucy when he bellowed, "TOM MOONEY, get in here right now!"

The summoned officer opened the door, looking ready to pounce. Lucy started to laugh at the ridiculousness of it all, and then she couldn't stop laughing. Dr. Wilson gently led her out the door, all the while yelling at Tom to open the station doors and help him get her into his car. Lucy's laughter had turned to sobs, and she felt as if she couldn't catch her breath.

"Lucy, it's okay. I'm taking you to the clinic. I think we need to get a better look at you, check out that lump, and clean the wound. You're also very dehydrated. Try to slow your breathing down."

As she hyperventilated between short sobbing breaths, Lucy tried to tell the doctor why she was crying. Dr. Wilson, however, was giving Officer Mooney an earful for waiting so long to call him. The doctor eased Lucy into the back of his sedan and wrapped her in a blanket.

"Lucy," he spoke softly, "you're having a panic attack. Have you ever had one before?"

She shook her head no and tried to follow his instructions for calming her breathing. She closed her eyes, attempting to concentrate on something good. First, she thought of her grand-parents, but that just brought the pain of losing them to the surface. She thought of the bookstore, always her happy place as a child. But the memory of someone being in there when they shouldn't have been made her upset.

Finally, she settled on something she could count on to make her smile, even if he was aggravating. Tor. She couldn't wait to go home and pick up that massive ball of fur.

Dr. Wilson kept Lucy for several hours, running tests and doing x-rays. He hooked up an I.V. to rehydrate her and gave her a vitamin boost as well. His gentle ways were just what she needed, and when she was feeling a bit better, he called Miss Hattie to deliver some comfort food.

The food arrived, hand-delivered by Miss Hattie herself, who insisted on seeing Lucy and serving her lunch right there in the office. Lucy's eyes welled up when she saw what was on her plate. A Jammie Sammie. Miss Hattie had strict rules about those special sandwiches. No one over the age of twenty-one could even order one. She always said some things were better left in childhood, and we all have to grow up sometime!

"Now don't you go blabbing to anybody about this, you hear? I'd have a town riot on my hands if anyone found out!" Miss Hattie gave Lucy a conspiratorial wink as she gave the doctor a grilled chicken salad without dressing. He didn't look anywhere near as enthusiastic about his lunch as Lucy did hers.

Lucy, feeling like a much-loved child, told them the whole story of going home, finding an intruder, apparently being knocked out, and waking up in the hold of a ship. They both frowned as she told them about Officer Mooney's questioning.

"The Coast Guard came on board and found me at the foot of the stairs. They told me the boat was stolen and belonged to the historical society. They put me in handcuffs until I talked to the captain, and I convinced him that I had no idea how to sail an old ship like that. He said he believed me and that it takes at least a small crew to sail. He was genuinely nice, but he said he had no choice. He had to turn me over to Officer Mooney. I don't think he wanted to. He said he'd be in touch in a few days for some paperwork."

Lucy knew Miss Hattie and Dr. Wilson would never suspect her of wrongdoing, so she felt safe in their company.

"There's one other thing. It may be nothing, but I had a very strange visit from Mrs. Butterfield. She accused me of doing something to my grandparents so I could inherit the bookstore. Can you believe that?" Lucy saw them exchange a glance and worried that maybe they could believe it, after all.

"Lucy, I want you to steer clear of her. She hasn't been quite herself for a few years now, and lately, she's been even more erratic and cantankerous," Miss Hattie said. "And the last thing you need is some crazy old woman stirring up trouble!"

Dr. Wilson agreed and added, "Lucy, you need to be careful. I don't know what's going on, but I'm going to send my son-in-law over tomorrow to install a security system for the bookstore. You'll have more peace of mind knowing an alarm will be sent to the police if anyone tries to break in again. I'll have more peace of mind too. I don't want any repeat business from you, thank you very much!"

Lucy smiled at him. She was grateful for these kind people who had known her grandparents and who were looking after her in their absence.

"Right then. Let's get you home," said Dr. Wilson. "I called the station and requested they send someone to meet us to make sure it's safe and to make a report. I'll drive you. Hattie, do you need a lift?"

Lucy and Dr. Wilson pulled into the long driveway of The Cozy Cat Bookstore to find two squad cars and an ambulance already parked there. After making sure Lucy was okay, Dr. Wilson ran ahead to see if anyone needed his help. Lucy stood back, taking in the scene.

Yellow police tape hung across her front door, and policemen milled around the front yard. EMTs closed up the back of the ambulance. Dr. Wilson talked briefly with the driver and then hopped into the passenger side. He gave Lucy a reassuring wave as the ambulance passed by her and turned onto the road.

Lucy jumped when the vehicle turned on its siren. Still confused, she approached the policemen stationed at the perimeter.

"Hello, I'm Lucy Patterson. This is my store. Is this about the intruder last night? And who was in the ambulance?" Lucy pinched the bridge of her nose with her thumb and forefinger. "Can this day get any worse?" she mumbled to herself.

The young officer with bright blue eyes and perfect teeth, who had been smiling as she approached, registered a look of surprise on his face and quickly drew his service weapon, pointing it straight at Lucy.

"Captain! Over here! I found her!"

Lucy did the only thing she could do at that point. She sat down on the grass and put her head on her folded knees. She fought off the panic in her chest and tried to breathe the way Dr. Wilson taught her.

"Franklin, holster that weapon!" The captain, seeing his most junior officer standing over a petite, visibly terrified woman, wasted no time in getting there. "What in the blazes do you think you're doing?"

"Sorry, Sir! Mooney said—"

"I don't care what Mooney said," he growled. "I'm your commanding officer, and this is my crime scene. Now put that weapon away!"

"Sorry, Sir," he replied and quickly complied.

"Miss? Miss Patterson? It's all right. Here, let me help you."

He extended a hand, and Lucy let him help her up.

"I'm Captain Harrison. I'm so sorry we frightened you."

Lucy looked up at the man and studied his face. He was tall, and his face had that tanned and weathered look of someone who spends a lot of time outdoors. He smiled at her. The smile traveled all the way up to his kind eyes. Lucy did a double-take. His eyes were the color of frosted sea glass—an unusual shade to be sure—but one she'd seen recently somewhere before. He immediately put her at ease.

Lucy gave him a small, tight smile in return.

"Captain Harrison, I've had an unbelievably bad day. Please, just tell me what is going on?"

"Miss Patterson, Franklin over here"—he nodded toward the sheepish-looking younger man—"was sent out this morning to check the place based on your report of an intruder last night. But when he arrived, he found the door open, the store tossed. An elderly woman was inside unresponsive. He called for backup and medical support, and we've been here ever since. The store is a mess, and it looks like a struggle took place. The woman inside suffered a cut and a large bump on her forehead. She's unconscious but stable." He paused and looked at Lucy. "Are you with me so far?"

"Yes, I think so . . . Last night someone was inside, and I went to hide. I think they hit me in the head too." She winced as she touched the still-tender spot on her skull.

Captain Harrison looked sympathetic.

"Am I a suspect in this too?" she asked. "This is just all just . . . too much."

"We're not ruling anyone out at this point, Miss Patterson. I can tell you, however, that the house is clear. You can go home, but only into the kitchen door and upstairs. The store will have to remain closed until our investigators finish. You must stay out of there. Do you understand?"

She nodded, but she felt as confused as ever.

"Who was it? Who was in there?" Lucy asked.

"A former resident of Hidden Springs, a retirement community about an hour from here, Mrs. Fuchsia Butterfield."

Oh no, Lucy thought. She wondered if she should tell him Mrs. Butterfield had been in the day before and the terrible things she'd said. Because the truth always comes out one way or another, Lucy figured she had to tell him.

"Please, call me Lucy. I must tell you something. It may make things worse for me, but I have to be honest."

Captain Harrison raised his eyebrows and waited.

"You see," Lucy sighed, "Mrs. Butterfield was in here yesterday. I used to know her a little bit from when I'd spend summers here with my grandparents. She was once friends with my grandmother."

"Go on."

"Well, she was pretty unpleasant. She accused me of doing something to my grandparents so I could inherit the store. But I would never! I loved my grandparents. They were always so kind and always there for me, and I could just never do anything to hurt them! I don't know why she would say such horrible things to me." Tears gathered in Lucy's eyes at the painful memory.

She told the captain the rest of the story—how she'd stayed calm and offered to make some tea, but while she was in the kitchen, Mrs. Butterfield had disappeared. She told him that she'd gone to dinner and told Miss Hattie all about it. He took down a few notes and then told Lucy to stay close and not leave town. He gave her another reassuring smile and asked Officer Franklin to escort her to the back of the property and upstairs.

Passing through the kitchen, Lucy could see the bookstore, which was the entire front of the old house, in complete disarray. Books and knickknacks were all over the floor. Police tape covered both interior doors that led to the front of the house.

Officer Franklin, now that he wasn't pointing a gun at her, seemed like a nice guy. He even apologized for upsetting her before.

Alone at last, Lucy looked out the bedroom window that faced the front yard. Officer Mooney had arrived on the scene. She watched as he and the captain exchanged heated words. She really didn't like that man. Lucy couldn't hear anything they were saying, but it was clear the captain was unhappy with him, and she smiled just a little when Officer Mooney, red in the face, turned on his heel and stomped off to his car. He peeled out of her driveway.

"Good," she said aloud. "And stay away too!"

Chapter
Four

*L*ucy loved a hot shower, even if the pipes in the old Victorian were a bit musical when she turned them on. Tonight, though, she just wanted to soak, so she grabbed a few things and headed to her grandparents' room. Once, it had been just a large, elaborate bathing and dressing room, but her grandparents had remodeled it to make it a cozy suite. She threw her robe on the antique iron bed her grandfather had pulled out of the attic. When he found the relic, there was a note attached to it penned in a beautiful script. It read, "Nanny's bed, should she return."

It was quite a mystery, and Lucy's grandparents loved anything with a story, so it became their bed of choice when they'd moved to the smaller room. Her grandmother, always whimsical, had added a floral garland twined around the bars on the footboard. And her grandfather, not wanting to be left out, had written a note on cardstock and attached it with a ribbon. It read, "Our bed, at least until Nanny returns."

Seeing the bed made up with a gorgeous old quilt and thick down pillows made her miss her grandparents even more. She filled up the "double dipper" cast iron tub, admiring the intricate carving on the claw feet. Her grandmother had been just as excited about the tub as she had been the bed—she told Lucy it was called a double-dipper because both ends were raised, with a dip in the middle. She'd added, with a wink, "That means two people can sit in there and soak together!"

Lucy, a teenager at the time, had blushed and groaned and asked her grandmother to keep her gross love stuff to herself. Now it just made her smile, and she was thankful they'd been so happy.

Soaking in the tub, with several droppers of lavender oil added to the hot water, Lucy finally relaxed. She let go of the stress as best she could and tried to enjoy the moment, feeling closer to her grandparents in their room and knowing they would want her to enjoy the things they loved. Like a little girl, Lucy even slipped completely under the water for a moment and counted to see how long she could hold her breath. When she came up, a feeling of peace settled over her. "Mmmmm," she sighed.

She let out some of the water and then turned the tap on again until there was plenty of steamy hot water to soak a while longer. Lucy had nearly relaxed herself to sleep when she noticed something strange. The steam from the hot bath had fogged up the mirror over the sink. Barely visible words appeared, slightly darker than the glass around them.

Fully awake now, Lucy sat straight up and read the inscription. "Meet me in the basement."

The message looked sloppy, as if it had been hastily scrawled. She wondered how old it was and if it was some sort of silly game her grandparents played. You never could tell with those two.

Still feeling violated after having the intruder the night before, Lucy also considered that it could be something more menacing. But no, no one could have guessed she'd take a hot bath in a room she wasn't living in. It had to be something older. Maybe it was a clue as to why her grandparents had gone missing?

Shaking a little, Lucy emerged from the tub and wrapped up in a soft, oversized yellow towel. Cold and tired, she had endured enough excitement for one day. She exchanged the towel for her robe, which was thankfully thick, warm, and long. Even though the police had checked thoroughly and locked up everything tightly before they'd gone, Lucy was still a bit nervous about being alone in the house. She quickly crossed the room, locked the door, and slid into Nanny's bed. The soft feather bed beneath the sheet gave way just enough so that it felt as if she were resting on a cloud as she fell asleep, and the well-made antique quilt was just warm and cool enough to keep her that way for many hours.

When she woke again, Lucy had the feeling someone was watching her, but that sensation quickly retreated. "Don't be silly," she said to herself.

She realized that she hadn't seen Tor when Officer Franklin let her back into the house. He had likely been in the bookstore hiding from all the commotion, or maybe he'd gone out the cat flap in the back door. She got up and stretched. Pulling her robe more closely around her, Lucy unlocked the door. When she opened it, Tor was sitting across the doorway, looking for all the world like a guard on duty. He purred when she scratched his ears, and he immediately began meowing and trying to lead her to his food bowl. Laughing, Lucy picked up the fine gentleman and kissed his head. He didn't like that much, but she didn't care.

"Victor Admetus Bombalurina, am I glad to see you!"

The next few days were a whirlwind for Lucy. The police combed every inch of the bookstore and even her home but found nothing to aid their investigation. They finally took down the crime scene tape and permitted Lucy to enter the bookstore and put it back into order.

Dr. Wilson's son-in-law did come by, as promised, and put in a new alarm system. When Lucy asked him how much she owed for it, he refused any offer of payment. He told her his father-in-law would skin him alive if he took so much as a penny.

"Besides," he told Lucy, "I thought the world of your grandparents. Your grandfather is the only reason I passed AP history."

Lucy smiled. Her grandparents seemed to make friends everywhere. Lucy did insist that the man pick a book to take home with him—it was the very least she could do by way of thanks. He quickly chose a hardback book about World War II from the clearance rack, mentioning that he'd never lost the love for history that her grandfather inspired in him.

A steady stream of visitors came by—with many genuine offers of help as well as the merely curious. So many that at the end of each day, she felt completely worn out. Among those who helped return books to their rightful places were many who had loved her grandparents, including the Ruth Circle of Presbyterian Women. Lucy loved the chatty women—all near her grandmother's age—because they not only worked hard, but they each found a few books they couldn't live without. Sales had never been better for The Cozy Cat.

In the middle of it all, Tor started acting strangely. He didn't like so many visitors at once, and the usually genial, gentle cat started to growl and run away when the doorbell rang. Normally, Tor was the self-appointed greeter at The Cozy Cat, checking out each person as they entered the store, as well as appropriating any available children for ear scratches and cheek rubs. But now he seemed slow to warm up. He was wary of adults and trusted only a handful of children who knew him well. Lucy began keeping him in her room at night because otherwise, he'd wake her up patrolling the house, mewling loudly, or running around madly, crashing into things. They both slept better together, she thought.

On a quiet morning about a week after Lucy had found herself captive on a ship, she woke up feeling hopeful. She wasn't sure why, but optimism flowed through her body from the minute she got out of bed. The air was mild and sweet when she opened her bedroom window, and it carried the spicy scent of the rosemary that grew almost unchecked in her grandmother's raised-bed, multi-colored garden below. Even the sunlight was gentle on her face, mixed as it was with the last traces of fog that were quickly burning away. A songbird in the bottlebrush tree near her window was similarly moved, and a cheerful melody overflowed the banks of its feathery little heart.

Lucy, drinking it all in, felt a sense of peace unfamiliar to her in recent days. For just a moment, she had the fleeting idea that if she went downstairs, she'd find her grandmother in the kitchen whipping up lemon-blueberry pancakes. Grandmother would make chicken apple sausages while waiting for the kettle to boil for her special morning tea—a blend of Earl Grey and dried lavender. Lucy savored the feeling as long as she could, dwelling on the memory of happier days until Tor demanded to be let out of her room. Before she turned away from the window, she said "Thank you!" to the little bird still singing his heart out.

Lucy's sense of peace and bliss evaporated immediately when she heard a man's voice reply from beneath her window. "You're welcome!"

*L*ucy nearly tripped over Tor three times before she could get downstairs. She knew the old house was locked up tight, and the alarm hadn't gone off, so she felt somewhat foolish over her fears. It was close to time to open the shop, and the man who'd spoken to her was probably a customer who arrived a few minutes early and caught her talking to the birds.

Still, Lucy's heart raced, and she felt particularly uncoordinated as she tried to unlock the front door. It didn't help that Tor wanted to be underfoot instead of racing off to hide. The bell above the door jangled as she opened it, but no one was there. Puzzled, Lucy stepped out onto the covered porch, scanning the driveway and the yard. She saw no one, so she turned to go back in. She jumped when she saw a man with an amused smile sitting in her grandfather's old rattan rocking chair.

"I didn't mean to alarm you, Miss. Patterson, I just came to bring you some paperwork, and to, uh, see how you're doing." He stood up and extended his hand to Lucy.

"I'm sorry, I didn't see you sitting there!" She felt the hot flush of embarrassment creep up her neck as she realized who he was. "I didn't recognize you out of uniform, Captain Fellowes." She shook the Coast Guard captain's hand and was surprised by how warm it was and how nice it felt. "Won't you come in?" she asked.

"Yes, thank you. Do you have somewhere we could sit and go over a few things? I just need a couple of signatures from you." He smiled down at her and added, "Oh, and these are for you." He picked up a vase filled with multi-colored pastel flowers from the table by the rocking chair. A gossamer blue ribbon tied around the vase truly set off the arrangement.

"For me?" Lucy asked.

It was his turn to flush, and Captain Mark Fellowes, who was accustomed to ordering dozens of sailors around, suddenly looked a bit shy.

"Well, that was quite a hard knock you had on your head, and I talked to Dr. Wilson who assured me you were all right, but I thought . . . you know . . . you might need some cheering up."

Lucy adopted the same amused smile she'd seen on the captain's face a few moments before. "Thank you. They're beautiful. Are these snapdragons? I love them. It was so thoughtful of you."

Lucy carried the flowers into the bookstore and gave them a place of honor on the oversized secretary. *Don't think I've forgotten about you!* She aimed her thought at the antique desk and made a mental note to look for the secret drawer again as soon as possible.

She led the captain to the kitchen and suggested he lay out the paperwork on the much-loved and well-used table. Like many of the furnishings in the house, it was old but so well made that it seemed it might last forever. The style was timeless, but her grandparents didn't know much about it other than it had come from the Midwest and had a maker's mark on the underside that read "C.I." Whoever C.I. was, he made quality furniture.

After she put the kettle on to boil, Lucy put some scones she'd baked the evening before into the warming tray. One antique her grandmother refused to tolerate was an ancient stove. The classic gas range looked as though it fit into the overall vintage scheme, but it was a top-of-the-line modern appliance with all the bells and whistles and made to look like an antique. It had six burners and cast-iron grates to support heavy pots and pans. Lucy's grandmother had been a serious cook, often whipping up large batches of food to share with others. Her cookie jar was legendary, and her hospitality was second to none.

Lucy stood at the stove while she waited for the water to boil. She could feel the captain studying her. He sat quietly while her thoughts wandered. She let out a sad sigh as the kettle whistled. Everywhere she turned was a reminder of her grandparents.

Lucy saw the look of genuine concern on his face as she brought the scones and butter to the table. She carried the tea over on a serving tray and wiped her hands on a tea towel as she smiled at him. "I'm fine, sorry. I was just missing my grandparents. It's this house—it's so full of the things they loved."

He flashed a smile at her that reached his eyes. Lucy was struck by how unusual the color was, like green sea glass polished by the sand and waves, with a lighter center that made it look as if his eyes were lit from within.

"Well, I have the perfect cure. Let's get this paperwork out of the way and go for a walk, shall we? I have the entire day off."

Lucy laughed. "The bookstore is open today. I can't just leave!" Secretly, however, she loved the idea of putting up a Gone Fishin' sign and playing hooky.

"Eat your scones, Captain. Some of us have responsibilities," she teased.

"Call me Mark, please."

She nodded and said, "Okay, then. Eat your scones, Mark. Some of us have responsibilities! Oh, and call me Lucy."

Less than an hour later, the papers were all signed and squared away, and the scones had all disappeared too. The bookstore bell sounded, and Lucy left Mark to put away the cream and stack the dishes in the sink while she went to check on her customer.

Miss Hattie had come in and was standing at the secretary looking at the flowers. She picked them up and turned them around, obviously looking for a card.

"What a snoop!" Lucy giggled and winked at the startled Hattie. "There isn't any card," she told her.

"Oh, I'm sorry! Curiosity got the better of me. These are beautiful! Did you get them from the flower shop downtown?" Hattie asked.

"No, these were a gift." Lucy smiled at her. "And no, I'm not telling you who they're from!" No way was she going to give Miss Hattie the satisfaction. She adored Hattie, but the woman wasn't known for playing it cool.

"Why aren't you at work," Lucy asked, "and what can I help you with?"

"Oh, it was such a lovely day I couldn't stand to stay in the kitchen. I left Hector in charge. He knows most of my recipes by heart, and he's been after me to make him assistant manager for some time now, so I thought I'd pop out to see you. I've missed you at the cafe—I've been imagining you holed up here starving without a decent meal."

Lucy walked over and hugged the older lady. *What a sweet friend*, she thought, *even if she is a bit of a mother hen!*

Just then, Mark emerged from the kitchen and saw the women hugging.

"Hey, can I get one of those?" he asked.

Lucy, feeling he was being a bit forward with his request, let go of Hattie and rounded on him. *Of all the nerve.*

Hattie, seeing Mark, let go of Lucy and made a beeline straight for him. He caught her up in a bear hug and spun her around before setting her on her feet again. Hattie grabbed his face and pulled his head down so she could plant a kiss on each cheek.

"Mark! I didn't know you were here! Are you on leave? Why haven't you stopped by?" Hattie pretended to pout, but she couldn't hold her lip out for more than a few seconds. "Lucy Patterson," she wagged her finger, "what is the meaning of this? Why have you hidden my boy in your kitchen?"

"*Your* boy?" Lucy was once again confused. "Hattie, I didn't think you had any children?" Lucy looked from one to the other of them, hoping for an explanation.

"Miss Hattie took me in when I was a teenager, Lucy. If it wasn't for her . . ." He looked at the older woman with total adoration and hugged her again.

Will wonders never cease, Lucy thought. She picked up Tor and curled up in one of the comfortable chairs by the window, content to pet the giant, purring furball as she watched her two friends catch up.

Chapter Six

$\mathcal{M}$ iss Hattie pushed Lucy and Mark out the front door of The Cozy Cat, promising to mind the store and keep an eye on Tor. When she'd learned that Mark was planning to take a walk and had invited Lucy to come along, there was no stopping her. Lucy thought she looked a little too pleased with herself, but Miss Hattie could manage everything well enough. Besides, Lucy had been longing to visit the redwood groves where she played every summer since being old enough to wander on her own.

She scraped her strawberry blonde hair up into a loose bun, knowing that if she didn't, the coastal fog would turn it into a mess of unruly curls. Mark, wise to the changeable weather, stopped at his car to put away the file of papers he'd brought for Lucy to sign. He also grabbed a sweater and a jacket from behind the seat. He pulled the gray cable knit over his head and offered the jacket to Lucy, who took it happily.

"I have a windbreaker inside, but I'm not going to risk the wrath of Hattie to get it!" she laughed.

"I wouldn't," said Mark, with a smile. "She isn't one to be disobeyed!"

The Cozy Cat Bookstore—Lucy's home—perched on the edge of town, slightly uphill from many of the downtown shops.

The summer she was ten, Lucy learned that a short, quarter-mile walk up the road leading out of town would bring her to a gate and a dirt road. A sign said, "Trespassers will be treated kindly as long as they pick up after themselves!"

A well-worn path led around the gate, and some civic-minded person had even provided a box where dog walkers could take a plastic bag for pet waste. It was typical of the friendly, eccentric village of Seaview.

Mark and Lucy walked quietly at first, each a little bit unsure of what to say. The path diverged from the dirt road and sloped gently upward through a grassy field dotted with dandelions and delicate purple flowers. A massive California oak stood sentry in the middle of the path that divided and went around the tree on both sides. Lucy had climbed it often as a child, using the low-hanging limbs as a ladder and nestling in it for hours at a time. The view from the base of the tree overlooked the whole town, but when she scaled the branches, the blue expanse of the Pacific was her reward.

Mark paused at the tree and turned around to look. Lucy stood beside him, admiring the panorama of the village. It was like something out of a storybook, which made it immensely popular with tourists during the summer. Everywhere a person looked, there were charming houses, many decorated with gingerbread trim, and even some of the more modern homes had added decorative pieces.

She told Mark the story she'd heard—that in the sixties, a group of teenage refugees and dropouts from the Summer of Love in San Francisco had migrated to the town and were taken in by an older couple with plenty of land. The teens learned various handicrafts from the man and his wife, and one of them became a real prodigy at making the trim. The young man used his skills to barter with almost everyone in the village. In just a few short years, he'd moved away with his bride—another teenager from the commune—with enough money for both to go back to college. Meanwhile, the town had become a photo-op favorite for visitors.

Mark whistled. "That's some story, Luce." He smiled at her and asked, "Is it okay if I call you Luce?"

Dazzled by his smile, Lucy said, "Sure, anything is better than Lucilla."

"Lucilla? Is that your name? I love it! Maybe I'll call you Lucilla instead of Luce!" Mark couldn't hide a trace of a smile, so Lucy knew he was teasing her. "Besides," he said, "my real first name is Lucius. Lucius Marcus Fellowes. Just think of it—Lucilla and Lucius!" He laughed.

Lucy laughed too. "Both of our names mean 'light.' So, I guess they do kind of go together!" Lucy blushed, realizing her words could be taken to mean something more romantic. "I didn't mean . . ."

Mark, not laughing now, gazed at her intently. Her hair was slipping out of the bun, and the loose pieces curled around her face. He looked as if he might kiss her, but instead, he tucked a curl behind her ear.

"I agree," he said. "They do go together. Beautifully."

Taking her hand, he pulled her to the other side of the giant oak where the path continued toward a stand of redwood trees bordering a nature preserve.

"Shall we go on?" he asked.

Lucy nodded, afraid to say anything else. Mark didn't let go of her hand.

The sun was doing its best to burn off the fog, but several low-lying patches remained. A thin wisp of mist shrouded clusters of California poppies that flourished at the edge of the meadow with their golden heads peeking through.

"I'd like to get a picture of that, but I didn't bring my phone," Lucy lamented.

"You can use mine. It has a nice camera on it. I upgraded because there's always something fascinating floating around in the ocean, and you never know when you might capture a mermaid." He grinned at Lucy.

"Not everything out there got there by choice!" Lucy felt a little off-balance remembering her recent ordeal.

"Yes, ma'am," Mark replied as he snapped to attention and saluted Lucy. "The Coast Guard is happy to be of service, in case you ever find yourself out there again!"

Lucy laughed. He was so charming, so sincere. And he made her feel safe. *This is new*, she thought.

The white mist was quickly fading in the sunny meadow, so Lucy snapped all the pictures she could on Mark's phone.

"I'm not sure how these will come out, but I appreciate the use of your phone, Mark." She tried to hand back his phone but he shook his head.

"Why don't you give me your number, Lucy?" he asked.

Lucy, not thinking, said, "I don't usually give my number out . . ."

Mark put on a serious face. "Well, then, Miss Patterson, how am I going to send you the pictures?"

Lucy laughed. "Of course! I'm sorry! I wasn't thinking. Old habits, you know." She thought putting her foot in her mouth twice in a single day was plenty.

She entered her number into his phone and handed it back to him.

"Would you like to see my spring?" she asked. "I'm not sure anyone else knows it's there."

Lucy pointed to a barely perceptible trail just off the beaten path that wound its way into the grove of redwoods. The majestic trees blocked out so much light that it felt almost like twilight under the trees.

"No matter how many times I see them, I'm always amazed," said Mark.

Lucy, looking straight up at the canopy hundreds of feet over her head, nodded in agreement. "Mmmm, I love this feeling. When I was a little girl, I'd come here and pretend I was a fairy or a tiny gnome because the trees are just so huge! I came with my grandmother once and a whole bunch of other little girls. We ran all over the forest, chasing each other and pretending we lived here. See that tree over there?" She pointed to a large tree with a wide clearance around it. "It took seventeen people holding hands to get our arms around it!"

Lucy spun in a slow circle, stretching her arms out to the sky, drinking in the sights and the smell of the damp earth.

"This is my happy place," she said. "It feels as though time stops here, and if you could only sit here long enough, you could hear the slow conversation of the trees."

Mark smiled at her whimsy. "You should be a poet."

Lucy groaned and rolled her eyes. "I have *reams* of terrible poetry hidden away. The last thing the world needs is me being a poet!"

"I'd read every word."

"Have you ever read *The Hitchhiker's Guide to the Galaxy?*" she asked.

"I don't think so. Why, should I?"

"Yes! You must. And then you'll know what I mean when I tell you that when it comes to poetry, I'm a total Vogon."

"I'll be sure to pick up a copy as soon as possible, then, if I can find it."

"You can borrow my personal copy." She laughed, and then added, "And all the sequels too!"

They continued down the trail to a spot where a giant

redwood tree lay on its side, the result of a long-ago fire that had burned into its core and finally weakened it enough to fall.

"This way," Lucy said, as she picked her way around the gnarled roots to the other side of the tree.

"The path is this way though," Mark nodded his head in the other direction.

"I know, but my spring is *this* way." Lucy leaned her head the opposite way. "It isn't far, but it's well hidden." She raised her eyebrows, "Are you coming?"

Mark hopped up and over the fallen tree. "Let's go!"

After nearly half an hour of working their way down a hillside into a ravine and alongside a small stream, Lucy put her hand up to stop Mark.

On a rock by the water lay a long, thick banana slug. They watched the vibrant creature inch toward a bush. Lucy had always liked the strange organisms. In an overcast forest of green and brown, a bright yellow banana slug was like a cheerful ray of sunshine. They carefully stepped over him and watched their footing a bit more closely after that.

At what seemed like the bottom of the ravine, a wider bank appeared. It looked like the forest primeval, Lucy thought, with giant ferns growing alongside patches of soft, dewy clover. She cut through the vegetation carefully, motioning for Mark to follow. As they approached the place where the hillside met the bank, Mark could see a carved-out stone depression with water bubbling up from its base.

"This is it. I used to play here for hours, lying in the clover and listening to the sounds of the water." The flow slipped over the edge of the rock basin, trickled in a thin rivulet through the grass, and joined the stream where it naturally widened at the base of the hill.

"Lucy, this is . . . well, magical. There's no other word to describe it. I didn't know something like this could exist."

"It's an artesian well." She was prepared to tell him all about the geology that caused the spring to occur, but Mark had other ideas.

He wrapped his arm around her and pulled her closer. He looked into her emerald eyes and said, "Thank you for sharing this with me. This is a sacred place to you, isn't it?"

Mark's words touched something deep inside her, constricting her throat and causing her eyes to well up. She nodded and closed her eyes against the tears threatening to fall. Honestly, she'd been through so much, and this place was so full of happiness for her that it seemed she had an artesian well inside too. It bubbled up and mingled with her grief and sadness, pushing it to the surface and carrying it away in a peaceful stream. She leaned her head against Mark's chest. He held her while she cried.

Chapter
Seven

*L*ucy heard the mail drop in through the ornate brass slot and land on the floor. Tor, who dozed in one of the leather wingbacks, opened one eye and went straight back to sleep. As she rummaged through the assorted flyers and junk mail, she noticed a small card written with an exquisite, lady-like script addressed to her grandmother. There were watercolor roses painted on both sides but no return address. It was almost more a work of art than a letter, Lucy thought.

A little wave of sadness washed over her as she thought of her grandmother. Perhaps there'd be a return address on the inside or a name she could find in her grandmother's contacts. Whoever it was that made such a beautiful card deserved to know her grandmother was gone. Lucy ran her fingers along the edges of the envelope, feeling the heavy, luxe stationery under her fingers. She started to open the envelope but suddenly felt a little strange about opening someone else's mail. She opened a desk drawer and put it inside, thinking she would deal with it after the store closed for the day.

It was a slow afternoon—warm and a little hazy outside. No one had stopped in since before lunchtime, and Lucy was feeling drowsy. She sat down in the desk chair and leaned back, wiggling into the seat to get comfortable. Her eyes felt heavy.

"Maybe I'll just close my eyes for a minute, Tor," she said to the sleeping cat. Tor's tail twitched in his sleep. Lucy's thoughts drifted here and there, touching on the strange happenings of the summer—the hidden drawer, the message on the mirror, and the break-in. She hoped Fuchsia Butterfield was recovering well after someone knocked her unconscious in the shop. Just before she drifted to sleep, Lucy wondered again about whatever had happened to her grandparents.

Lucy woke up with a start to the smell of vanilla cookies and the sound of the oven door closing in the kitchen. Her heart raced. Had someone broken in again? The fog of her unintentional nap lifted, and Lucy decided she should be more careful in the future not to doze off with the door unlocked. She slipped out of the chair and crept along the wall until she came to the kitchen entryway. Someone was taking books off the shelf and rifling through them, then dropping them on the table. She peeked her head around just in time to see Miss Hattie put an index card in her pocket. Lucy saw a tray of cookies on the table.

"Hattie!"

The older woman startled at Lucy's voice and turned around slowly.

"Hello Lucy, I was just . . ." She broke off and looked down at the floor. "I was just trying to find one of your grandmother's recipes!" She looked up at Lucy, her paperwhite cheeks burning with two bright pink spots.

"I'm sorry, Lucy." Miss Hattie pulled the index card out of her pocket and crossed the room. She handed it to Lucy.

Lucy, somewhat bewildered, took the card. It was her grandmother's recipe for the special tea blend. She knew it was popular and that her grandmother had kept the recipe to herself—to the annoyance of any number of hostesses in the town of Seaview. Lucy only had enough of the blend for a cup or two remaining in her carefully hoarded stash, so she threw her arms around Hattie and kissed her twice, once on each cheek.

"Thank you, thank you, thank you! You darling, I was so afraid the recipe was gone forever!" Lucy beamed at Hattie. "I can't believe you found it. Where was it?"

Hattie, surprised by Lucy's reaction, pointed to the table. On top of the stack of books was a leather journal with the word "Receipts" engraved on top.

It dawned on Lucy, who'd overlooked that book a hundred times, that it wasn't an accounting book at all. "Receipts" was the name given to recipes long ago. The book was an antique, and as she flipped through it, Lucy saw there were recipes written by different people throughout the book. Lots of yellowed notes and newer index cards sat wedged in between the pages. Some of the earliest recipes dated to around the time the house was built. A few had even earlier dates.

Lucy felt as if she'd found a treasure.

"Hattie, this is wonderful. But what are you doing here?"

Hattie smiled at Lucy, sure now that Lucy wasn't angry, and said, "I saw you sleeping, and I thought I'd make some of the vanilla pudding cookies your grandmother used to make. Some of the children have been asking for those, and *that* recipe I have. I thought you might like some yourself.

"Oh, I would. I really would!"

Lucy and Hattie carried the warm cookies and the last two cups of her grandmother's tea to the cozy window seat just off the main rooms of the bookstore. It was an hour before closing, but a warm summer rain had begun to fall, and Lucy supposed no one else would be coming into the shop. Hattie seemed to be in a nostalgic mood, which suited Lucy simply fine. She'd been longing to talk to someone on a deeper level about her grandparents and all the precious memories she had of them.

"It's just so hard, Hattie." Lucy looked down at her teacup with the Mayfair pattern on it. It had been her grandmother's favorite. "I expected to spend the summer with them, maybe the last full summer I could spend here before I started a new job. But instead, I feel as if I'm alone, and there are too many questions. I can't even think about moving forward. I don't want to do anything else—just stay here and keep the bookstore going."

Hattie stirred her tea, responded with a sympathetic murmur, and waited for Lucy to go on.

"I know it sounds insane," Lucy said, "but I have this strange hope that they'll just show up, and it will all have been a bad dream." She looked at Hattie, hoping for some sort of sign that Hattie felt the same way.

"Lucy, that's understandable. Your grandparents loved you very much. But I think you need to accept the fact that they're not coming back. I know it's hard, not having any closure, but it's been so long now. I think if they were still—"

"Please don't finish that sentence, Hattie. I can't bear to hear it out loud." Tears welled up in Lucy's eyes.

Hattie leaned over and wrapped an arm around Lucy.

Lucy was grateful for the gesture and nestled into Hattie's shoulder. If anyone understood what she was feeling, it was Hattie. She'd been one of her grandparents' dearest friends for so long that the lines between friendship and family had blurred long ago. They sat huddled together there, listening to the sound of the rain and watching the glossy leaves dance in the wind.

When the storm had passed and the sun began to peek out from behind the rose-gold clouds, Hattie left Lucy with a gentle squeeze and an invitation to come to dinner at the cafe. Lucy, still in her reverie, nodded but didn't make any promises. She might want to skip dinner, she thought, and wrap herself up in one of her grandmother's afghans and spend the evening on the porch—the spot her grandparents had both loved.

Tor had the same idea, Lucy discovered, when she made her way out to the matching rocking chairs on the porch. He was curled up as cozy as you please on her grandfather's chair, so she went and sat in her grandmother's. It was approaching the time of day she loved most. Lucy had always thought this was the most magical moment—when the day held on and seemed to caress the earth and everyone on it with a promise of a swift return. There was a deep peace found in watching the day surrender to the night and gently acquiesce to the coming rest.

Just as she felt the sweetness of the evening fall over her with the tree frogs singing and the crickets chirping and the scent of the night-blooming jasmine filling the air, the antique streetlight flickered to life with a golden glow and a low hum. The light fell in a circle around the base of the lamp, broken only by the silhouette of a man standing at the end of the sidewalk. She felt her heart jump and begin hammering as he saluted her with a finger to his forehead before turning and walking away.

Lucy slept badly, tossing and turning and fighting her way out of disturbing dreams. Around 4:30 a.m. she heard the morning birds break into a happy song, announcing the coming of the new day, even though it was still dark to human eyes. Lucy was comforted by their cheerful optimism, but she knew there was no way she could fall asleep again now.

Tor sat on the windowsill, his tail swishing back and forth, watching something outside. Lucy joined him at the window and scratched his ears and under his chin. He rewarded her with a rumbling purr, and when she stopped, he pushed his head against her hand to get her to continue. She was grateful for his affection and companionship in the old house. It made her feel much less alone. She scooped him up and carried him downstairs, enjoying the feel of his soft fur and warm, fluffy body in her arms. Just how old was Tor? She counted back the years she could remember him being in the bookstore and decided he was at least eight years old, but he still seemed healthy and happy.

Lucy was halfway down the stairs when she stepped on a creaky one. She hadn't bothered to turn on any lights because the moon was still up, and nearly full, so the tall windows above the landing provided enough light by which to see. She heard a muffled noise downstairs. Tor wriggled frantically to get free while meowing for Lucy to put him down. She let him go, and he dashed down the stairs toward the bookshop.

Lucy was initially afraid but then angry. Whatever was going on—with the break-in, the mysterious happenings, the feeling of some unknown person watching her—she was tired of it and had about enough. She crept back up the stairs, then grabbed her phone and a heavy cast-iron poker from the set beside the fireplace in her room. *I'm not going to be a victim any longer.*

She crept down the back stairs this time—the narrow wooden steps that led to the kitchen. *I won't be caught by surprise coming down at the very back of the house.* Lucy paused for a moment to enter 911 on her phone. Now she only had to hit the call button, and someone would be on the other end of the line. She also turned on her phone's flashlight and put her thumb over the light to hide it until she needed it.

Another noise came from somewhere near the front of the house—a scraping sound she couldn't identify. Tor meowed from the same direction. Lucy hoped the cat was all right. If anything happened to him, she didn't know what she'd do.

Lucy reached the bottom of the stairs and crept on her tip-toes into the kitchen. She paused. Not a sound.

The moonlight didn't reach this corner of the house, so she carefully shone her flashlight around and saw nothing unusual. Hiding the light again, she moved toward the front of the house.

Tor was no longer meowing, and she had no idea where he was. She was afraid of tripping over him, so she glided across the floor rather than stepping normally. As she passed through the dining room, Lucy stubbed her little toe on the leg of a chair. She stifled the pain. Now would be a bad time to make noise. Hitting the chair had already made a slight noise, and she didn't want to give whoever—or whatever—was in the house a warning that she was coming. She gripped the poker a little more tightly and started forward again.

Just before she reached the open french doors that led from the dining room, she heard something else—the scraping sound again, followed by a dull thud, and then another scrape. Lucy froze. Tor yowled and hissed. Lucy's heart pounded so loudly in her ears she could hear nothing else. She knew there was a light switch on the wall just ahead of her. It would flood the dining room, the reading room, and the hallway with light if she flipped all three switches simultaneously. She was grateful for one modern thing in the old house—the wiring. Her grandmother had insisted on it bringing it up to code long before Lucy was born.

She took in a deep breath and released it slowly to calm her nerves and made sure the call screen was still open on her phone. Before she could lose her nerve, she switched the lights on.

No one was there but Tor.

She ran quickly to him, and seeing he was okay, she sprinted into the bookshop, turning on all the lights as she went. She'd blown her cover by turning on the first light, so she ran from room to room, switching on lights and holding her poker in the most menacing way she knew how.

Lucy found nothing out of place and no one downstairs.

She was beginning to feel a bit foolish. *Perhaps I imagined the whole thing,* she thought. But then she saw Tor.

Cobwebs and a thick layer of gray dust covered his coat. She thought he looked very offended as he tried to bathe himself. *There was nowhere in the house he could get that dirty so quickly,* she thought. The attic stayed locked, but even that crowded space was cleaner than Tor appeared to be.

She gathered him up again, and after checking the locks on the doors and windows, Lucy decided she'd better help him with his bath. The early birds had stopped singing by the time she wrestled him into the shallow, warm water, and the sun barely peeked over the hills in the east before she finished sponging off the very annoyed cat.

Chapter Eight

*L*ucy sat at her grandmother's desk making a list of supplies to pick up at the Esperanza Street Farmer's Market. She waited for the cute little girl with soft brown curls and big blue eyes to make up her mind on a trio of books. Any longer and Lucy might be too late to get what she needed.

Around four o'clock, the winds usually picked up, and vendors started winding down to close the market. The forecast called for chilly temperatures and a thick marine layer of fog for the evening. Every summer, there were a handful of nights like this, and Lucy thought the fog was beautiful. Sometimes it got so thick it turned the world into a ghostly white landscape—the kind where a person couldn't see more than a few feet in front of their face but sounds carried strangely for miles.

The little girl's mother finally decided to buy her all three books. Lucy thanked them for stopping by and told them to be sure to say goodbye to Tor, who sat on a table on the porch waiting for ear rubs. The little girl—her curls bouncing—ran out of the store to give Tor some much-needed love. He'd been extra affectionate all day and stayed close to Lucy. She was glad—she enjoyed the company after the long and strange night they'd had.

Lucy had just about reached her wit's end with it all. She'd even briefly considered selling the bookstore and moving back to the town where she'd attended college. One or two of her old friends still lived there, and she'd always loved the atmosphere of the place. She also considered calling her parents—wherever they were this month—to see if they wanted a visitor. Still, she knew with their busy schedules they'd feel obligated to entertain her or, perhaps, guilty if they couldn't. And that was even if they were reachable at all. She often had to wait for them to call her from a satellite phone.

"I'm going to have to stick it out, Tor, and make the best of it. Whatever is going on, I'm sure we'll figure it out. I can't possibly leave you, anyhow." Tor gave her several lazy blinks, and then she added, "Or Mark. I can't possibly leave Mark." She blushed for having said that out loud, and to a cat, no less!

Lucy put Tor inside and locked the shop behind her. She had her market bags on her arm, but before she reached the end of the drive, a car wheeled in and stopped just in front of her. It was Miss Hattie, who was more than a little flustered.

"Lucy, no time, get in the car! We have to go right now. Fuchsia is awake and she's asking for you!"

"Wh-what?" Lucy stammered. "Why would she want me?"

"Your guess is as good as mine, but the police are already there. Come on!" Hattie leaned over and opened the passenger side door. Still dazed, Lucy slid in, even though she was fairly sure she didn't want to go.

Hattie sped down the street and turned onto the municipal highway that led to the county medical center.

Lucy and Hattie filled out visitor information cards and made their way to the fourth floor and Fuchsia's room. Officer Franklin, the young policeman with the perfect skin and teeth, stood outside the door.

"I'm sorry, ladies, but you can't go in. You should stick around though. Officer Mooney wants to have a word with you." He nodded toward Lucy.

He sent them to a family waiting room, where they found a disheveled man trying to entertain two young children and feed a toddler. He looked at them in anticipation but slumped a bit when he saw that they weren't nurses coming to give him an update. The toddler began to cry, and the two younger children chose that moment to have a dispute over the possession of a handheld electronic game.

Hattie and Lucy exchanged a look and stepped in to help. Lucy distracted the squabbling children with the offer of a story, and Hattie took the toddler in her arms and fed her oat rings and blueberries from a plastic bowl. The tired father mumbled a thank you and sat down in a dusty-pink recliner. He tried to relax and close his eyes, but worry lines crossed his face.

Lucy loved children and enjoyed reading stories to them from a stack of books that had seen much better days. A couple of times, she had to improvise or tell the story from memory due to missing or torn pages. She made a mental note to talk to someone about the needs at the hospital and how she could help. Hattie had soothed the toddler, now finished with her snack, into a light doze, so she carried her over and laid her in her father's lap. They'd both rest a little easier that way.

Lucy found the remote for the television and put on a quiet show for the children. It was one of her favorites as a child—a gentle story about a small bear who lives with his mother and father in the forest and has a wide variety of animal friends. He even had a little human friend who had a doll named Lucy, so she'd loved the show even more for that reason.

It wasn't long before Officer Mooney, a scowl on his face, came looking for them. Hattie saw him coming and headed him off—no way was she going to let him wake up the toddler or the father. She motioned to Lucy, who slipped away from the children and met him in the hall. Lucy noticed he was out of breath, and he had sweat stains on his shirt.

Before Lucy could say a word, Officer Mooney spat at her, "You might be off the hook for assaulting Fuchsia Butterfield, but you're not off the hook altogether. She's gone missing, and I'd be willing to bet YOU had something to do with it!"

Lucy rolled her eyes. She was over this whole thing and more than a little fed up with the officious Mooney.

"Why do you think that, Officer? I barely know the woman, and I've been at home all day in the bookstore, with customers who can vouch for me. And another thing, I don't appreciate your tone. You seem to have had it in for me from the beginning. I'm going to call an attorney. Enough is enough!"

"I'd advise you, Miss Patterson, to tread very carefully. If you barely knew the woman, why was she asking for you? And why did she leave you this?" Officer Mooney reached into a bag, pulled out a book wrapped in string, and waved it in Lucy's face.

"I have no idea," Lucy said. "But since it has my name on it, don't you think you'd better give it to me?"

"Not a chance," he replied and slipped the book into a clear, plastic evidence bag. "I need you to come down to the station right away. We need to have a long talk."

Hattie, face flushed with indignation, said, "I'll drive her to the station, but we're stopping to get a lawyer first!"

She led Lucy down the hall and away from the sputtering and angry policeman who decided to let her go with that promise.

Hattie drove Lucy over to the only legal office in town. The weathered wood shingle still hung from the roof of the porch, announcing the services of Samuel D. Stevens, Attorney at Law.

It was here that her grandparents' friend had spent his entire career practicing law. Lucy remembered him as a funny old man who liked to smoke cherry tobacco in his pipe, which he had to do on the porch because her grandmother wouldn't let him in until he'd finished. Lucy hated smoke, but she'd loved the smell of that pipe tobacco.

"Come meet the new guy, Lucy. I think you'll like him, and he's a family friend. He's Samuel's grandson. He's only been practicing a year, but he seems to know his stuff."

"I hope so! I have a feeling Officer Mooney has already tried and convicted me and is just waiting to hand down a sentence." Lucy frowned. "I wish his grandfather hadn't retired. I know my grandparents thought he was a wonderful lawyer."

Lucy and Hattie made their way inside the office. The first floor of the cottage served as both office and meeting space. An antique bell announced their arrival.

"Hello! I'll be there in just a minute! Hang tight," a male voice called out to them from the back room. It was followed by, "Just another minute!" And then, "Actually, could you come back here? I need a little help!"

An impressive picture window overlooking a small but beautifully landscaped garden lit up the back room. What Lucy noticed most, however, were the dust motes dancing in the air. She coughed a couple of times before she noticed him. A man was sitting on top of a bookshelf, one of many that lined the walls. A ladder lay on its side on the ground. Lucy didn't feel inspired with confidence.

"As you can see, I'm in a bit of a jam. I could just jump, but I already injured my knee once this week. Do you think you ladies could prop the ladder back up for me?" He smiled, and it was so charmingly self-deprecating that Lucy and Hattie couldn't help but giggle.

"Hold on, Lucy," Hattie said, her eyes full of mischief. "Do you really think we should help him—for free? Maybe we should negotiate a fee while he's stuck up there!"

"Hattie!" Lucy gave her a warning look. He might be a new lawyer, but she desperately needed his help. She looked up at the young man, who had smudges on his cheek and forehead, and felt relieved to see he was smiling.

"Sure, Hattie," he said. "For you, all my services will be doubled! For her, well, I think we can arrange something. You're Lucy, aren't you?"

Lucy nodded. Did everyone here know her name and business? Of course, they did. It was a ridiculously small town, after all.

"Yes, I'm Lucy, and I need you to come down from there. I'm due at the police station any minute, but I don't want to go back there without representation!"

She and Hattie lifted the ladder and propped it against the shelf, then held it while he scrambled down. He wiped his hands on his pants and reached out to her.

"Hi, Lucy, I'm Sam. Samuel D. Stevens, same as my grandfather, but his *D* stood for Daniel and mine is David. You can call me Sam. Nice to meet you. Now tell me, what is it they're saying you did this time?"

Lucy smiled. She could tell he was already on her side.

Lucy and Hattie sat in the conference room with Sam. Mooney had tried to keep Hattie out, but she wasn't having it. He also asked Lucy repeatedly why she thought she needed a lawyer if she had nothing to hide, but Lucy, as instructed by Sam, didn't answer. He didn't let Lucy answer most of the officer's questions, which didn't sit well with the older man.

"It will be better if you cooperate, Miss Patterson. This is your last chance to tell your side of the story. We know you had something to do with the disappearance of Fuchsia Butterfield."

He moved some papers and pulled out the book Lucy had seen earlier. It was *A Witness Tree* by Robert Frost. The thick paper and rough-cut edges caused Lucy to wonder if it was a first edition. She started to reach for it, but Mooney pulled it away. On the front cover was a sticky note that said,

To Lucy,
I'm sorry.
The truth lies beneath.
—FB

He opened it and jabbed a finger at a couplet. "What exactly does this mean? Is this why you had to get rid of her? She knew too much?"

Lucy tensed to respond, but Sam put a hand on her arm and said, "How is my client supposed to know what it means when she doesn't even know what it says?"

Mooney, leaning back in his chair, appraised the trio. His lips twisted into a sneer. He turned the pages to face them. Lucy could see two faint pencil lines underlining a bit of the text. She pursed her lips, thinking that even such minor wear could affect the value of the volume.

Mooney turned the book back to himself and read, "We dance round in a ring and suppose, but the secret sits in the middle and knows." He glared at Lucy and said, "This little poem is the only thing marked in the whole book. There's nothing else. So tell me, what does that mean to you?"

Sam leaned over and whispered in Lucy's ear, "Does that mean anything to you?"

She shook her head no and said, "Nothing at all. The book might have some value, but I'd have to look it up to be sure. Otherwise, I really couldn't say."

Sam looked at Mooney and said, "Nothing. It means nothing to my client. Now, unless I'm mistaken, no one knows if Mrs. Butterfield is missing. Isn't it possible that she walked out of the hospital on her own? And since my client has an airtight alibi, I don't think you have evidence of anything."

Hattie nodded vigorously, and she had the names and phone numbers of Lucy's customers handy. She and Lucy had prepared the list at Sam's office while Lucy told him the whole crazy story. So she pushed it toward Mooney.

He took it. "You'd better believe I'll be checking with each one of these people to see if your story holds up!"

Sam stood. "Now, if there's nothing further, and unless you're charging my client with a crime, I think we're done here." Mooney started to answer, but Sam cut him off, saying, "And I think you have something that belongs to my client. There's no evidence of a crime, and you've had plenty of time to examine it. Keeping it now would be theft."

Mooney's face turned red. He slammed the book down on the table and stood up suddenly, causing his chair to crash to the floor behind him. "You listen to me—"

Before he could finish, the conference room door opened, and Police Captain Andy Harrison strode into the room.

"No, you listen to me," he said to Mooney in a quiet but firm manner. "I told you to let this go. There is no evidence of any wrongdoing here, and Mrs. Butterfield herself cleared Miss Patterson this morning. She was certain that Lucy is not the person who attacked her."

The two men, both in blue uniforms, stood toe-to-toe. Mooney, furious, worked hard to control himself as the captain nodded toward Sam, Hattie, and Lucy. Mooney turned to the three and said, "You're free to go."

Sam picked up the book and offered his hand to Miss Hattie, who was grateful for the assist. Lucy followed the two, not making eye contact with Officer Mooney. She was still afraid of what she might say.

She did, however, look up at the captain to say thanks. Before she could, he said, "We're still investigating the incident with the Mendocino Maiden, Miss Patterson. It seems obvious to me that you were the victim in that case, but if you were involved—maybe colluding with someone—we will find out." Mooney smirked at her, but the captain gave him a warning look.

"Your grandparents were good people, and I think you probably take after them. I looked up to your grandfather, especially. He was a great man who helped a lot of troubled kids in this community. I'm sorry for the stress this whole thing has caused you, and"—he looked again at Mooney to make sure he wasn't going to say anything else—"we appreciate your cooperation."

Lucy nodded. That was the best she could hope for right now. She looked at the captain for a few seconds longer than necessary. Something about him made her feel safer. He reminded her of someone with the unusual shade of green in his eyes. Suddenly feeling awkward, she looked away and quickly joined Sam and Hattie.

Chapter Nine

*H*attie insisted that Lucy and Sam come to the Lace
Curtain for dinner, but as they drove past Laurelyn
Street, they saw the market was still going. The fog was holding
just offshore, and the winds were milder than forecast. Lucy
asked Hattie to drop her off, and Sam decided to join her, both
promising to meet her at the cafe after some quick shopping.

Lucy was a little flustered that Sam seemed eager to join her.
He was a friend of the family, so to speak, and he had Miss
Hattie's seal of approval. Still, Lucy was mentally exhausted and
didn't feel like making small talk or discussing her case. She just
wanted to take in the sights and smells of the market, to savor
the visual feast of the abundant and colorful fruit and lush vegetables. She especially loved to stop at the baker's booth and
try new things or at the lavender seller's tent. It smelled heavenly inside, and she always came home with something—a bar
of lavender oatmeal soap or a small bottle of lavender essential
oil. The climate was perfect for growing the fragrant purple
flower on that part of the coast. Some thought it even rivaled
the famous lavender fields of Provence.

Sam, however, didn't intend to make small talk, and he
didn't want to talk about her case. Instead, he took her by the
arm and directed her to the sidewalk, away from the lively market

that covered two blocks in the center of the street. He looked around to see if anyone was close enough to overhear. Lucy narrowed her eyes. She dreaded what he might be about to say and planned to make it clear that she wasn't available if that's what he had in mind. Besides, she was his client. It would be completely unprofessional if he'd tagged along just to ask her out.

"Lucy, I wanted to talk to you alone," he said.

She raised her eyebrows and waited. At least he was direct!

"I don't know if you know this, but you were already my client before you walked in today. Well, sort of. Your grandparents had a long-standing account with my grandfather, and there are certain ongoing obligations I have to your family, legally speaking, since I took over his practice and his clients. There are several things I need to speak with you about. But first, you should know that there is a substantial account balance."

Lucy's heart sank. She didn't have any capital to pay off debts her grandparents might owe. She'd have to sell the shop after all and hope it was enough. She closed her eyes and sighed.

"I'm so sorry, Sam, I didn't know." She looked up at him and said, "I'm not sure what they owed you, but I will do the best I can for you. And here I've added even more to the debt by hiring you to represent me today. I really didn't know."

"Oh, no, Lucy, you have it all wrong! The account balance isn't owed, it's more like a retainer. There is a sizable account for any legal costs accrued by your grandparents, The Cozy Cat Bookstore—even you and your parents are named on the account as beneficiaries of the legal fund."

"I don't understand. Why would my grandparents do that?"

"I don't know, myself," he replied, "and I've written to my grandfather about it. I'd call, but the island he's on lost their phone system during hurricane season last year. The mail still works, but it's a bit slow. But no, you don't need to worry. The retainer and the legal fund are more than enough to cover anything you might need. So, in truth, I'm at your service." He smiled and made a small bow in her direction.

Lucy laughed, almost giddy with relief. She wanted to stay right where she was and run The Cozy Cat. It was her home, and she loved it.

He laughed. "In fact, I was planning to come to see you before you came to see me. There are some packages held in trust for you. There's also a document, but there are restrictions on when it can be opened. I don't know what it says, but it's securely encased in a locked box and even sealed with wax. It can be opened in just over two weeks."

Lucy's head reeled. "Why not sooner?" she asked.

"Legally, I'm bound to not open it until the time your grandparents chose. It would be a serious breach to do otherwise. There are very precise instructions, and opening it early might have major consequences. You might be able to challenge that in court, but I think it's better to just wait. Two weeks isn't that long!"

Lucy thought two weeks sounded like a lifetime. Sam gestured toward the closest farm stand, and they walked over together. A few of the merchants were packing up already, but Lucy found everything she needed. At the end of the day, the prices often dropped by a decent margin, as the farmers would rather sell it for a bit less than have to pack it up and take it home with them. Sam wandered off in search of flourless chocolate tarts from the Flour Child Bakery booth, and Lucy stopped by the lavender tent for some bath bombs. She thought a good dinner and a long soak might be just what she needed.

Lucy left the Lace Curtain Cafe feeling rather full. Hattie had cooked up a wonderful Irish stew for Lucy and Sam, her "extra special recipe," she'd said with a wink. Lucy decided that meant it had real Guinness stout in it as well as bunches of thyme from Hattie's garden. It was delicious, and Lucy promised herself that the next time she was in Hattie's kitchen, she'd go snooping for that recipe. Hattie couldn't complain, considering Lucy caught her doing the same thing in her grandmother's kitchen!

As if the stew and cloud-like biscuits weren't enough, Sam pulled out the chocolate tarts to share. They were amazing but extraordinarily rich. The center was more like a chocolate ganache than anything else.

Lucy was looking forward to walking home and working off some of the richness she'd enjoyed at dinner. She loved the long days of summer. The sun hadn't yet set, but it hovered just above the looming cloud bank that was moving closer to shore. There was a crispness to the air she relished, breathing it in as deeply as she could. Nothing was better than a salty sea breeze to make her feel alive. She stood at the corner of the street, looking out over the ocean, watching the waves roll in and crash on the shore. Seaview was a wonderful place to live, she thought, even with all the strange things she'd encountered.

She set off toward home, taking a different route than she usually did. It wasn't the fastest way, but this way, she could see more of the wildly colorful gardens the town was famous for. The houses in this section were colorful too—pinks and blues and yellows, each with white gingerbread trim, set in the middle of their riotous gardens like jewels. The houses attracted a lot of tourists during the busiest part of the summer Hometown Days celebration, so Lucy was happy to have the gardens all to herself. She even stopped to take a few pictures with her phone of some gladiolus in every possible color, all growing together in a raised box.

Lucy rounded the corner, then stopped.

Ahead, Mark stepped out of his truck. She called out to

him, but her voice was lost in the wind. Mark reached into the cab of his truck, pulled something out, then wrapped it in his jacket. He scanned the area around the building as if looking for someone.

It was a rustic building with a wide wooden porch and gray weathered siding. Mark ran up the three stairs and peeped in through the window. Lucy watched as he moved to the door and tried to open it, shoving it with his shoulder. When that didn't work, he stuck his arm in his rolled-up jacket, broke the glass on the door, reached inside to unlock it, and made his way inside.

Lucy turned back to go the other way. Had she just seen Mark commit a crime? What else could he have been up to? Lucy pulled out her phone and looked at it. She didn't want to call the police—she didn't have the best relationship with the police at this point. She started to put her phone away but then thought about Miss Hattie and how close she and Mark were. Hattie would know what to do. She fumbled through her contacts, the wind chilling her fingers. California summers could be colder than Indiana winters.

Hattie didn't answer, so Lucy sent a text, asking her to call her as soon as she got this message. Lucy decided that she trusted Mark. If he had to break into a building, there had to be a good reason. She waited to see if Mark would come out, but the sun had disappeared due to the heavy fog moving in.

Lucy made her way up the street in the deepening twilight, trying to be quiet but quick. Just before she reached the old building, she heard a noise and hid behind an evergreen bush. A motorcycle sped out from a shed behind the abandoned structure and disappeared toward the highway. Lucy had a bad feeling in the pit of her stomach. Throwing caution to the wind, she ran up the wooden stairs and through the broken door. The sign said "McCoy's Pawn Shop and Trading Post," but the shop was empty except for built-in bookshelves and a display counter.

Lucy's voice caught in her throat. She didn't see Mark anywhere in the dark building. She found a switch on the wall, but when she flipped it, nothing happened. It was difficult to see anything, so Lucy felt her way forward.

"Mark? It's Lucy," she whispered. "Are you in here?"

Lucy tripped on something and went sprawling on the floor. She landed hard on her hip and right hand, but her left hand pushed on something soft. She tried to stifle the pain and not cry out, but someone else did. She leaped up and hobbled away.

"Oh no, no no no!" she said. Turning on the flashlight on her phone, she saw Mark crumpled on the floor on his side. It had been his foot she'd tripped over.

Mark, in a comical Ricky Ricardo voice, said, "Lucy, you have some 'splainin' to do!"

"Me? I don't think so!" Lucy reached out to help Mark get up from the floor. "I saw you knock out the glass and break in, and then someone on a motorcycle came tearing out from behind the building. I was worried something was wrong!"

"You just happened to be here, and you just happened to see me? How is that possible, Lucy? Why are you here?" Mark and Lucy hobbled out the door together. The streetlights were just flickering on, and the nearest one cast a warm glow on Lucy's face. His eyes searched her face as he said, "It seems a little too coincidental, Lucy."

"What do you mean, coincidental? Just why are you here, Mark, and why did you break in?"

"I'm in the middle of an investigation. That's all I can say about it." He reached up, touched the back of his head, then winced. "Someone hit me in the head and ran out the back, and the next thing I know, you're coming in the front and crash landing on me." He looked at her again, still scrutinizing her. "What did you say you were doing here, again? I mean, why were you in this neighborhood?"

Lucy told him about her day, starting with the events at the hospital, hiring Sam, Mooney's interrogation about the book and note from Fuchsia Butterfield, and finally, dinner at Hattie's. "It was a nice night, so I decided to walk home the long way around and see some of the gardens. I haven't been able to enjoy the summer as much as I'd like," she said.

Mark gave her a meaningful smile and said, "Well, I've been enjoying the summer a great deal—at least parts of it." His voice was deep but silky, and she found herself blushing. She hoped he couldn't tell in the soft light. He leaned forward and said, "Lucy . . ."

"Yes, Mark," she murmured, tilting her head ever so slightly. She could smell his cologne—a rich, warm scent, and it was intoxicating.

"Lucy." His eyes burning with a strange fire. "Can you give me a description of the person on the motorcycle?"

Astonished, Lucy just laughed. "I really can't. I wish I could, but"—she paused for effect—"I was hiding in the bushes!"

Chapter
Ten

*M*ark drove Lucy home, and she invited him in. She unpacked her bags from the market and was sad to see that the beautiful raspberries she'd bought hadn't fared too well during her exciting evening. They weren't even worth freezing for a smoothie, so she tossed them out and put the kettle on. Mark hadn't eaten, so she made a quick tray for him with cheese and crackers, slices of cucumber and tomato, and peaches from the market. She added some aged prosciutto she'd been saving for something special.

She told Mark about the strange noises she'd heard the night before and how exhausted she was from not getting enough sleep. Mark insisted on going through the entire house for her peace of mind and his. After he gave the all-clear, they settled on a comfortable velvet sofa. Lucy was glad for the company, but she still felt a little bit like an awkward teenager when he was around. Tor, being ever the busybody, sniffed the tray and decided there wasn't anything on it he wanted, so he settled down on the sofa between Lucy and Mark and promptly went to sleep. Clearly, Tor felt safe in Mark's company too.

At Mark's urging, she promised to lock up the house tightly and set the alarm system as soon as he left. And she did just that, texting him to let him know she was safe and sound, and the alarm was armed. She cleared up the tea tray and quickly put the kitchen in order. She couldn't wait to soak in a hot bath with the lavender bath bomb she'd bought at the market, and she was looking forward to another look at the book of poetry that Fuchsia left for her.

We dance round in a ring and suppose,
But the Secret sits in the middle and knows.

The faintly underlined words rolled around in Lucy's mind as she lay neck-deep in the lavender-scented water. Her muscles were just beginning to relax after a day filled with too much stress. The calming lavender oil and the hot water were just what the doctor ordered. Lucy drifted off into a light slumber as she pondered what possible meaning Fuchsia wanted her to take from those two lines. *Robert Frost*, she thought, as she slipped into a place deeper in her subconscious, *was far too subtle.*

Lucy dreamed that she was standing on a cliff overlooking the ocean on a bright day, surrounded by a group of little boys and girls. The girls wore white dresses with navy blue sailor collars, and the boys wore stockings and white, knee-length pants paired with a sailor's blouse. The children held hands and made a circle around her. Slowly they began to move, whispering something in unison. They chanted the words from the poem, growing louder and faster with each revolution.

"We dance round in a ring and suppose, but the secret sits in the middle and knows!" Lucy felt disoriented by the spinning circle of children, so she sat down in the grass. But as is often the case in dreams, the scene changed around her, and she felt herself falling in a dark place until she landed in icy water far below. Lucy woke with a start, realizing she had slapped the now-cold bathwater with both of her arms as if she were breaking her fall in the dream. She laughed at herself for falling asleep in the tub and scaring herself in the dream.

"I've got to get more sleep," she said to no one in particular. "Otherwise, I might start going mad and talking to myself!" She giggled. "At least I can still crack myself up. Otherwise, I really would be crackers!" She eased herself out of the chilly but still fragrant bath and wrapped herself in a towel.

"Maybe I'm the secret," she thought. She shook her head. "If I'm the secret, I've kept it even from myself!"

Lucy awoke feeling happy and refreshed in the morning. Her grandparents' bed was so comfortable, it was hard for her to get out from under the pile of quilts and down comforters. But the morning sunshine was inviting, streaming in the window to mark the pattern of the lace curtains on the floor. She crossed the room and opened the window. A gentle breeze greeted her, but she was too late to catch the songs of the morning birds. The sky was a glorious blue, though, and she knew it was going to be a warm and lovely day.

The ladies on the Hometown Days committee had asked to meet with her and to use the reading room for planning purposes later in the morning. Lucy was happy to oblige. The same group of women had overseen the event for as long as she could remember. Her grandmother served on the committee when Lucy was a child, so she knew most of the members somewhat well. The committee had asked Lucy to add an event for children to this year's schedule, and she was pleased with the idea she'd come up with. She hoped the ladies were equally excited about it.

She quickly set up card tables and covered them with her grandmother's old Battenberg lace tablecloth. It had an ivy pattern running through the lace, so she pulled out china tea-cups and a tea service from her grandmother's collection to match. She put a kettle on to boil and made a pot of coffee. Hattie was bringing brunch items, and a committee member who owned the ever-popular Honey's Bakery in town planned to bring baked goods to share. The owner of Honeys had earned the nickname "Honey" as a child, and it stuck. Lucy hoped beignets were on the menu. Honey claimed hers were as good as the famous ones in New Orleans. Lucy didn't know about that, having never tried the others, but she drooled at the prospect of a fresh, hot beignet from anywhere.

Just before The Cozy Cat was set to open, the committee trooped in, full of good spirits and loaded down with tasty food. Lucy ran to the kitchen to grab a couple of extra serving trays and the cream and sugar. She noticed a three-tiered serving piece in the corner and gave it a quick wipe. *It will be perfect for the pastries and add a nice touch to the table*, she thought. The ladies had everything laid out and ready to go in mere minutes.

Between bites of a heavenly breakfast strata, Hattie said, "Lucy, let's not stand on ceremony. Why don't you go ahead and tell the women your ideas for Hometown Days?" Lucy drooled at the sight of the beignet on her plate but agreed. The sooner her part was over, the more time she'd have to sample everything while others spoke.

She stood up and said, "I'd like to do a fairy book faire. I think it would be nice to set up a fairy garden party under the trees beside the community garden, with books as the theme. I'd have a big cake decorated like a fancy royal book and a fairy tea. We'd do fairy tales with a storyteller a few times a day, and the kids could dress up and have pictures taken with fairies. We could have magic bubble games, fairy arts and crafts, and a write-your-own-fairy-tale-ending contest."

Lucy sat down and picked up her beignet. No one said anything for a minute or so, and she thought perhaps her idea was a dud. But then all the women started talking at once in animated tones.

"Oh Lucy, that sounds wonderful. I'll bake the cakes, one for each day, and cupcakes, too," offered Honey.

"This will be very popular. We need to gather some volunteers for you," one of the women said.

"The children are going to love it!" another said.

"Are you sure about this, Lucy? It isn't too much to take on right now?" That question came from Hattie, who looked a little concerned.

Lucy bit into her beignet and sighed happily. The sugary treat melted in her mouth. She replied, "I think it will be just what I need. It will distract me from worrying about other things that are out of my control. I'm looking so forward to it." Lucy took another bite. "And can I order several boxes of these for the fairy tea? They'd be perfect for the kids, and I will tell them the powdered sugar is special fairy dust!"

Honey beamed. "Of course! I'll make them myself and send you fresh ones every few hours or so!"

Satisfied that she had the blessing of the committee, Lucy loaded her plate and poured a cup of tea. She listened as the ladies went to work at nailing down details and assigning tasks. She finally had to tear herself away to serve a customer in the shop, but it seemed to Lucy that this would be the best Hometown Days in years.

Hattie and Honey stuck around after the others had gone, clearing up and cleaning the dishes. Lucy appreciated their help—the bookstore seemed twice as busy as usual. Hattie popped in to tell her that she had put all the leftovers away in the fridge. "The vote was unanimous that you should keep them," she said. Lucy was over the moon—all the ladies were excellent cooks, and not just the two women who made food for a living. Everything she'd sampled that morning was delicious.

A little girl with curly red hair asked for help finding a book to read, so Lucy went with her to the children's section.

"I want a book that talks about gold mines and their tunnels," she told Lucy. Nothing came to mind to fit that description, but Lucy did find a book about animals who dig below the surface and make tunnels, dens, and warrens. The little girl seemed happy with that, and her mother did too. The little girl looked up at Lucy as she rang up the purchase. "I want to know what's underneath!" she said.

"Me, too!" Lucy said. "And thank you. You've given me an idea!"

After they left the store, followed out by Hattie and Honey, Lucy put up the Back in 30 Minutes sign on the door and locked it. Sometimes she used that for a lunch break if she needed it, but today she had a different plan.

"Underneath . . . what lies beneath . . ." she muttered to herself. She found a flashlight in the kitchen and headed down the basement stairs. *Maybe what lies beneath has been beneath my feet all along.*

The basement under the old Victorian home was fascinating. It had been off-limits to Lucy as a child, so it still held an air of mystery for her now. She'd only been down there a couple of times and only into the first room. It held antique furniture wrapped for storage, a fuse box, and in one corner was an old pantry area with a root cellar reachable by opening a wooden hatch and descending a set of stairs. Her grandmother once said that it hadn't been used as a root cellar in many decades, not since the advent of supermarkets. Beyond the first room was a series of smaller rooms that surrounded the main area, almost like a square, with doorways leading to them on the four walls.

She tried the doors to each of the rooms but found them locked tight. The doors were solid oak, and each had a vintage cast-iron lock painted a cream color but worn in places to show the dark metal beneath. She had no idea where the keys might be. Lucy sighed. Only one avenue was open to her at this point. She made her way through the furniture maze to the corner with the pantry. It was mostly empty, holding only a handful of mason jars of miscellaneous items.

There were several boxes in the area, one of them covering the wooden hatch that led to the root cellar, so Lucy took time to make room for them elsewhere. The hatch had an inset wooden handle that lay flush until raised up at right angles to the wooden planks. *Clever,* Lucy thought. *Throw down a rug and no one would know the hatch was here.* She pulled the hatch up with a hard yank but was surprised at how easily it swung upward. The hinges were well-oiled and almost felt as if they were on a spring. It held itself in an upright position, so Lucy crouched down and shone her flashlight down the stairs.

She couldn't see far, but she did locate a light switch just a couple of stairs down. She stepped down the first few stairs and flicked it on. A single, swinging light bulb, suspended by a wire from the ceiling, lit the room. It chased the shadows into the corners but did nothing to make the room feel warm or welcoming. Lucy eased down the stairs, expecting them to creak and groan under her weight, but the stairs seemed solid and almost new in construction. Her grandparents had given her the idea that the cellar was decrepit and dangerous, but Lucy could see it was clean and well organized.

"What's this about, then?" she spoke aloud. Hearing her own voice in the room was somehow comforting. Why would her grandparents put so much work into the musty, unused root cellar? Lucy noted a set of shelves lining one wall. The wall itself was rock, while the others were covered with wooden paneling.

From her perch on the bottom stair, Lucy could see the shelves were not quite against the wall, probably owing to some natural outcropping of rock. "Still, worth looking around since I'm down here," she told herself.

Lucy shone her flashlight into the space behind the bookshelf. The solid rock wall looked unremarkable, but Lucy spied something on the floor in the narrow space behind the shelf. She reached in but couldn't quite touch it. She leaned her body against the side of the shelf and pushed a little harder, thinking just a few centimeters more and she'd have it. Instead, the entire shelf moved, swinging out and away from the wall, causing Lucy to stumble. She landed hard on her knee and knew that it would have a nice bruise tomorrow.

Picking up the piece of paper, Lucy stood up and dusted herself off. It was just a scrap of paper, but Lucy could tell it was quite old from just the feel of it—brittle, thick, rough-rubbed edges. There was only one word on it, in an italicized handwritten script, although it looked as if there was meant to be more that had been torn off. "Illuminate," it read.

Lucy tucked it in her pocket and looked again at the rock wall. Why would anyone make a big set of shelves swing away from a rock wall? She touched the surface of it, but the rock was rough. She held her flashlight up and shone it directly on the surface of the wall. Something seemed a little odd about it. There were depressions in the rock, something that seemed normal enough, but the more Lucy looked at it, the more the pattern emerged to her eyes. The depressions seemed too evenly spaced to be natural and formed an almost perfect circle around the rock wall, probably three feet in diameter.

"Curiouser and curiouser," she murmured. The words from the children in her dream came back to her mind as she pondered the shape. She couldn't unsee it now. "We dance round in a ring and suppose . . . the secret sits in the middle and knows . . ."

Almost instinctively, Lucy reached up and pushed her fingers into the depressions, one by one. As she reached the last one in the circle, she heard a noise. It sounded faint and far off, like rock grinding on rock. It lasted only a moment, and then it stopped.

Lucy's heart pounded in her ears as she waited to see what would happen next. She stood there, unmoving, for what felt like a lifetime, but she knew it was only a few minutes. She thumped on the rock wall with the butt of her flashlight—nothing. She pushed on the wall. Again, nothing. Feeling foolish, Lucy stepped back and pulled the shelves back into place.

"Maybe not today," she said to the room, "but soon, I will figure you out." She turned the light off behind her as she ascended the stairs. She closed the hatch, and instead of putting the boxes back where she found them, she dragged over the heaviest piece of furniture she could find. It was an old cedar trunk, covered in plastic sheeting and wrapped in a mover's blanket. After she was sure it covered the hatch and didn't look out of place, she sat down on it. She wasn't sure exactly why, but she felt better knowing the root cellar was hidden from view.

Lucy heard the doorbell as soon as she came upstairs. She locked the door to the basement behind her and went to open the shop. She turned the sign around in the window and opened her door. *Apparently, the best way to drum up business is to be unavailable for half an hour.* She laughed to herself. It was good to see some of her regular customers coming into the store. It made things feel normal, at least for the moment.

*L*ucy stayed busy over the next week between working regular hours in the shop plus gathering art supplies and everything else she needed for her fairy garden party book faire. Several people came by and dropped off boxes for her, saying Hattie or Honey or another committee member had sent them.

The little girl who came in the week before for a book on tunnels came back with her mom, and they gave Lucy a large bag filled with fairy wings and tulle skirts and flower crowns, as well as some elf ears, felt vests, and boys' costumes with brown trousers shredded at the bottom. Her mom explained that there had been a children's production of A *Midsummer Night's Dream* in the neighboring town, and the costume designer there had sold them for a song—and an invitation to the fairy tea.

Lucy felt overwhelmed by the kindness people were showing. One evening a few nights before the festival, several men showed up with ladders and strings of fairy lights, which they hung throughout the community garden and in all the trees.

She spent an afternoon adding strings to pieces of crystal from an antique chandelier in the attic. Then she hung them from tree branches all around the garden so, day or evening, the fairy garden would sparkle and twinkle like magic. Volunteers set up tables for her, and cushions came in by the box load to scatter over the grass. Lucy found some lovely gauzy organza tablecloths in her grandmother's stash that would be perfect for a party—pink, green, yellow, peach, and rose. She pulled several boxes of books from the shelves—everything she had on fairies and fairy tales, as well as many books about nature—plants and animals, ocean and forest.

The morning of the festival, Lucy woke up early. She'd been too excited to sleep well, so she figured it would be nice to make some tea and relax a bit before her volunteers showed up. They were coming at eight o'clock, and the festival began officially at ten o'clock. It was already a nice temperature outside, so she carried her tea out to the front porch. From there, she could see a good portion of the garden and a bit of the woods that bordered it. Lucy smiled to herself. *It's going to be a wonderful day.* She couldn't wait to see the happy faces of children enjoying the book fair.

A high school student had volunteered to do some of the story times, and several other girls had signed up to help with face painting and general crowd control. A couple of shade awnings had already arrived. Lucy was grateful that someone thought of it because the weather forecast called for a warm and sunny day.

Just as she was gathering up her tea things, Lucy saw a flicker of motion at the edge of the garden. A man—well dressed and tall, scurried from the garden into the trees. Lucy didn't like the look of that. Why was someone out there so early? She didn't recognize the man, and with all the trouble she'd had with strangers and mysterious visitors, she thought she should call someone right away, especially since the entire area would soon be filled with children.

She went in and picked up her cell, thinking that she would call Police Captain Andy Harrison. Of everyone who worked there, she felt the most comfortable with him. The phone rang a few times, and then a friendly-sounding dispatcher picked up. Lucy gave them her name and asked for the captain, but he let her know Captain Harrison wasn't in today. He was setting up the police booth for the festival. Lucy walked back outside with her phone in hand and saw the back of a uniformed police officer disappearing into the same spot in the trees. *They must already be on top of it.* She thanked the dispatcher and declined to leave a message. She was glad someone was on watch.

With only a few minutes before her volunteers arrived, Lucy rushed to get ready. It was time to go full steam ahead. Tor made an appearance, coming through the cat door, looking quite pleased with himself. Lucy stopped and stroked his ears and scratched under his chin, which set his motor running. She opened a can of his favorite food and filled his water dish in the kitchen. "You behave today, Tor. Lots of people will be around, and I hope you come say hello." Tor just blinked at her slowly and went to eat his breakfast.

The sun was burning off the soft overnight fog. The day promised to be beautiful. It would be a lot of work, but Lucy relished the chance to be involved with the festival. She wanted to make it even more magical than she remembered from her childhood.

Lucy was dragging a large box of books from the foyer to the porch when her volunteers arrived. She had two volunteers help her carry out the books and set them up on the child-sized bookshelves scattered around the garden. Three girls came in wearing cutoffs and tees, carrying bags with their fairy costumes to change into. Lucy sent them upstairs to her grandparents' room to hang their dresses until they were done setting up. Sam,

Lucy's lawyer, arrived next. Mark followed closely behind.

"I thought you were out to sea, Mark!" Lucy couldn't hide her delight.

"And miss the festival?" He laughed and kissed her cheek. "Every year we get permission to come into port and set up a recruiting station during the festival. Several of the crew take turns manning the booth and talking to interested young people, and the rest get some much-needed shore leave."

"I'm so glad you're here." Lucy felt her cheeks grow red as she realized Sam was closely observing the pair with an amused look on his face. "But are you here to work?"

"Lucy, I'd do anything for you. I pulled some strings to get myself assigned to be your volunteer today. It helps that Hattie loves me so much!"

Lucy gleefully handed him a box and told him where to take it.

Standing back, Lucy took in the scene. The food tables were set up under the shelters, and there were bookshelves scattered around, with books displayed next to flowers and branches and pinecones. Strings of flowers decorated the tea tables, and the organza tablecloths gave a dreamy pastel look to the garden. Flowers bloomed nearby, and boxes of costumes and wings and crowns occupied one corner. The face painters were organizing their stations, and all the girls had changed into their long fairy dresses. With crowns of roses and other flowers woven together, the young ladies looked the part.

The first food delivery had been set up, and Hattie had seen to it that the delivery folks knew exactly how to organize it for Lucy's ease. All that remained was for Lucy to change. Sam and Mark were sitting on a loveseat under a tree. They'd helped themselves to a few of the treats from Honey's Bakery. She couldn't blame them. Her stomach growled madly, so she planned to change and get back quickly before all the beignets were gone.

A few minutes later, Lucy emerged, transformed into a fairy queen, complete with crown and wand. She'd saved a costume from a Halloween party in college—one based on the character of the good witch in the Wizard of Oz. It was pink, fluffy, and magical, and she was grateful it still fit! Mark and Sam both stood up and applauded as she approached.

Mark said, "Oh, the kids are going to love you!"

Sam added, "They're not the only ones!" He gave a cheeky wink.

"Okay, that's enough," she said, blushing. "Don't you have anything to do? Girls, can you come over here for a minute? We have some non-fairies in the garden."

Mark saw the girls approaching with elf ears and leafy crowns and pretended to make a run for it, but Sam jumped in front of him, guarding him like a basketball player.

Lucy was helpless with laughter as the girls finally caught her wayward elves and crowned them. They were just in time to meet a group of about a dozen children walking up the sidewalk with their parents.

"Welcome to the Fairy Garden Party Book Faire," Lucy greeted them. "Come, have some tea with me!"

Lucy sat down on a wrought iron chair and clutched a feather pillow to her chest. Looking around, she saw Sam saying goodbye to two little girls and their mother. The girls were bouncing up and down, holding flower crowns and a bag of books. *Good*, Lucy thought, *they'll be readers for life!* She looked around for Mark but didn't see him anywhere. Maybe he'd gone up to the house to use a real bathroom instead of the portaloos tucked into an unused corner of the garden.

Lucy yawned. Then her stomach growled. She'd been so busy entertaining children all morning that she hadn't stopped to have anything to eat herself. There weren't many people lingering right now, and the two children who remained were both older and curled up on cushions, reading books.

She dragged herself up from her seat and over to the food tables. The pickings were slim, even though regular deliveries of goodies had arrived throughout the day, brought by committee members. Lucy's stomach gurgled, but nothing looked appealing to her. Her phone rang then, and she pulled it out to see who was calling. It was Hattie, so she quickly answered.

"Hi, Lucy. I've been getting glowing reports about your booth all day long. You're the hit of the festival! Mark was here. He just left. He called me and told me you hadn't stopped to take a break all day! He's bringing you something to eat, so just hold tight, my dear, the cavalry is on the way!"

Lucy laughed. "I think you mean the Coast Guard, Hattie! Mark's in the Coast Guard, so he can't be in the cavalry!"

Hattie told Lucy she planned to send a group of high school boys over to help her carry things indoors for the evening. Lucy glanced at the time on her phone, shocked to see that it was already five o'clock. Time had flown by much faster than she'd realized. No wonder her stomach protested!

The teen girls wandered over and asked Lucy what they could do now that everyone had cleared out. She directed them to start packing away the paints and costumes.

Sam, who had stopped to pick up books left sitting on picnic tables and blankets, made his way over to Lucy.

"Hey, Luce. Is it okay if I call you Luce?" He smiled warmly at her.

She suppressed a quick smile. Mark had asked her the same thing, recently. "You can call me anything you like, Sam. I wouldn't have made it through today without your help."

"I like the way it sounds. Luce. It just rolls off the tongue. Can I call you 'Lu' too?" Sam's eyes were full of mischief.

"You can call me Lu, but not Lu-Lu," she laughed. "And please don't call me Lucilla!"

"Oh, wow, is that your first name? Lucilla?"

Lucy could see the wheels turning in Sam's mind as he tried to think of a witty remark.

"Yes, that's my first name! My middle name is Phoebe. And yes, they both mean 'light.' Kind of redundant of my parents if you ask me!"

"That's super pretty, Luce. I like it," he replied. "I bet they just couldn't decide which one was nicer, so they gave you both. And"—he paused—"you do kind of glow."

Lucy's cheeks grew red. Before she could reply, he added, "Maybe tomorrow you should wear more sunscreen!"

Lucy punched him in the arm and smiled.

"Sam, you're the little brother I never wished for!"

"Gee, thanks!" Sam pretended to pout. "Oh, by the way," he said, "I do need to talk to you about some legal matters. Do you think you could stop by the office tomorrow evening as soon as we're done here? I have some things to show you. I'll even pick up dinner from the cafe so we can meet and eat. Deal?"

"Sure. Can you tell me what it's about?"

"Better to wait. Just head over about six-thirty or so. That should give us plenty of time to eat and take care of everything before the concert in the square. I hear we have a Three Dog Night tribute band opening. Wouldn't want to miss that. And the committee outdid themselves this year. They got Cali-Train to play for the main event."

Lucy couldn't believe it. Cali-Train was one of her favorite bands. She was surprised they'd play for such a small venue, but Sam told her one of the band members had grown up spending his summers in Seaview. He explained that the mayor had offered the band a vacation package for themselves and their families during the festival. And one of the local ranches with several guest cabins had offered them nice lodging for their stay. Several of the band members had kids, Lucy knew, so she hoped she'd get to meet a few of them in person.

Mark arrived just then with a box full of dinner entrees and sides, and with him came several members of the high school wrestling team. The teen girls quickly took charge and showed them what to carry into the bookstore for the evening. The boys took the opportunity to show off their strength as they tried to outdo each other carrying boxes. The girls exchanged glances and kept giggling. Within just a few minutes, the teens had cleaned up and cleared everything away. One of the boys even grabbed the two plastic bags of waste and recycling as the group all left together. One of the girls hugged Lucy as they said goodbye, and Lucy thanked them for working so hard to make a magical day for all the kids.

Sam pulled up chairs to one of the tables and sat while Mark unloaded the feast sent over by Hattie. There was a container of pulled pork that smelled as if it had been on the smoker only minutes before. Plus three different barbecue sauces, soft buns, pickles, sweet coleslaw, Hattie's famous loaded baked potato salad, baked beans with pieces of bacon on top, and a large glass bottle of lavender lemonade. Lucy groaned with delight and called dibs on going first. Mark and Sam joked about not coming between a woman and good barbecue, and neither objected to letting her serve herself first. Mark said he and Sam had both stopped long enough to eat a sandwich during the day, and tomorrow, they were going to make sure she did the same.

"It's no good if the fairy queen faints during story time," Mark said.

Lucy couldn't argue. Her mouth was full of the best thing she'd ever eaten. She didn't even care that she had Carolina sauce dripping from the corner of her mouth. Hattie's special southern barbecue was heaven.

Chapter Twelve

*L*ucy stretched up on her tippy toes and then rocked back on her heels. There were going to be fireworks later out over the water. The launch tubes were set up on a floating barge and detonated by a remote.

Sam had gone home to change, and Mark had to be out with his ship to patrol the coast near town. Every year, lots of people went out to watch the fireworks in small boats and kayaks, and it never failed that at least one tourist would fall into the water and need help back to shore. Lucy knew she could see the fireworks from home, so she decided a hot bath and a little rest was in order. Then she could put on her comfortable pajamas and robe, make some hot chocolate, and watch the fireworks from the widow's walk atop one section of the roof on the original Victorian home.

Lucy settled into some cushions on a built-in seat in the cupola. Enclosed on three sides, it was a cozy spot to look out over the dark ocean. She'd heard many tales of ships lost at sea while sailor's wives watched in vain for their husbands to return, which gave the structure its sad name—widow's walk. She'd asked her grandmother about it, who was quick to reassure Lucy that no sad widows had ever walked on this particular roof because every expected ship had always come in.

Wrapped up in a cozy robe and blankets against the cool sea air, Lucy had no more than begun to sip her hot chocolate when the fireworks started. The wind carried the excited cheers of all the folks sitting on the beach and in the town square below. Lucy was grateful for the solitude after such a long and busy day. She sighed, half with contentment, half in fatigue.

Under the light of an especially bright and rapid series of colorful explosions, Lucy caught sight of some shadowy movement across the lawn. As the light faded, so did her view, and when the next bursts lit the sky, she thought she saw someone dart from the edge of the lawn into the woods. Her heart skipped a couple of beats, but she reminded herself the house was locked, and the alarm was on. She thought perhaps it was just a deer or her tired eyes playing tricks on her. *Either way, I'm safe here. I'll tell Mark about it tomorrow.*

The next day was even busier than the last. Word of mouth had spread about the Fairy Garden Party Book Faire. The committee sent Lucy twice the helpers, and Hattie sent her twice the "fairy food" for the little people. Sam brought word that Mark had urgent Coast Guard business and wouldn't be able to help, but Lucy didn't have time to be disappointed. Around noon, Hattie herself appeared with a lunch tray and dragged her into a corner of the shady part of the garden.

"Don't bother protesting, I'm not going to take no for an answer. Sit here," Hattie said, pointing at a petite wrought iron bench surrounded by miniature rose bushes. "And give me your wings!"

Lucy thought about resisting, but knowing Hattie, she realized there wasn't any point. Besides, she'd caught sight of the tray Hattie held and decided she didn't want to protest at all. Something smelled amazing, and Lucy's stomach growled loud enough for Hattie to hear it.

"See? Your body is telling you to stop and eat!" Hattie laughed. Lucy handed over her wings and her wand and told Hattie to have fun.

"Take your time, Lucy," she said. "You need a rest as much as you need food. Besides, I've always wanted to play dress-up and be a fairy. I promise I won't scare the children too much!" The twinkle in her eyes told a different story, making Lucy laugh.

"Thank you for lunch. I'll eat every bite," Lucy promised.

Lucy opened the containers on the tray and found a chicken salad sandwich with bacon, sun-dried tomatoes, and spinach mixed in, served on a soft half-whole wheat sandwich bread made especially for Hattie's cafe. There was a small bowl of creamy broccoli cheddar soup to go with it, as well as an assortment of cut vegetables—red bell peppers, cucumber spears, carrot sticks, mushrooms, and sugar snap peas. There was a peach nectar iced tea, too, that had a hint of cinnamon in it. Lucy thought it was wonderful and did as she promised—she inhaled every bite. She sat back on the bench and closed her eyes, savoring the feeling of being satisfied and surrounded by the sweet-smelling roses.

This part of the garden was one of the oldest parts, situated nearest to the back of Lucy's house. The trees here were big and provided abundant shade. Tangled brush and young saplings had overgrown part of the garden. Lucy could just see the vine-covered remains of the old summer house peeking out from between the branches of heavy vegetation. She wondered why her grandparents left it that way, nearly completely reclaimed by nature, when the rest of the grounds and gardens were immaculate. There was even a wall of blackberry bushes growing up around one side that got just enough sun to feed the birds and other animals some delicious berries throughout the summer.

Lucy sat for a minute longer, listening to the sounds of Hattie reading a book in funny voices and children's laughter. She smiled to herself. Hattie was an all-around talent, from cooking to making characters come alive.

Just as Lucy was about to leave with the remains of her lunch, she heard another noise. It was the slow, unmistakable creak of a rickety hinge opening. She froze, realizing that someone must be inside the summer house. If it were one of the children who had wandered back there, it could be disastrous. She had no idea what kinds of broken glass and rusty nails or slithering creatures might be in there. She was about to call out when she saw a man dressed in a camouflage hunting jacket and olive pants emerge from the far side of the summer house and dart across the lawn. He ducked into the woods and disappeared.

Lucy's heart hammered—he must have been the man she thought she'd seen the night before. She was going to have to tell someone. Hopefully, one of the town's police officers could come by and check it out. She knew they were incredibly busy with the festival happening, and perhaps it was nothing but a squatter, but Lucy had more than enough of the strange things happening around her. If needed, she'd drag an officer out there since someone was lurking where they had no right to be, and there were kids all around.

Lucy found Hattie surrounded by a group of giggling children. She was playing an improvised game of duck, duck, fairy with them, only she was using her wand to choose a child to be the chaser of the loser from the previous round. The kids loved it—most of them had their faces painted or wore flower or leaf crowns in their hair or had picked something from the costume basket to wear for the game. A visiting photographer captured action shots for the local paper.

Hattie spied Lucy and gave her a big wink.

"Okay, fairies, gnomes, trolls, and satyrs, everyone on your feet! It's time for the fairy fleet of foot contest! Everyone, line up beside me. When I say go, race to the rock wall at the end of the garden and back, and then the fairy queen herself will have a prize for you!"

The children scrambled into position, a few looking profoundly serious about the event and others just going along for the fun of it. Lucy noticed one little fairy in a yellow, gauzy dress who hung back from the crowd. When Hattie shouted for the children to go, the little girl sat down on the grass looking forlorn. Hattie came over and gave Lucy her wings back and pulled out a tiara from a box stashed under a table.

"Here, Lucy, this was my homecoming queen tiara. It hasn't seen the light of day in, well, too many years! I thought it would go great with your flower crown! Oh, and when the kids come back, I have fairy cakes just over there on the table in the big pink box. You be the fairy queen and give them their prize. I've got to run—there's a food shortage at the police and fire services booth."

"Hattie, while you're there, would you mind asking Captain Harrison to stop by sometime later this afternoon? I need to tell him about some strange men running across my lawn yesterday and today. One came out of the old summer house and ran into the woods just a few minutes ago. It worries me with so many children here."

"I will, Lucy. You be careful, and don't go anywhere alone, please. You've had enough trouble this summer."

Lucy couldn't argue with that. She noticed the little girl in the yellow dress was still sitting alone in the grass, so Lucy made her way over. All the other children would be back in a minute, and she wanted to see if she could help her join in and enjoy the party.

"Hi, I'm Lucy. What's your name?"

"I'm called Caro, but my real name is South Carolina," the little girl replied, looking down at her shoes.

Lucy bent down to the girl's level and smiled at her.

"What a fantastic name! Would you like to be my helper? I really need a junior fairy queen!" she asked.

"Can I be a junior fairy princess instead?" she countered. Her eyes had lit up at the prospect.

"Absolutely. In fact, you get to wear the crown!" Lucy took off Hattie's tiara and placed it on the little girl's head. "Now come with me and we'll go get the prizes ready!"

By the time the other woodland creatures made it back from the garden wall, Lucy and her helper had pulled all the fairy cakes out of the box and set them on the table. There was a large glass beverage dispenser filled with lavender lemonade in a stunning shade of violet. Caro's smile lit her whole face as she stood on the serving side of the table. She helped Lucy serve cupcakes to the racers until several of the other girls complimented her on her crown and her dress and asked her if she'd like to come over and sit on the princess pillows and look at books with them.

She hugged Lucy and asked if she could be excused.

Lucy hugged her back. "You're the best junior fairy princess I've ever seen." The little girl skipped off with a new friend, hand in hand. Lucy smiled as she watched her go. *Someday, I want a little girl of my own. And I hope she's half as sweet as Caro!*

A man approached her, interrupting her daydream, to ask about buying books.

She gave a last glance at her little helper and turned to answer him. Momentarily stunned into silence, Lucy recognized him as the lead singer of Cali-Train.

"I, uh, hello. I'm Lucy," she said. "Can you repeat the question?" She hoped she didn't look as starstruck as she felt, knowing that the band was well known for being down-to-earth people who lived anything but a rockstar life.

"Sure." He smiled. "I'm Ned. Are all the books for sale? My daughter has a stack of them she'd like to take home. By the way, thank you for letting her help you. She can be so shy sometimes and has a tough time making friends. I appreciate you letting her wear your crown."

"That's your daughter? Caro?" Lucy hadn't seen her famous father nearby when she'd been talking to her. "I had no idea. She seemed like she just needed a little encouragement. She's such a sweet girl!"

"Thank you. I was hanging back by the bookshelves. I hoped if I gave her a little room she might join in the games with the other kids. I was about to come to her rescue when I saw you approach her, and you were so good with her I thought I'd wait and see. Do you have children?"

"No," Lucy blushed a bit. "I'm not married, no kids. At least, not yet."

"Well, you're a natural. You'll be a great mom."

Lucy felt a little heat behind her eyes and a small lump trying to form in her throat. "Thank you. That means a lot."

"Now about those books. Are they for sale?"

"Oh, yes, absolutely!" she replied.

"Okay, I'll take them." He waved his hand over toward the reading area populated with several small groups of children looking at various books.

"Sure thing, have Caro bring over the ones she wants, and I'll ring them up for you," she said.

"No, I mean, I'll take all the books. Everything you have out there. I'd like to buy them all and let Caro keep what she wants, and then we'll give the rest away to the other children. Fostering a love of reading is one of the best things you can do for kids. I have a foundation that provides children with books online. Can I give you a card? Maybe we could work together on some ideas for future giveaways." He smiled and waited for her reply.

Lucy was speechless again. She decided Cali-Train was now her favorite band of all time. "I'd love to do that," she replied. "Are you sure you want to buy all the books?"

"Absolutely. I'll just tell the kids to bring up the book they want and maybe we can keep a tab open? I'll send Caro over

first, so I can take her stack of books back to the tour bus. It'll
be a great distraction for her since we have a long drive tomorrow, and she's already read everything she has twice. If there are
books are left over, could you just box them up and donate them
to the local library for us?"

Lucy was thrilled. Not just because the incredible act of gen-
erosity meant her bookstore would be in the black this month,
either. It was the thought of seeing all the kids' eyes light up,
getting to take home a free book of their own.

He summoned Caro and paid for her stack of books with
cash. For the rest, he left a credit card on file for Lucy with the
name of his foundation. Lucy told him she would give him the
friends and family discount since it was such a large order, and
he thanked her, telling her his foundation was a nonprofit, and
every dollar saved would go toward more books for more children. Caro returned Hattie's crown and gave Lucy another hug.

"Will you come to Daddy's show tonight? If you do, look for
me. I'm going with my mom and my brother. I'll look out for
you," Caro said in a sweet tone. "I can't wait to tell my mom I
met the fairy queen!"

Chapter Thirteen

he afternoon went by in a blur as the word spread about the free books. Lucy limited each child to one and had to ask a few parents not to take books meant for the children when they tried to go through the line. Most were pleasant about it, but one woman raised a bit of a ruckus, declaring that if they were free, it shouldn't matter who took them. Lucy kept her cool, though, and explained that it was only one book per child.

A few minutes later, Lucy noticed the same little girl coming back through the line with another book, so she decided to take matters into her own hands.

"Hi sweetie, I see you have another book there! Since you already have one, this one will be nine dollars and ninety-five cents plus tax." She didn't want the girl to be upset or feel bad about her mother's behavior, so she added, "I'm glad to see you love books so much! I love to read too!"

"My mom didn't give me any money. I'm not sure what to do," the little girl answered.

"Oh, I'm sure she meant to! I'll hold this here for you, and you can go ask her. Don't worry, I'll keep it right here. And if your mom decides not to buy it, it will go straight in the library box, and you can check it out for free there in a week or two!"

The little girl didn't return and neither did her mother.

Good! Lucy thought. She didn't want to have to deal with the woman's sullenness over the matter any longer. True to her word, she stuck the book in a box for donations, hoping the little girl would visit the library and read it to her heart's content.

Just before the end of the day, her helpers started gathering up the leftover children's books and reported back to Lucy that there were fewer than a dozen. The young men from the high school came back to help. The one who bragged he was a math whiz got the job of adding up all the totals and applying the discount. Even with the lower rate, the sales were over fifteen hundred dollars. Lucy was excited to think about browsing the distributor's catalog to restock The Cozy Cat's inventory for children.

She rang Caro's father to tell him the total before she ran it through on his credit card to make sure it was all right. He thanked her and told her that she'd let him off easy. He was delighted the giveaway had been such an enormous success. With the business end settled, Lucy packed up everything she could for the next day, assisted by the small army of volunteers Hattie sent to help her.

Then it hit her. There was still one more day of the festival, and she was out of children's books! She supposed she would have to tell Hattie that the fairy book party would have to wrap up a day early. She gave Hattie a quick call and sketched the situation out on her voicemail. There was nothing else she could do, but perhaps they could continue with the face painting and tea party events.

She called Sam, who'd only left half an hour before, to postpone their dinner meeting. She was hoping to catch part of the Cali-Train concert and asked him to save a spot for her if he was going to be there. She was curious to know what he had for her, wondering what sort of mysterious objects her grandparents left her, but that would have to wait. She needed to come up with a new plan for the fairy garden party book faire, and fast.

Lucy quickly started brainstorming games and activities the kids could do with items she had on hand. She put together a "fairy ring toss" game and found a few fun live-action role-playing—or LARP—games for fairies online, complete with a storyline to read to the children. Lucy remembered there was a box of foam swords in storage—a promotional item sent a few years before for the launch of the latest book in a popular series about wizards and knights—so she added those to her supplies. They would have a battle royale to save the fairy queen and her court.

Satisfied that she had done all she could do, Lucy grabbed a jacket and her water bottle and headed for the town square. The place was already packed with people on blankets and in camp chairs, with children running and playing games along the side where there was a small playground. There were vendors and food trucks along the street that bordered the other side of the square, so Lucy bought a hot panini sandwich and a cream puff for her dinner. She wandered through the crowd a bit, wondering if she'd find Sam or anyone she knew with an extra corner of a blanket she could share. She was just about to give up when she saw Hattie waving frantically at her from near the front of the crowd. She and Sam had set up early and had saved her a prime spot!

Cali-Train was a hugely popular band and put on an incredible show. The happy, energetic music they played was simply perfect for the summer evening. As the sun finally set behind them and twilight turned to darkness, strobing blue and purple lights lit up the stage and crowd. Lucy couldn't believe how close they were to the band and she enjoyed dancing with the crowd and singing the catchy tunes at the top of her voice.

Halfway through the concert, they slowed it down and sang a

medley of nostalgic tunes. A few of the band members' children came up on stage and helped with the singing. Lucy was happy to see Caro there, holding her dad's hand and still wearing the flower crown she'd picked out at the fairy faire. Caro spotted Lucy and waved at her, then blew her a few shy kisses, which Lucy pretended to catch and hold to her heart. The little girl pointed to the side of the stage where Lucy saw a lovely woman who was unmistakably Caro's mother. The woman lifted both arms to Lucy in a kind gesture and mouthed "Thank you!" to Lucy, warming her through and through.

Sam drove Lucy home and made sure she was safely inside before he left. Lucy, exhausted, fell into bed and went straight to sleep with her clothes on. She slept so soundly that she never even knew when Tor jumped up on her hip to curl up and sleep on top of her.

It seemed no time had passed when her alarm chimed insistently, punctuated by the sound of someone ringing the doorbell over and over and her phone ringing at the same time.

"What in the world . . ." Lucy sat up too quickly and felt a bit of vertigo as she reached over to shut off the alarm. She accidentally knocked it off the nightstand as she grabbed for her phone, turning the radio on as the clock lodged itself between the bed and the wall. The doorbell, in the meantime, continued to ring. Ignoring the clock radio—a relic of her grandfather's— Lucy grabbed a robe and headed downstairs.

Tor was sitting on the top of one of the leather chairs but looked ready to bolt away. He let out a long meow to Lucy, informing her that he was not happy with the level of racket going on. Lucy's phone had gone to voicemail but started to ring again just as the doorbell did. She didn't know which one to answer first so she did both, pulling the door of The Cozy Cat open and shouting hello into the phone at the same time.

On the doorstep was Hattie, with a bag in one hand and her

phone in the other. Hattie said hello, and Lucy heard her echo in both ears. Hattie was also the person on the phone!

"Hattie, what's going on?!" The lack of sleep combined with her early alarm and the unexpected visitor was making Lucy feel discombobulated.

Hattie set about making coffee and putting fresh pastries on a plate. She told Lucy her plan. Lucy quickly agreed to it and ran to take a shower. As the warm water eased the tension in her shoulders, she said to herself, "Leave it to Hattie to come up with a plan to kill two birds with one stone!"

Lucy hurried to dress and pulled her damp hair up into a french twist secured by a wide-toothed clip. She looked in the mirror and decided she was going nowhere without a quick swipe of lipstick and a little mascara to combat the fatigue showing on her face. Satisfied that it was as good as it was going to get, she slipped on comfortable shoes and ran down the stairs.

Hattie stood in the doorway of the bookshop giving directions to a group of older men and women. Lucy had to smile. Only Hattie could marshal a small army of volunteers at the crack of dawn on the last day of the festival. There were two vans in the driveway—one filled with boxes and the other open and now empty—for the volunteers.

Lucy counted. There were already thirty boxes of books on her wide front porch.

"Hattie, how did you pull this off? And how many more boxes are there?"

"There's just a few more boxes in the van. They're almost done! When I called Maisy, who oversees the Friends of the Library program, she thought it was a marvelous idea and called all her regular volunteers. This will help the library so much! They had a lot of donated children's books in storage, and business has been slow in the little bookshop they run as a fundraiser for the library. If your team can sell the paperbacks for fifty cents and the hardbacks for a dollar, I think they'll go fast. Oh, and Maisy offered to split proceeds with you so you can do something nice for your high school volunteers. I heard they've been working hard!"

"That's amazing, Hattie. I think my volunteers would say they're already being richly rewarded with treats from you and with Honey's pastries! I think we'd rather give the entire amount back to the library. I'll spring for a pizza party for the teens. They'll love that."

The library volunteers finished unloading, and several stopped to thank Lucy and wish her luck. They piled into the two empty vans with Hattie leading the way. The coffee Hattie had brewed was waiting, and the aroma drew her inside. There was a plate of Heavenly Cinnamon Buns, for which Hattie was famous, waiting beside the coffee pot. Lucy groaned with delight. "*This* was worth getting up early!" she said to herself and to Tor, who looked with interest at the cinnamon bun Lucy was devouring.

Shortly before the high school volunteers were scheduled to arrive, there was a knock at the door. Tor took off like a shot to the front of The Cozy Cat and perched on one of the leather chairs, peering out at the person on the porch.

Lucy heard Tor hiss and let out a growl, completely out of character for the normally laid back, friendly feline. Lucy peered out the window herself before opening the door. She was relieved to see that it was just Officer Franklin, and he didn't appear to be holding his weapon. Lucy had largely forgiven the handsome young officer for drawing his gun and pointing it at her after someone attacked Fuchsia in the bookstore. Still, she was a bit wary as she greeted him.

"Good morning," she said, "what can I do for you?"

"Morning, ma'am. Captain sent me to check on you. You called and didn't leave a message? He wanted to make sure everything was all right here."

"Oh, yes! I was just going to tell him about a couple of strange incidents—I've seen a man I don't know a couple of times on the property here, once going into the woods behind the garden and once coming out of the overgrown summer house. With all the kids here this week, I was worried, especially after everything else that has happened. But I saw an officer go into the woods shortly after the man did, so I assumed you guys were aware and keeping tabs. But I just don't like having someone in the summer house— it's full of old rusty things and broken glass—and since it's mostly hidden from view, it has me worried. If something happened to a child . . ."

Officer Franklin nodded but looked a little pale. "Did you get a good look at this man?"

"No, not really. The first time was from up on the roof during the fireworks, so it was dark and far away. The other times it was only the back of a person I saw, and they quickly disappeared. I'm afraid I wouldn't be any help in identifying them."

Officer Franklin wrote a couple of notes in his book and thanked Lucy. "I'll give this information to the captain. I'll ask him to step up patrols and to send someone to check out the summer house situation. I'll come by myself while the kids' events are going on, just to make sure all is well."

Lucy was relieved. It would be nice to have another set of eyes keeping watch. She offered Officer Franklin coffee and a cinnamon bun, but he was on duty and couldn't stop longer. She quickly wrapped up one of the cinnamon buns in plastic and insisted he take it with him. He didn't even try to resist. Hattie's Heavenly Cinnamon Buns were irresistible.

The day flew by. Word about Lucy's event had continued to spread, and Lucy could swear there three times more children than she'd had on the previous two days. The children loved the games she'd designed for them. The foam swords turned out to be extremely popular, and all day long there were hordes of elves and fairies and goblins strategizing and battling to save or kidnap the fairy queen.

Released from their other duties, the young men from the high school wrestling team were free to spend the day where they liked. Before the day was over, Lucy counted almost as many helpers as she had children. The girls had also invited friends to come help. They gave Lucy frequent breaks from being the sought-after fairy queen, and several of the boys took over the role-playing game and organized small armies. Lucy smiled. *Teenagers are still very much kids at heart.*

Many parents came, as well, snapping up "bargain basement prices" on the books available. One local parent told Lucy that she was buying as many as she could fit in a suitcase because she was taking a cruise and stopping over at an island where local residents needed books. Destroyed by a hurricane, the only library for children had great need and little purchasing power, so several people in her cruise group were gathering books to deliver to them.

Hearing that brought tears to Lucy's eyes. Imagining children with no access to books was a painful thought. By the end of the day, there were only two small boxes of books left unsold, so Lucy added up their value and put her own money into the lockbox. She had one of the boys set them inside the store for her. She knew Hattie could connect her with the lady who was gathering books for the cruise to send with her. She smiled at the thought of the island kids seeing their little library start to fill up again.

*L*ucy woke up gradually the next morning. First, she heard the songs of the morning birds before she dozed back to sleep. She found herself wandering through a previous dream where children danced in a circle and sang the verse from the poem that Fuchsia Butterfield had underlined for her. She tried to stop the children and ask them what they were singing, what it meant, but in the way of dreams, they couldn't hear her. She remembered falling in the dream and tried to warn the children that the ground might give way, she couldn't say the words no matter how she tried. Then one of the small girls disappeared as if the earth had swallowed her up, and the other children began to scream. Lucy screamed with them and woke herself up.

Tor, who was not a skinny cat, sat on her hip, staring at her. She reached out to pet him and pull him next to her. With Tor for comfort, she quickly brushed the scare off and fell asleep once more. Lucy's alarm woke her next. She'd changed it to the gentle chiming sound of harp strings. She knew she could afford to sleep in a little bit this morning since the Hometown Days festival was finally over, but Tor was quite sure the alarm was for his breakfast. He insisted with many meows that it was time she got up to feed him. His purrs and nudges and plaintive cries were enough to convince her that she was finally up for the day.

Lucy was sore from all the games and physical labor of the last few days. Most of the town would be sleeping off the festivities this morning, she imagined. She carried a cup of coffee with a spoon of chocolate hazelnut butter swirled into it to the front porch and changed her sign to reflect an afternoon opening. Lucy smiled to herself, thinking she'd earned it over the last few days. After coffee, a nice long shower sounded perfect.

She forsook her grandmother's rocking chair and settled instead on the top stair of the porch next to the gorgeous hydrangea bush blooming in fresh, lively blues. She leaned in to study the blossom next to her, looking at it from the back side. She'd never realized how beautiful hydrangeas were from behind! It looked like a whole miniature world inside, or maybe a fairy's bedchamber. Then she saw it and squealed. Two nictitating eyes looking back at her. The small green frog, whose hiding place she'd discovered, jumped out at her. She managed to hang on to her coffee, but only just. The frog leaped away into the grass and disappeared, but not before croaking his displeasure at her intrusion.

After her shower, Lucy took extra time to pamper herself. She exfoliated with a Japanese cloth she'd bought online, and then worked a fragrant body lotion into her skin. Her thirsty skin welcomed the green tea and chamomile face mask that soothed and hydrated. She even dabbed on some under-eye cream. Lucy didn't have any true wrinkles yet, but smile lines had started to form at the corners of her eyes. She didn't mind them so much, but it felt good to take care of herself for a change.

Lucy had dressed for work in the bookstore, choosing a simple cotton summer dress with blue roses scattered across it. She pulled from her jewelry box a pair of blue sodalite earrings, a gift from her grandmother, which matched perfectly. The box was on a table under a window in the back corner of the room. As she closed the box, something outside caught her eye. It was that man again! Crossing the yard quickly from the direction of the garden, he soon disappeared into the wooded area behind the house.

Lucy had had enough. She was going to find out once and for all what was going on and why he was there. She grabbed her hiking boots and pulled them on, quickly doing up the laces. She grabbed her phone on the way out and called Hattie. She didn't have time to look for the card with Officer Franklin's number, but she wanted someone to know where she was going and why. She left the details on Hattie's voicemail as she crossed the yard in the direction she'd seen the man take.

Lucy stepped into the trees, her heart pounding in her ears. It was quite shady as the planted and ornamental trees gave way quickly to native stands of oak and redwood. She looked around but didn't see the man she hoped to follow. Just then, she heard a noise several yards away and crept toward it. She inched around a large redwood until she could see the man pulling some branches and greenery away from something on the ground. Lucy remembered that there had once been an arbor at the back entrance to the estate. But it and the fence that joined it had long since succumbed to the forest. The man appeared to be dragging the remains of the arbor off to one side.

When he finished, Lucy saw what looked like a cellar door built into an incline on the ground. He opened the door, and Lucy pulled back as he took a quick look around. She heard the door close behind him, so she peeked around and saw the way was clear. She quietly worked her way over to the door. It looked old and heavy, with antique iron hinges and fittings. She pulled out her phone and took a picture of the door, then sent it to Hattie along with a text detailing what she'd seen and where she was going.

She knew she probably shouldn't open the door and go in, but she felt compelled. This was yet another secret. She was starting to believe her grandparents had hidden many things from her, but it was on her property, and she needed to know where it led and why someone was trespassing to gain access to it.

Lucy waited a few more minutes just out of sight of the door in case he returned. She was sure she didn't want a confrontation. Finally marshaling her courage, she raised the door and shone the light from her phone into the dark space. A set of wooden stairs led down into the darkness. She couldn't see much beyond the stairs themselves. They appeared to be old but solid and well-crafted. She struggled with the heavy door but managed to hang on to it once she was inside and closed it softly.

Her heart hammered again, so she waited a few minutes until it slowed, breathing silently in through her nose and releasing it slowly. When she felt close to normal, she set out from the bottom of the stairs into what appeared to be an underground tunnel.

Lucy walked a few paces and inspected the walls of the tunnel. They were solid rock, but in a few places roots appeared to be growing through them. The rock was cool and in one place, a bit damp. It seemed to her that she was in a natural but narrow cave. The floor consisted of packed dirt and smooth rock. She kept her light low and let her eyes adjust to the dimmer light, but after she hit a tree root in the ceiling with her head, she felt foolish.

"What was I thinking?" she muttered softly. "This is nuts." She turned around and went quickly back the way she'd come. It seemed shorter going back than it had going forward, and she was relieved to see the wooden staircase sooner than she expected. She climbed the stairs and pushed on the door, but it wouldn't budge. She took a deep breath and pushed with all her strength, but still, she couldn't lift it an inch.

"Oh no. No, no, no!" she whispered. She was well and truly

stuck underground. What if the man came back and found her? What if he didn't, and no one found her? She covered her eyes with her hand and tried to fight down the feeling of dread. Lucy knew the tunnel had to go somewhere, and since she couldn't get out where she was, she decided to go further into it. Maybe there would be another way out, and she could avoid running into the unknown man. She couldn't hear anything—it was eerily quiet. She decided to go as quietly as she could, hoping to hear him before he heard her.

Lucy walked for quite a while, or so it seemed. According to her phone, it was only thirty minutes so far, but they were long minutes to Lucy as she made her way through the tunnel. It was straight, with only a few bends and curves to navigate. In one spot, the tunnel widened and the ground sloped away, but with her phone's flashlight, she could see that it met solid rock just a couple of yards below. Water had collected there, making a dark pool, its surface smooth as glass.

There were no side tunnels or other openings near the surface, so she kept going. She was glad she'd left Hattie all the information on voicemail, but there was no telling how long it would be until Hattie discovered the message.

Lucy wasn't sure when things changed, but she realized she was smelling something familiar—the ocean. There was a faint, fishy smell in the air, and the walls of the tunnel collected a fine layer of moisture. In front of her, the way narrowed as the side-wall of the tunnel curved around into her path. She was afraid this was as far as the tunnel went, but that didn't make sense.

The man she'd followed had not retraced his steps, and there was no way he could have gone past her. She went up to the wall and could see a narrow opening behind it. The ceiling of the tunnel also dipped down, so going into it would mean ducking and shimmying sideways into a blind space. She didn't like it, but she knew the only way out had to be through.

She took a couple of breaths and felt her way forward. The floor sloped down a bit, so Lucy held on to the wall with both hands as she pulled her body around the wall and found footing. She was able to pull her phone from her pocket and use the light again with her hand free, but before she did, she realized she could see faintly. Natural light was coming in from somewhere.

Ahead, she could see an inky, dark chamber off to the right. Chilly air coming from that side of the tunnel brushed her skin. She shuddered. What if he was in there? She quickly made her way forward, and after she went around another cramped protrusion in the tunnel, she no longer needed her phone at all. Her eyes grew accustomed to the brighter light.

She laughed quietly in relief. *The proverbial light at the end of the tunnel.* She could see a bright opening in front of her, but it was tight, and there was yet another wall to shimmy around. She emerged into the daylight only to realize she was on a cliff above the ocean. Her breath caught in her throat—she was higher up than she realized.

Looking around, Lucy didn't see an obvious path down to the beach, but she did see what looked like an easy way to climb up the cliff. With her legs shaking, she scrambled up the rocks to the grassy cliff above. She could see no one nearby so she lifted herself up onto the grass and laid down. A shaky sob escaped her lips, along with a small prayer of gratitude for being above ground again. What she did not see, however, was the captain of a Coast Guard ship watching her through binoculars from the deck of his ship.

Lucy lay on the grass for a few minutes, watching the clouds pass overhead and listening to the sound of the ocean roaring and crashing below—shaken and more than a little unhappy with herself about the decisions she'd made. She needed to call Hattie and tell her where she was and that she was okay. She'd silenced her phone in the tunnel as a precaution, but she hadn't had any signal since she went underground. Her phone's battery level was flashing, indicating that she'd soon lose power altogether. Her stomach sank when she saw that she had missed fifteen calls and had notifications for texts and emails. Hattie was probably worried sick. Knowing that just added to the heap of guilt and regret she felt.

She quickly enabled battery saver mode on her phone then sent off a quick text to Hattie.

"I'm okay. Followed tunnel, came out on cliff. I'm above the cove near the Shore Trail, I think. Going to work my way down. Phone almost dead—will come over as soon as I can."

She hoped that would be enough to reassure Hattie as she set off down the trail, along the bluffs, and down through the park that bordered the shops overlooking the ocean. It was a beautiful day and a beautiful walk. The filtered rays of sunshine piercing the trees and the colorful wildflowers along the path helped Lucy regain her equilibrium. Her legs were still a little shaky, however, and fatigue was setting in. Her stomach began to gurgle before she reached the end of the trail. She hoped Hattie wasn't mad at her because she desperately needed some lunch. *And a hug*, she thought.

Lucy emerged from the trailhead to see not only Hattie but also Mark waiting there. She couldn't hear what they were saying, but Mark's face looked flushed and red, and Hattie had a hand on his arm. She looked tense and upset. Neither of them had seen Lucy yet. She considered ducking back into the trees, but she knew she'd have to face the music sometime.

As she walked toward them, she heard Mark say, "I know what I saw! She has to be involved."

Hattie replied, "Don't be ridiculous! Look at my phone!"

Lucy cleared her throat and waved at them.

"I'm so sorry! I didn't mean to worry you, Hattie! And Mark, I'm so sorry. I had no idea that Hattie would call out the Coast

Guard!" Lucy smiled weakly, knowing that her attempt at humor wouldn't go over well.

Mark peered down at her, and Lucy didn't like what she saw in his eyes.

"Lucy, I saw you on the cliff. Exactly why were you there? I need you to tell me the truth."

Lucy bristled. She'd always told him the truth. He had no reason to question that. Mark was clearly angry, and Lucy had no idea why. She knew what she'd done was foolhardy, and she was sorry she'd worried Hattie, but something in Mark's tone made her feel defensive and a little edgy.

"I don't know what you mean. I had no idea where the tunnel would come out. I'm just glad it came out somewhere! I was trapped in there. I never saw the man I was following, but there's a dark chamber close to the exit that he might still be hiding in. I was in a hurry to get out!" Lucy put her hands on her hips and gave Mark a defiant look. Whatever he was thinking, she wasn't having it.

"What do you mean, you were trapped?" His voice sounded odd in her ears. Tight, and stressed, she thought.

"I mean trapped. As in I couldn't get out. I went through the door and walked inside for a while, and then I changed my mind and tried to go back out the way I came. But I couldn't open the door no matter how hard I tried. So, I had to take my chances and see if there was another way out. Thankfully there was!"

Hattie interjected. "I told you, Mark. Just listen to the voicemail! Lucy has no idea what you're insinuating!"

"What exactly are you insinuating, Mark?" Lucy's eyes narrowed. She didn't like this new side of Mark. She could feel her blood pressure rising. In fact, she was beginning to feel a little light-headed. She turned to Hattie.

"Hattie, I don't feel so well . . ." Lucy could see the trees swaying oddly across the parking lot from where they were standing.

"Lucy!" Hattie shouted.

Suddenly, she felt Mark's arm around her, and then he was scooping her up.

"Oh Lucy," he whispered into her hair. "I believe you. I'm sorry."

She closed her eyes and leaned into his chest. *He smells like a sea breeze*, she thought. Lucy considered telling him to put her down, but she felt weak. Instead, she said, "I think I need a sandwich."

Chapter Fifteen

*M*ark settled Lucy into Hattie's car. Hattie was on the phone ordering her second-in-command to wrap up several items for pick-up and leaving instructions for the rest of the afternoon.

"I want you to go home and eat something substantial. Then just take it easy. I need to get back to the cutter and make some arrangements. I'll be back later, around dinnertime. We need to talk, Lucy."

Mark looked over Lucy's shoulder at Hattie. She was off the phone now, so he asked, "Can you stay with her until I get back?"

"That's my plan," she said. "I don't like any of this. I plan to call Andy Harrison and get him to come over as well."

Lucy liked Police Captain Andy Harrison, but she hoped he would come alone and not bring that dreadful Mooney with him. Not only was he irritating and boorish, but he also treated Lucy like she was a master criminal every time she saw him.

Hattie swung by the Lace Curtain Cafe with Lucy. One of the waitstaff was at the door with two big bags of food, which he put in Hattie's trunk. She rolled down the window and thanked him for being so quick. Lucy recognized him as one of the boys from the high school wrestling team who had helped her with the book faire, so she smiled and waved and added her thanks.

He beamed, presumably happy to help Lucy again and happy to score points with his boss.

Hattie had ordered a feast, and Lucy didn't mind one bit. She dug into a lobster macaroni and cheese dish that was incredibly creamy and delicious, a whole piece of smothered chicken, and stewed greens with bits of bacon. There was a large salad, but Lucy ignored it in favor of the "soul food with a twist" lunch. There was an entire carton of Hattie's special cornbread—the kind with diced smoked gouda and sweet onions baked in. The top was slathered with creamy herb butter. Lucy wished she had more room, but one piece was all she could manage.

A couple of customers came into the bookstore while they were eating. Hattie wouldn't let Lucy leave the table, insisting on serving them herself. Lucy noticed that Hattie only made herself a small plate of mostly salad and veggies with a piece of cornbread.

"Are you on a diet, Hattie?" she teased.

"What? No!" Hattie laughed. "It was biscuits and sausage gravy for breakfast. That's my weakness. I had to go back for seconds! Sometimes I wish I weren't such a good cook!"

"I'm not sorry you're such a good cook." Lucy chuckled and patted her midsection. "I feel so much better now."

Hattie looked her over and gave a satisfied nod. "You needed a lot more than a sandwich! I'm guessing you walked a good five miles today and had a bit of a scare too."

Lucy couldn't deny she'd been scared. The adrenaline from being trapped underground with no sure way out—plus an unknown man trespassing on her property—was wearing off now, and she felt exhausted.

Lucy wasn't sure when she'd dozed off, but she woke to find herself curled up in one of the leather wingback chairs under a throw and with Tor asleep on her lap. She eyed him suspiciously. "Since when did you become a lap cat, Tor?"

The handsome feline's ears twitched, but that was the only sign he gave of hearing her. She petted him, causing him to stretch and roll over. He yawned and flopped over again before standing up and looking at her with blinking eyes. He started to knead the fuzzy throw covering her, purring like a kitten. She patted his head and scratched under his chin. She loved this sweet side of Tor, even though he didn't show it often.

She heard something in the kitchen and stiffened. Remembering her earlier trespasser, she put Tor on the floor and crept toward the back of the house. The dining room was dimly lit due to shade tree shadows, so she carefully made her way past the table and chairs, avoiding a creaky spot on the floor. She heard lowered voices but couldn't make out what they were saying.

Lucy stood just outside the kitchen. She let out a long, silent breath she didn't know she'd been holding. The voices belonged to Mark and Hattie. Lucy's tight shoulders relaxed, remembering that Hattie was staying with her until Mark returned, and Mark was here now. Relieved, she started to make her way into the kitchen, but as she did, she caught wind of what Hattie was saying.

". . . told you, she would never be involved with smuggling!"

Mark had started to reply but stopped when he saw Lucy standing there. She could feel the heat rising in her face—she was both hurt and angry. How could Mark think she was capable of criminal activity?

Lucy turned straight around and hurried back to the front of the house.

"Lucy, wait!" Mark hurried after her.

Lucy made it to her grandmother's desk in the front of the bookstore before she stopped. She rounded on Mark, eyes flashing.

"Wait for what? For you to accuse me of some outlandish thing?" Lucy sank into her grandmother's desk chair and ran her hands through her hair. She was fed up with always being a suspect in some crime she knew nothing about.

Hattie followed Mark into the room. "Lucy, it isn't what you think. I played your call from earlier for Mark. He believes you. I played it for him because I thought it might help his investigation."

"What investigation? Lucy's eyes narrowed. What Mark said now might very well determine their future—if they even had one.

"Lucy, I can't get into all the details. I'm collaborating with a team from other government agencies investigating a smuggling operation. Somewhere along the coast in this area, we believe a group is operating a smuggling ring. There have been rumors for a long time—years even—but only recently have we seen signs of activity we can trace. We've been watching the area you emerged from today for a few months now. I believe you were there for the reasons you said you were, and if anything happened to you . . ." Mark's jaw clenched tight. "I don't want anything to happen to you, Lucy," he said softly.

Lucy regarded him for a long minute. He was sincere. She could tell. Hattie stood behind him, hands pressed together, nodding her head.

"It's true, Lucy." She took one of Mark's hands in her own and reached for Lucy's hand with the other. "I love both of you dearly, and I know you both have things you need to say to each other. I'm going to leave you two to talk." She gave each of them a meaningful look in turn. "I expect you to talk and really listen to each other. Enough is enough if you ask me." Hattie put Lucy's hand together with Mark's and let them both go.

Lucy decided it was time to trust Mark and allow him to do the same.

"Mark, there's a lot I need to tell you. Maybe you can stay for dinner?" She was enjoying the feeling of warmth flowing through his fingers to hers.

"I would love to, Lucy. I would love to stay." His thumb caressed the back of her hand. "Hattie called in an order for dinner while you were sleeping. We both want you to take it easy tonight."

Lucy turned to Hattie. "I can't let you keep feeding me all the time! I'm eating all your profits!"

"No, Lucy, you're not. I thought you knew. Your grandparents invested in the Lace Curtain years ago. They were my only stockholders, so to speak, so their shares will eventually come to you. They saw me through some very lean years. They wanted to just make a gift of the money, not even a loan, but I couldn't let them do that. I insisted they become part owners. They never would take a cent of the profits, though, so over the years I've been reinvesting their portion of the profits. I'm not sure what it all comes up to, but Sam—Senior not Junior—kept account of it as the lawyer in charge of their trust. I'm sure Junior could fill you in on the details anytime you want to know."

Lucy shook her head. "I don't understand. Why didn't they tell me? Why didn't you tell me?" It was too much to take in. She let go of Mark's hand and rubbed her temples. "It's been an exceptionally long day. Hattie, if what you say is true, it sounds to me as if they didn't want you to pay them back. Neither do I. So please, just don't do that anymore. Keep all the profits for yourself. Maybe I can sell you back those shares? Legally I'm not sure what we have to do, but I'd be willing to sell them for a few Jammie Sammies. What do you say?"

Hattie's eyes welled up and soon spilled over. "I think you are just like your grandparents, that's what I think." She leaned in and kissed Lucy on both cheeks. "We'll discuss terms later, my dear. I'm headed over now to pick up dinner so we can eat our profits together, okay?" Hattie looked up at Mark and gave him her warmest smile. "Look after our girl. I'll be back in two shakes!"

Hattie picked up her bag and unlocked the front door, letting herself out. Tor sniffed the air as she went and decided to follow her out. Lucy watched him go and turned to Mark.

"Why don't we . . ."

Mark pressed his mouth to hers. Surprised, she stiffened, but as he wrapped both arms around her more tightly, she melted into them. He kissed her slowly, giving her time to warm up to the idea. She was soon kissing him back, even though she still felt a bit shy about it. He took this as a promising sign and kissed her more enthusiastically. Just when Lucy decided she wanted to stay locked in this embrace forever, Mark pulled away and studied her.

"Lucy, I just want you to know, you mean everything to me." His eyes were shining with emotion.

Lucy felt weak and her legs trembled under her for the second time that day. "I feel the same way about you. I can't even remember my life before you were in it."

True to her word, Hattie was back quicker than Lucy liked. *Probably a good thing*, she thought. Hattie bustled in with her packages and gave them a curious look. This time Mark blushed, and Hattie raised her eyebrows at him. Then she set about unboxing the dinner she'd brought back with her. Lucy was only slightly disappointed there were no Jammie Sammies included when she saw the feast Hattie laid out.

"It's something new I'm trying," Hattie said.

"It looks delicious and smells even better, but what is it?" Lucy's stomach growled, even though she'd eaten a substantial lunch, thanks again, to Hattie.

"I call it yellow chicken and rice. It's an Indian-inspired curry but probably not authentic enough to claim that title. Besides, I know some of our old-timers will never even try it if it has a fancy name. There's jasmine rice to spoon it over, and a spiced potatoes and peas dish. I brought some garlic flatbread too. It's loosely based on the naan bread I had last year at a little Indian restaurant up the coast. I hope you two like it!"

"When have I ever not loved something from your kitchen, Hattie?" Mark squeezed her arm. "I'm starving." He sat down and began scooping rice onto a plate.

Lucy decided to join him and loaded up on vegetables first. "Sit down, Hattie. Eat with us."

"Well, I hadn't planned on staying. I need to get back and close up the cafe. Lucy, I was hoping maybe you'd come to stay over with me tonight. I don't like everything that's been going on, especially now that you've had strangers roaming around. I know you have an alarm system, but I just don't feel good about it." Hattie frowned. "Has Captain Harrison been here yet?"

Lucy shook her head no. She'd just taken the most heavenly bite of chicken and she was determined to savor it.

"Maybe you should call him again, Hattie?" Mark said, between bites.

"I'm not sure what else he can do. I told Officer Franklin about the other incidents in the summer house during Hometown Days and the stranger on the lawn during the fireworks, and he promised to step up patrols."

"Lucy, why didn't you tell me about the other incidents?" Mark looked upset.

"It's just been so busy, and I honestly thought it was being handled. Officer Franklin assured me it was all under control. It just didn't occur to me to tell you." Lucy felt contrite. It wasn't that she didn't want to tell Mark, it was just that so much was going on, she could hardly keep track of it herself!

"Well, that's it. I think you should stay with Hattie for a few nights. I'm on leave for a couple of days so I can stay here and see what if I can catch whoever it is that's messing around." Mark put his fork down. "I don't like the idea of you staying here by yourself."

Lucy could feel her stubborn streak rising. "I'm not going anywhere. This is my home, and I need to be here. Tor needs me. The bookstore needs me. I'm not letting anyone scare me off." She softened her tone and continued. "I appreciate both of you so much. I don't know what I'd do without either one of you, but I have to stay put. If I give up ground here, I don't think I'll ever feel safe." She smiled at them each in turn. "If you both want to stay with me here, however, I have plenty of space."

"I think that's a great idea, Lucy," Hattie said. "I'll go help with closing, pack a bag, and be back around eleven if that's okay? I can sleep in the room next to you and Mark can sleep downstairs on the sofa." The older woman looked sternly at Mark, who had the grace to blush once more.

"Yes ma'am. I wouldn't have it any other way." Mark grinned at Lucy, who didn't entirely believe him.

Hattie packed up the empty containers and headed out with another warning look at Mark. He grinned back at her this time and told her he'd be eagerly waiting for her return. Then, more seriously, he told her to call before she left so he could watch for her, which warmed Lucy's heart.

Hattie met Captain Andy Harrison coming up the steps as she was going down. Lucy heard her promise to call him tomorrow and fill him in as well, so she went over to open the door, and Mark went with her.

The two men looked at each other awkwardly for a moment before Mark stuck his hand out. "Captain."

"Captain," Andy Harrison replied as he shook the proffered hand.

Lucy smiled at the sight of them. Both tall and trim, with sandy hair and green eyes. Seeing them together, Lucy realized they both had the same sea glass green eyes, the very unusual shade she'd been noticing lately. Shaking off the coincidence, Lucy mimicked them both with a mock-serious tone. "Captain."

Lucy was delighted when they both caught her inflection and turned to her, replying "Captain!" in unison. She couldn't help but laugh, and neither could they.

"Won't you come in, Captain Harrison?" Lucy emphasized Harrison and gave Mark a sassy look and a wink.

"I'd be delighted, Captain Lucy," he replied, also her an exaggerated wink. Then his tone turned all business. "I hear you had quite an upsetting adventure this afternoon. Hattie gave me an earful, but I'd like to hear it from you firsthand. Is there somewhere we can talk?"

Lucy thought of her dinner growing cold on the table. "Have you eaten, Captain? We just sat down. But Hattie delivered enough food for a family of five. Would you like to join us?"

He started to decline. "I'm on duty—"

"Which means no, you haven't eaten because you're here working through your dinner hour to squeeze me in, right?" Lucy smiled. "I insist. Think of it as a public service. I need *help* to finish this feast, and your job is to protect and serve, right?"

Captain Harrison decided not to fight Lucy on it because she was right on every point. "I can't turn down dinner from Hattie's kitchen. And I missed lunch today, as well, so thank you. What are we having?"

Chapter
Sixteen

*O*ver dinner, Lucy described the day's events again, how she followed the trespasser and found the tunnel, was locked in, and eventually came out on the cliff above the ocean. Captain Harrison asked a few questions and jotted some notes in his notebook.

Between the two captains and Lucy, there were no leftovers to put away. While Mark cleared the table and put the dishes in the sink to soak, Lucy took a sip of water and looked at the police captain over the rim of her glass. She could see he was working himself up to give her a lecture. She knew because she'd seen that look twice already today, once from Hattie and once from Mark.

"Before you say anything, I know what I did wasn't smart. Following a strange man into a dark hole in the ground . . . it's the thing you scream at people *not* do in the movies. But I was just so fed up with this lurker. Even the extra patrols Officer Franklin ordered made no difference. It seems like people are coming and going at will." Lucy gave him a defiant look. "I know it was stupid. I just wanted to get to the bottom of it!"

"I'm sorry, did you say Officer Franklin ordered extra patrols? When did he do that? It's the first I'm hearing of it." Andy Harrison looked genuinely confused. "*Why* did he do that?"

"Because of the man in the summer house during the fairy book faire and running across my lawn while the fireworks were going. You sent Officer Franklin out when I called during the Hometown Days, remember?"

"I remember that you called, but I never heard anything else about it. It was a busy week. Franklin never mentioned anything about an intruder or needing to step up patrols. Maybe he went to Mooney with it thinking I was too busy. Let me get back to you on that. In the meantime, do you have a place to stay? When Hattie called me earlier, she was adamant that she didn't want you to stay here alone. And I agree with her." He looked toward the kitchen where Mark was still doing dishes. "Is he . . . ?" He let the question trail.

"He's staying here tonight, but it isn't what you think." She blushed at what he might be thinking and pressed on. "He's sleeping downstairs to keep a watch out, and Miss Hattie is coming back after closing to stay upstairs with me." She grinned. "We'll be well chaperoned, I promise!"

Andy Harrison laughed. He liked her. Lucy could see it written on his face. And Lucy liked him, as well. She felt strangely at home with him.

Satisfied that things were under control and that he had a good handle on it, Andy Harrison stood and thanked Lucy for dinner.

"Thank Hattie! She's been feeding me a lot lately." She rubbed her stomach contentedly. "Mark, Captain Harrison is leaving!"

"Why don't you call me Andy? Most folks do." He patted Lucy on the shoulder. "Try not to worry. We'll get to the bottom of this. Tomorrow I'll come out personally with a team and we'll look over everything. Is after lunch okay for you?"

Mark dried his hands on a dishtowel as he spoke up from the kitchen door. "I'd like to be there too, Captain."

"Any time after lunch would be great." Lucy nodded. "The more, the merrier!

Mark smiled at Lucy and motioned for the police captain to go ahead of him. "I'll walk you out."

The two captains walked out together. Lucy was struck again by how similar they were. While the older Captain Harrison was an inch or so shorter than Mark, they had the same square shoulders, the same long limbs. From behind, someone could easily mistake one for the other.

Lucy cleared crumbs from the dining room table and set out fresh bowls of food and water for Tor, who had been scarce during dinner. Mark hadn't yet returned, so she went to her grandmother's desk. She hadn't been keeping up with accounts as well as she should have lately. She quickly checked her personal bank balance and the bookstore's account. Each account had just a modest balance but enough that she wasn't worried. At least not this month.

She opened one of the desk drawers for a pen. It snagged on an envelope, so she pulled them both out. It was the letter that had come for her grandmother. She'd forgotten all about it. Lucy turned it over in her hands. It was beautiful, with watercolor roses hand-painted on both sides of the envelope. It was neatly written in an old-fashioned style. She toyed with the idea of opening it, but then Mark came in, so she dropped the letter on the desk and greeted him with a smile. Hopefully, this time, Hattie would take longer than two shakes before she came back.

Lucy stretched and yawned. The sun shining through her curtains was cheerful and inviting, so she threw back the quilts and rolled herself off the high bed. She opened the window and took in a deep breath. *Is there anything more beautiful than*

a summer morning? Lucy smelled bacon even through her closed door, so she jumped in the shower and dressed quickly. She'd slept so well that she was an hour and a half late for The Cozy Cat to be open. "Some hostess I am," she muttered to herself. "My guests are cooking their own breakfast and probably minding the store too!"

Lucy flew down the back stairs to the kitchen where she expected to see Hattie. Instead, Sam was there, turning bacon on a foil-lined sheet tray.

"Sam? What are you doing here? Where's Hattie?"

"I don't know, Luce. Mark let me in, then put me in charge of the bacon. I think he's ringing someone up in the bookstore." Sam smiled at Lucy. "So, Captain Mark, hmmm?"

Lucy laughed and punched Sam, who pretended to be seriously wounded.

"It isn't like that, and you know it! He and Hattie both spent the night last night. I've been having problems with trespassers."

Sam finished flipping the slices of bacon and returned the tray to the oven. "Luce, I don't like the sound of that. Are you okay?"

"I am. And I'm being very well looked after. Matter of fact, I'm afraid I'm being too well looked after!" Lucy patted her tummy and smiled. "I smell coffee!"

Sam poured her a cup before she could do it herself. "It's my recipe. I hope you like it. I put a few secret ingredients in it. Can you guess what they are?"

Lucy sniffed the coffee appreciatively. "Mmm, smells like . . . vanilla? And cocoa powder?" She added a bit of cream to cool the coffee off and stirred in a couple of spoonfuls of sugar. She took a sip and let it roll over her tongue. "There's something else, but I can't place it. What is it?"

Sam beamed. "You got two out of three. I'll tell you what the third ingredient is, but you can't tell anyone! Deal?"

Lucy quickly agreed. This coffee was yummy and something she was sure she'd like to have again in the future.

Sam leaned in and whispered, "It's nuts!" He winked at her and waited.

"Nuts as in plants or nuts as in crazy?" Lucy asked.

"Nuts as in macadamia nuts. I chop a few of them up and smash them and add them to the coffee grounds. I learned that trick from my grandfather, but I have no idea where he learned it!"

Lucy took another sip. "This is so good, Sam! You should be a barista. I mean if you weren't already a barrister. But hey, if business is slow, you could be the Barrister Barista or the Barista Barrister! Would you have to pass the "bar" for that or just pass the cream?" Lucy giggled. Sam looked a bit pained, but Lucy was cracking herself up.

"Seriously, Luce? Is that the best you've got?" Sam laughed. "But speaking of barristers, that's why I'm here. I need you to come down to the office today. But you should come alone. It's about your grandparents' estate and the packages waiting for you. I can also go over the will with you today too if you want.

"Oh, yes, I'm sorry I've had to keep postponing our dinner. So much has been going on." Lucy frowned. "But I'm not sure I can come in today. The police will be here anytime to look around. I have to show them where I've seen the trespassers."

Sam nodded. "Mark filled me in a little bit. He said he thought they might not need you the whole time and said I should stick around and eat brunch. I think maybe he just wanted to pass the tongs to someone else!"

The timer for the bacon dinged, so Sam grabbed the potholders and took the tray out. Lucy pulled out a porcelain plate and lined it with paper towels for Sam to drain the bacon.

"I better go check on Mark. I feel bad leaving him to do my job while I loaf around in the kitchen drinking coffee! Thanks, Sam. I'll be right back."

Lucy found Mark seated on one of the big leather wingback chairs reading a book to a toddler sitting beside him on the arm of the chair. One hand around the child and one hand holding the book, he turned pages deftly with his fingers. He smiled when he spotted Lucy and held up a finger for her to wait as he finished reading.

"'Put that down, Puppysaurus Rex! That car is not a toy! Be a good boy!' But Puppysaurus Rex didn't want to be a good boy, so he put the car down and roared. Then off he ran to find his cave, knocking down trees in his way! 'Puppysaurus Rex, stop that now. I'll give you a treat, your favorite thing to eat!' Puppysaurus Rex thought long and hard and decided that being a good boy wasn't so bad, so he stomped off to live in the little boy's yard. The end!"

Mark handed the book to the toddler, a sweet-faced boy of about two and a half or three. The little boy took the book and ran off with it, calling for his mama to come see.

Lucy spotted her over in the cookbook section. She turned and mouthed "Thank you!" to Mark and smiled at Lucy, then carried her selections to the counter. "Three cookbooks and one *Puppysaurus Rex*, please. I love this store. We live in the next town over, and I've never been here before. Do you always have readers available?" She looked hopeful.

"I'm sorry, we don't usually. But I'm always happy to pitch in and help where I can. I like to keep the kids happy so the parents can shop. We have a play area for littles over in the corner if you ever want to take advantage of it. I'm so glad you came in today. I hope you come again." She handed the lady her receipt. "We do have a bookstore cat. His name is Tor. I don't see him right now, but he loves children. Maybe come back and pet the kitty next time?"

The young mother picked up her bag and led her son to the door, calling back, "Oh for sure, we'll be back!"

Mark put an arm over Lucy's shoulder. "Did you find Sam? I had him take over in the kitchen. Everything but the bacon is on the table already. And before you ask, I made breakfast, not Hattie! I hope you won't be disappointed!"

"What I'll be is spoiled!" Lucy laughed. "Sam? Are you ready to eat?"

Sam came in from the kitchen carrying a platter of bacon and a tray with coffee mugs, a carafe, sugar bowl, and creamer, so Mark and Lucy rushed over to help him.

Unburdened, he said, "Good food, good meat, good Lord, let's eat!"

Mark raised an eyebrow, but Lucy just laughed and said, "Amen!"

Chapter
Seventeen

*A*fter Sam left for his office, Mark and Lucy found themselves alone again with no chaperones but Tor and the occasional customer. Mark called Captain Harrison's office and discovered that they'd hit a snag and wouldn't be coming by until a little after two o'clock, so Lucy settled in at her desk and Mark settled into a chair at a table nearby. Many times, she'd seen her grandparents sit in the same places, and the familiarity of it tugged at her heart.

Mark had been clear that he intended to stay until he was sure she was safe. Lucy loved having him around, and not just safety's sake. She started to tell him so but could see he was concentrating while reading something on his phone, so she turned to her desk and began making it neat. She picked up the rose-covered envelope again, deciding to open it this time. Perhaps there was an address inside or something she could use to identify the sender to let them know the letter never reached her grandmother.

It was such a beautiful envelope that Lucy opened it gently with the letter opener to preserve it. The heavy paper was suitable for watercolors and had held up well. There was a faint postmark, but it wasn't legible. She eased the folded letter from the envelope. It was written on heavy cream paper with a single small rose painted in one corner. The lines were a bit slanted, and the words looked as if the pen had fits and starts from a low ink supply. The letter continued on the next page, followed by an oversized signature. It simply read "Mariana Marshall." No one Lucy had ever heard of.

She glanced over at Mark, who was engrossed in reading something on his phone, and decided to read the letter, even though it felt a little bit like an invasion of privacy.

> *My Dearest,*
>
> *How I long to visit with you once again. I thought of inviting you over for Easter dinner, but I was too tired to cook. My daughter Carolina and her husband Gilbert came to visit and brought their new baby, Kiri. I'm just batty over her! You should see her. She's a doll, just don't wake her! I do hope we can connect. I'm in a new relationship. I can't wait for you to meet him. He's super and keeps me financially afloat. Hopefully, I'll see you soon!*
>
> *All my love,*
> *Mariana Marshall*

Lucy frowned. The tone of the letter sounded like an old, dear friend, if a somewhat scattered one, but Lucy had never heard of her. She decided she would look for Mariana's contact information later and slid the letter back into the envelope. She tidied up her desk and slipped the envelope into the ribbon on a corkboard as a visual reminder.

Mark, meanwhile, had finished reading. He stretched and put his phone away.

"Lucy," he said, "I just want to be up front and let you know that the team running the joint investigation with us has decided to join the local law enforcement officers today. They're coming to look at your tunnel and the summer house too. I told them you aren't involved in anything they're looking into, but they may have some questions for you anyway. It would be best if you just agreed to cooperate with anything they ask. That won't be a problem, will it?"

Lucy trusted Mark. "If you think it's all right, it's fine by me. I didn't even know about the tunnel. They are welcome to do whatever they need to do. I don't want to hike back through that tunnel though!"

"I don't want you to do that either! I don't think they will ask you to. In fact, they may ask you to be off the property while they look things over. I got a text saying they'd be here soon. Is there anything else you want to talk to me about before they get here? Anything else I should know?"

Lucy weighed her options. There were things she hadn't told Mark. But none of them seemed to connect to whatever operation he might be involved with, at least in her mind.

She shook her head. "I'm not sure. I mean, it's an old house and there are lots of quirky things about it . . ." Lucy trailed off as her eyes raked over the antique desk. Did she want to tell him about the secret drawers? Or the hidden chamber in the basement? As far as she could tell, the basement was enclosed and didn't connect to any tunnels, secret or otherwise. Her grandparents had never even told *her* about any of these things. It seemed wiser to her to find out why they hadn't before she shared that knowledge with anyone else, even someone she was beginning to care for deeply.

"Okay, Lucy. We can talk about it more later. I'm sure if there was anything the police needed to know, you'd tell them." Mark gave her an inquisitive look.

"Of course, I would." She returned his gaze and tried not to think too hard about whether she would or wouldn't.

"That's what I told them." Mark smiled and reached for her.

Lucy walked into his arms and put her face on his chest. She didn't want to do anything to betray his trust in her, but some things, she thought, were better kept secret. At least for now.

Lucy stood toe-to-toe with the revolting police officer Tom Mooney. She could feel her temperature rising but she stood firm. She wouldn't take the bait. He was trying to goad her, the odious little toad.

"No, you may *not* go in for a look around. That wasn't part of what I agreed to, not at all." Lucy set her jaw and crossed her arms. She'd had just about enough of this man who seemed determined to blame her for anything and everything.

Mooney's eyes darted toward the open door behind her and then narrowed as he leaned in a bit too close for comfort. "If you didn't have anything to hide, you'd let us in to look around. It seems like all roads lead to you, Miss Patterson." Mooney spat off the side of the porch, which made Lucy's stomach turn.

"You're not coming in. Period. Not even to buy a book! You're banned from the bookstore, and I know I'm within my rights." Lucy was seething. While Captain Harrison and Mark and the rest of the investigative team had searched the summer house with Lucy, and she showed them the door to the tunnel, Officer Mooney had hung back. When Lucy returned, she found him rifling through her desk. She yelled at him, demanding that he leave immediately. She was so angry that Mooney backed out as far as the porch, temporarily cowed by her demeanor.

"I'm here legally," he whined. "We have permission to search."

Lucy's eyes narrowed. "You have permission to search the grounds, not the house. And I gave that permission. I did not give you permission to go through my personal things! I'm calling Sam, and when Captain Harrison gets back, he's going to hear about this!" Lucy turned away from the angry officer to pull up Sam's number. She knew Mark would not have any cell signal down in the tunnel, and it would be some time before he returned. Before she could hit the call button for Sam, Mooney knocked the phone out of her hand and spun her around.

Lucy couldn't believe it!

"Miss Patterson," he spat, "I'm arresting you for striking a police officer." He yanked one of her arms behind her and started to slip on the cuffs. "Go ahead and tell Captain Harrison anything you like. I know you're guilty, and all I need is probable cause, which I won't have any trouble getting while you're cooling your heels in a jail cell." He smirked, as if anticipating his discovery of whatever Lucy was hiding.

"I never hit you! Let go of me!" Lucy knew if she struggled, he would likely use force and use it gleefully.

Just as Mooney was putting the other cuff on Lucy, Officer Franklin, the youngest member of the force and the one who'd mistakenly pointed his weapon at Lucy in the past, walked around the side of the porch. "That's enough, Mooney. Let her go."

"Franklin, what are you doing here? Why did you leave your post? You're supposed to be guarding the summer house." Officer Mooney licked his lips and started over. "It's a good thing you're here though. You can take her to lockup and start the paperwork for me. I'll stay here and watch over things until the captain gets back." He tried to sound authoritative, but Lucy could see Officer Mooney was sweating now.

"Officer Franklin, I'm glad you're here! Officer Mooney was inside going through my desk! I yelled at him to get out, but I never hit him. He's lying about that!" Lucy appealed to the younger man, hoping he would have the ability to calm things down and call Mooney's bluff.

Mooney tightened the cuff on Lucy's arm, causing her to yelp.

Officer Franklin walked up the sidewalk and up the stairs. "I said let her go, Mooney."

"I'm the ranking officer here. Don't you forget that! I will write you up for insubordination!" Mooney glared at the younger officer, his sending vibes of "How dare you question your superior?"

"I saw the whole thing. She didn't hit you. She didn't do anything at all. You're on the wrong side of this thing, Mooney, and I will not cover for you. Now let her go before she decides to press charges for unlawful detainment and assault on her person and property." He nodded toward Lucy's phone lying several feet away. He spoke again, with a dangerous edge to his tone. "Open the cuffs and then go pick up Miss Patterson's phone and hand it to her. Then I want you to apologize. Now."

Mooney's face, already red with anger, trended toward purple. Lucy thought he might explode or have a stroke. She did not expect him to comply, but that's exactly what he did. He uncuffed her and picked up her phone, brushing it off before handing it to her.

"This was just a misunderstanding," he said to his colleague. "I wasn't really going to arrest her. I just wanted to scare her into admitting what she's hiding.

"That isn't an apology, and even if it were, I'm not inclined to accept it!" Lucy spun on her heel and went inside, where she locked the door and put up the closed sign behind her. She pulled the curtains across the windows and headed for the back. She could hear Mooney and Franklin arguing, so she shut the dining room windows on her way and pulled those blinds too.

She passed through the kitchen and locked the back door before she let a single tear fall.

She called Hattie and left a message. Then she called Sam and told him all about it on his voicemail. Her legs were shaking, so she turned the kettle on and sat down. A nice cup of tea was just what she needed. She picked a strawberry, chamomile, and lavender tea hoping it would soothe her. Officer Mooney was way over the line. She couldn't wait to report him! She pushed it away from her mind and concentrated on drinking her tea.

Before she finished with it, Sam returned her call. He was as outraged as she was, which made her feel vindicated. He offered to come over to her, but she decided she would go to him instead. *After I make sure all the doors and windows are tightly shut and locked*, she thought.

Lucy was glad there was no sign of the loathsome Mooney as she backed out of her drive, but before she reached the street, Officer Franklin appeared and whistled for her to stop. She considered ignoring him but none of what happened was his fault. She rolled her window down. "Yes?"

"I hate to impose, Miss Patterson, but would you be headed toward the police station? Mooney has the keys to the patrol car, and I need to get back to the office to take care of a couple of things. He's stationed himself near the door in your backwoods, and I don't want to have to ask him for the keys. I'm sure he's there waiting so he can tell his side of the story to the captain first." He pressed his lips together. "But I meant what I said. I will not cover for him. What he did to you was wrong, and I know the captain will want to make it right."

Lucy couldn't blame him for not wanting another confrontation with the belligerent Mooney, so she motioned her head for him to get in. Sam had advised her not to speak to anyone until she got to his office, so Lucy turned on the radio to avoid having to discuss the situation. Unfortunately, The Doobie Brothers were singing "I Shot the Sheriff," so she switched it off. She didn't want to give herself any ideas!

Wisely choosing not to comment on the song, Officer Franklin gave Lucy a lingering look, causing her to check her loosely pinned up hair and fair complexion in the rearview mirror.

"Miss Patterson, may I call you Lucy?"

She glanced at him but didn't answer.

Apparently, he took her silence as permission and said, "Lucy, I know everything is up in the air right now, and a lot is going on with the investigation—not just our investigation but the larger investigation too . . ." He shifted in his seat. "But I was thinking, maybe when this all blows over, we could go out to dinner sometime?" He smiled at her in what he surely thought was a charming manner.

Lucy hit the brakes hard, causing him to throw his hand out and brace himself. She took a deep breath. He hadn't actually done anything wrong, had he? Just because it was completely inappropriate and unprofessional and bad form to hit on someone who has just been through an emotional ordeal . . . Her thoughts trailed off. No, she was right to be angry. Why did men presume it was okay to approach women this way?

"Lucy! What are you doing?" He sounded upset, but Lucy just resumed driving as if nothing were wrong.

"Squirrel," she said.

She didn't answer his request for a date, and he didn't ask again.

Chapter Eighteen

*L*ucy settled into the corner of a red leather sofa while she waited for Sam. She admired the changes he'd made around the small sitting area in the front room of his practice. It was cleaner and more modern than it had been before but still retained the original charm of the house. Sam had been busy outside too. The paint was fresh—a sunny yellow that fit in well with the other historic homes and businesses in the quaint downtown area—and the gingerbread trim looked like new with a bright coat of white. There were blue and purple hydrangeas blooming outside, which made the whole place look very appealing. Lucy wasn't surprised that she had to ask a couple of tourists with cameras taking pictures of the charming place to let her in the gate.

Inside, Sam had filled an antique white porcelain pitcher with blossoms from the hydrangea bushes. They were gorgeous, but something moving caught Lucy's eye. It was just a little ladybug, so she put her finger in its path, and when it climbed onto her hand, she carried it gently outside to place it on one of the bushes.

Sam came through the office door to get Lucy just as she slipped out. He followed her outside. "Not running away, are you? You just got here!" He grinned at her.

"No, just relocating a stowaway from the flowers inside. I love ladybugs—they're so cheerful—but I didn't think it would be happy inside for long." Lucy took in the beautiful day—the bright blue sky with just a few cotton-ball clouds, the perfect sea air with a slightly cool breeze, and beautiful flowers blooming everywhere. It would be nice, she thought, to spend a day just strolling through town and looking at all the gardens and window boxes, and even wildflowers that seemed to spring up everywhere they could. *But business first.*

She followed Sam back inside and through to his private office. He motioned for her to sit at a table situated next to a window with beautiful sheer curtains and a jacaranda tree blooming outside. He'd done a wonderful job in this room too, cleaning, organizing, and rearranging his grandfather's old office. It was inviting and comfortable, a mix of modern office equipment and beautifully polished antiques. Before Lucy could compliment him on his good taste and decorator's eye, Sam carried over a large box from his desk and dropped it on the table in front of her. It was a bit dusty, which caused her to sneeze several times in a row.

"I'm sorry, Luce! I did dust this thing off, but I think it's been in storage for quite a while. He brought over a box of tissues for her and then went into the next room and came back with two ice-cold bottles of mint lemonade, a local specialty sold at the DeLiteFull Deli housed in a pink cottage across the street. Lucy thought the name was a bit ridiculous but everything the little vegan deli made was delicious.

"Thanks, Sam." She flipped open the metal stopper on the reusable bottle and put in a paper straw Sam handed to her. "This is the best lemonade I've ever had! I wish they sold it by the gallon!"

"Me too, Luce! It's probably better that they don't. I'd be floating." He patted her on the shoulder and gave it a small squeeze before he sat down. "Are you okay? I was with a client when your call came in earlier, but you sounded so upset on the voicemail. I can help you file a complaint at the station if you want. It makes me so angry to think of that bully putting his hands on you!"

"I'm okay. I think I will talk to Captain Harrison first. Maybe if I tell him what happened he can handle it in a way where I don't ever have to see that horrible man again. But if it comes to that, yes, I would love to have your help. Right now, I just need to cool down and not even think about it. Plus, I can't wait to see what's in the box!"

Sam smiled and put his drink on the windowsill out of the way. "Well, let's get right down to it. First, I must tell you that I opened the letter addressed to me by my grandfather, written when I agreed to take over the practice. It has some surprising information about the packages and your grandparents' estate. Let's start by unwrapping the parcels. There are three of them, and they're numbered." Sam pulled out a sealed package from the box wrapped in brown paper. He set it on the table and pulled out two similar packages. Using a penknife, he carefully slit the tape on the first package and unfolded the paper to reveal six identical books, each with the word "Ledger" stamped on the side.

Lucy reached for one of the books. "May I?"

Sam nodded quickly, "Oh yes, everything in this box belongs to you. Please, go ahead."

Lucy picked up the book on top and began flipping through it. It was a series of numbers for an account that began in the late 1970s and continued until 2018. As she browsed through each of the other books, Sam opened the other two packages. They were all filled with ledgers of the same binding. Lucy turned back to the first page, but there was no information other than an account number at the top, followed by a list of what looked like deposits and withdrawals.

"Sam, I don't understand. What is all this?" She gestured toward all the other ledgers, about fifteen in total.

Sam picked one up and paged to the beginning. He pointed at the account number at the top, which was different from the account number in the book Lucy held. "According to the letter left to me, these are your grandparents' accounts. Each one is unique—see this? It's a routing number. Each one corresponds to a different account, and somewhere there should be a key." Sam fished around in the box and pulled out an envelope bearing his grandfather's letterhead. It was heavy cream paper, and a red wax seal secured the flap. Sam held it out to Lucy, but she waved for him to open it. He used the flat edge of his knife to pop the seal off intact, then handed the envelope to Lucy.

There was a handwritten note from her grandmother attached to a printed report. Tears sprang to Lucy's eyes as she took in the familiar script. The ache she felt at the loss of her grandparents and the frustration she had over not knowing what happened to them was never far from the surface, even if she managed to keep it well hidden most of the time. She took one of the tissues from the box and dabbed her eyes. The letter was addressed to Lucy and her parents. Sam watched Lucy closely, so she pulled the report out and leafed through it. In it, she saw the names of several local businesses followed by a series of numbers.

She held it up for Sam to see. "Do you know what this is about?"

Sam nodded. "There was some explanation in the letter I have. It's a key to the accounts that your grandparents held as part-owner, investor, or shareholder in several businesses. My grandfather was not only your grandparents' legal counsel, but he also managed most aspects of the Patterson Trust. Each of those accounts and ledgers corresponds to a different business."

He picked up one of the books and came around to Lucy's

side of the table. "See here?" He matched the account number to one in the printed report. "This is the account ledger for The Seaview Messenger, which, as you know, is the local paper. If you look here,"—he flipped to the end of the ledger—"you can see how much money is in that account." The number he showed her was a substantial amount.

Lucy spent several minutes looking through each of the books, figuring out which business they corresponded to. She hesitated when she came to the ledger for Lace Curtain Cafe. Hattie was family. She skipped to the last page. The amount stunned Lucy. There were over two million dollars in that account alone.

Lucy looked at Sam. "I don't understand, is this the amount they have invested? Or just what?"

Sam carefully slid the book out of Lucy's hands and put it on top of the stack.

"I can answer questions for you, but you need to decide on a couple of matters, first. Are you happy for me to continue in my grandfather's place—to have legal access to the matters of your grandparents' estate, the Patterson Trust, and your personal inheritance? I understand if you want to hire someone you know better or who is an outside party since we've only known each other for a short time.

"I am happy to continue, and I will do everything in my power to serve your needs in the same way my grandfather did, but I want to be transparent with you, Lucy. It serves me financially to keep you as a client. I didn't know this when I took over the practice, but a sizable portion of the operating costs have been underwritten by your grandparents over the years."

Lucy studied Sam. He seemed serious and very earnest. He was correct. She hadn't known him that long. But what she did know of him, she liked. Her grandparents had trusted his grandfather with a great deal, all of which was news to Lucy.

Growing up, there had never been any conversation about businesses or accounts. If anything, she assumed her grandparents were well off enough to own the house and bookstore and that they made a little profit every year that they saved and invested for retirement.

The bookstore accounts, which Lucy had access to when she took over, had enough to operate but not a lot of margin. Her grandparents had never been frivolous with money either. Her grandfather had driven the same beat-up station wagon for a decade past its prime and only retired it when the repair costs were greater than the replacement. Even then, he bought a secondhand vehicle.

Lucy decided she trusted Sam. She didn't have any siblings, but if she could choose one, she thought she'd choose him.

"I would be grateful if you would, Sam. I feel completely lost with all this. And baffled. Do my parents know about all this?"

"I don't know. Perhaps not. I have a document here signed by your parents that entrusts you with the entirety of your grandparents' estate and all matters concerning their property and business. It was signed along with my grandfather and gave him power of attorney to act in your interests and that of your grandparents' estate until such a time as you made other arrangements. Basically, in the simplest of terms, if you wish me to continue in this role, you just need to sign one piece of paper. At that point, I will be free to advise you on the particulars. And by signing, it means that you and I will be the managers of the estate and the trust. It also means we are both bound by the express wishes, terms, and conditions your grandparents built in."

Lucy's brain was on information overload. She wished she could discuss it with Hattie or Mark, but she had a feeling she should make this decision on her own. Her parents were unreachable, that she knew. Their work carried them to places where they didn't always have access to communication with the outside world. This month, they were on the remote island Tristan da Cunha, which was about two thousand miles from anywhere. Her parents were delivering much-needed medical supplies and working with an international medical aid group to bring specialists to the island for a short rotation.

"You mentioned the Patterson Trust. Is that what this is? All these accounts?" Lucy was trying to make sense of it all. "Or is it something different?"

"The Patterson Trust is a separate fund. I haven't had a chance to look over all the particulars yet. You and your heirs are the beneficiaries of this trust, and if anything happens to you before you have heirs, the remainder goes to various charities. My grandfather is listed as the trustee. It is set to be accessible on your next birthday." He paused to gauge whether she was able to take in more information. "Lucy, it's a substantial amount. Taken care of properly, it will last a long time." He reached over and patted her hand. "I know you'd rather have your grandparents here, but just look at it this way. They put this aside for you so they could be there for you financially for a long time to come."

Lucy was determined not to cry again, but her throat was painfully tight, and her eyes filled with tears despite her wishes. Sam was right. She'd give everything she had to have her grandparents alive and with her again. She knew they adored her and knew that they would do anything for her. Still, why hadn't they told her about any of this? How many other secrets had they been keeping from her? Lucy shook her head. She needed some air.

She stood abruptly and made a beeline for the back door of Sam's office. The backyard wasn't big but had a privacy fence made of redwood that enclosed it. As she came through the door, a flicker of movement caught her eye. It was the back of a man's suit as he zipped around the corner of the house and went through the side yard gate. Lucy shouted for Sam.

Sam hadn't followed her outside, giving her some space and time to process things. He was there in a flash when she cried out. She pointed at the side yard and told him a man had just gone out that way. Sam took off after him but returned to Lucy a few minutes later when there was no sign of him on the sidewalk or anywhere in the street in front of the office.

Lucy felt sure it was the same man she'd seen before. Was he stalking her now? Had he been listening outside the window while Sam went over everything with her? She felt sick and sank into a wrought iron chair that was part of a bistro set on the lawn. She put her head in her hands on the tabletop. Sam ran inside to lock the front door and bring Lucy the rest of her drink.

"Here, Luce. Drink this." He nudged the bottle against her arm. She didn't respond. He pulled out his cell phone and dialed Hattie's number. When it went to voicemail, he left a short message asking her to call him as soon as she could. He sat down next to Lucy and waited, putting a protective hand on her back.

Lucy's cell, left on the table inside the office, started to chime. When Lucy didn't move, Sam went in to get it. It was still ringing as he brought it out to her. Mark's name flashed on the screen. Lucy hadn't even looked up, so Sam took the liberty of answering it for her.

"Hello, Mark. It's Sam. Lucy is here at my office. She's . . . indisposed. Where are you?" Sam listened to the reply and added, "Yes, I think that would be best. We're in the back. Come through the gate on the side of the house." He paused. "Yes, perfect. We'll see you then." Sam set the phone down beside Lucy and put his arm across her shoulders. "Mark will be here in about ten minutes. He's down at the station."

Still overwhelmed, Lucy lifted one of her hands and squeezed Sam's. She was grateful for her friends.

*M*ark didn't come through the gate alone. Hattie and Police Captain Andy Harrison trailed him. He nodded to Sam, who moved aside quickly. Mark knelt beside Lucy, who still had her head down on the table.

"Lucy, hi, what's going on?" He pulled her hair back from her face and tenderly stroked her cheek with the back of his hand.

Lucy let a small sob escape from her throat as she turned in her seat and wrapped her arms around Mark, burying her head in his neck.

Sam spoke softly, "She's had a really hard day. First, she was abused and manhandled by Officer Mooney, then we reviewed her grandparents' estate, which can be upsetting under the best circumstances. She came outside for a minute and saw a man in the backyard, potentially listening at the window. He ran away as soon as she came outside. She thinks it may be the same man who has been sneaking around at her house. Then she just shut down—I think she might be in shock."

"What do you mean, she was abused by Mooney?" Captain Andy Harrison demanded. He looked at Mark, whose face flushed bright red while his fist clenched at his side.

145

"I will play you the voicemail she left me," Sam offered, "but look at her arm. I've been watching that bruise darken since she got here." Sam nodded toward the arm Lucy had stretched across Mark's back. There were defined bruises where someone had gripped her quite hard.

Mark gently patted Lucy on the back and disentangled himself from her tight embrace.

"Lucy, let me see." Mark gingerly held her arm up for inspection. Lucy hadn't realized there were bruises, even though her arm had been sore since the confrontation that morning. Andy Harrison and Hattie both leaned in to look more closely. Mark swore softly.

"Sam, would you and Hattie stay here with Lucy? I need to go. I'll be right back." Mark looked Lucy in the eyes. "He isn't going to get away with this. Stay here."

Lucy tried to protest, to tell Mark she wanted him to stay there with her, but Captain Harrison interrupted.

"Stand down, Captain Fellowes. He's my officer. I'll handle this." The police captain squared up to the Coast Guard officer. It was apparent that neither man wanted to give ground. Hattie pushed her way between them, putting a hand on each man's shoulder and gently nudging them apart.

"I think we'd better listen to the voicemail and ask Lucy what she'd like to do," Hattie suggested.

Everyone decided to go to the station together after Sam played Lucy's voicemail and Lucy went through the events of the morning again with Captain Harrison. Mark wanted Lucy to file charges. Hattie declared herself Lucy's moral support and refused to budge from her side. Sam came along as counsel to Lucy. First, he locked away the books and other documents they'd been reviewing. Lucy was again thankful for her friends, but she decided she was more concerned about the man who seemed to be following her than she was about the awful Officer Mooney.

In the end, Officer Mooney was not at the station and was unreachable, so Lucy gave an official statement but decided to defer filing an official complaint. She was certain that whatever Captain Harrison had in mind for him would be punishment enough.

"Before we leave, how did the investigation go?" she asked.

"I can't comment on the investigation, but I can tell you that we're finished with our search on your property. We didn't find anything useful in the summer house. It appears there was once a basement with a tunnel that probably led to your house, but it looks as if that was sealed up a long time ago. The other tunnel we determined to be partly man-made but mostly an old lava tube. At the far end near the beach, there is a chamber, but the floor quickly drops out, and there seems to be nothing below except seawater coming in from somewhere.

"For safety, we're going to seal it off. If you wouldn't mind, we'd like to secure the tunnel on your end as well, at least for now. We also recommend that you consider tearing down the summer house. It's a hazard and falling apart anyway. We can send some public works crews to do that since it is partly on the land your grandparents set aside for the community gardens."

Lucy was more than happy to have them do that. Perhaps it would deter whoever was creeping around on her property from returning. She shuddered and agreed.

Mark, with a grim look on his face, decided it was time to go. He put an arm around Lucy.

"Please keep us posted about the situation with Officer Mooney." Mark nodded to the police captain. "I need to get

Lucy home now, but I want you to keep him away from her altogether." Mark's eyes still flashed with anger.

"I will. I promise," he replied. "Lucy, here's my cell phone number. I want you to call me directly if anything else happens, day or night. Don't hesitate to call me." He handed her a card.

Whatever anger Hattie had been biting back over the situation came out when she added, "Andy, you see to it that Mooney stops harassing her. You and I both know he's past his sell-by date, and early retirement might be the best thing for everybody."

Lucy and Mark made their way out to his truck. Hattie and Sam decided to meet up at the Lace Curtain Cafe and bring dinner back to Lucy's house for everyone.

Lucy was quiet on the ride home, and Mark left her to her thoughts. He turned on the radio to a light classical station, which Lucy liked because it was both soothing and cheerful. She rested her head against her seatbelt and closed her eyes. Thankfully, it was a short ride, and she couldn't remember ever feeling happier to be home.

"I'm staying over again, Lucy, just to make sure no one else bothers you," Mark said.

Lucy was in no mood to argue. She was growing accustomed to having Mark around and knew she'd miss him when his leave was over. She looked at him for a long minute and smiled.

"I think it's a good idea," she said. "Would you like to stay in a room upstairs? It would be a lot more comfortable."

"As long as Hattie doesn't object," he said. "I can't afford to be on Hattie's bad side." He rubbed his stomach and playfully raised his eyebrows.

Lucy laughed. "I don't think Hattie has a bad side!"

They decided to have dinner outside since the evening was so nice. Lucy was thrilled to have something positive to focus on after such a difficult day. Channeling her energy into making dinner nice was the perfect way to lift her own spirits. She pulled out an old quilt for a tablecloth and draped it over the outdoor dining table. There were "twinkle lights," as her grandmother called them, on the back patio and wrapped around a few of the trees in the backyard, so Lucy switched those on. It was still light outside, but they would make a pretty setting if people lingered as she hoped they would. She added candles to the table and a few hanging lanterns to trees with branches close enough for her to reach.

Next, she picked some rhododendron from a bush over-loaded with blooms and put a few stems each in several milk bottle vases she found in the kitchen. Lucy thought they looked very festive on the table. It had been a long day and she had too much to process, but all she wanted now was just some sort of normalcy and the comfort of enjoying an evening with friends.

Mark, who had been on the search teams earlier in the day, opted to take a quick shower. Lucy gave him a bedroom with an en suite bath on the other side of the room Hattie had stayed in. It was the room farthest in the house from her own. She knew she didn't have anything to worry about with Mark. He was a complete gentleman and understood intuitively that Lucy was not ready for a more physical relationship. Not that she hadn't thought about it . . . Lucy quickly returned her thoughts to set-ting up for dinner so she wouldn't be thinking about Mark.

She made coffee and poured it into an insulated thermos and filled up a tray with sweeteners and a pitcher of cream and cups and spoons and carried it outside. She set it up on a conve-nient table on the patio so it would be easy to get to after dinner. Satisfied, she went in to wait on Mark and prepare the bookstore for the next day.

Lucy unboxed a few new arrivals from the book distributor and set them up on a display table. Tor, who had been sleeping in a wing chair when she came in, came over to sniff the books and check out the now-empty boxes. Lucy scratched under his chin and behind his ears, promising to give him more attention later. She dusted a few tables and straightened the rug by the door before checking the lock. She let Tor keep one of the boxes since he had curled up in it and fallen straight to sleep.

Lucy looked around her and sighed. Twilight was falling. The warm glow of the lights and the candles combined with good company and delicious food made for a perfect summer evening. She picked up her glass and swirled the last of the California rosé. It was sweet and pink and came from a local vineyard. For a day that had started so badly, it was ending so very well.

Hattie brought over the coffee tray and poured a cup for herself and Mark. Sam waved her off, and Lucy did the same. She had enough adrenaline still in her system that caffeine might keep her up all night. Hattie sat down and fingered the quilt on the table.

"Lucy, I love what you've done with the table and the yard. It's so cozy and pleasant. Do you mind if I steal this idea for the back garden at the cafe? I've been wanting to do something with that space for ages, but until now, nothing seemed right." Hattie pointed to the lanterns hanging from several branches. "I might do this too, but I'd have to use battery-operated tealights."

Mark stretched and stifled a yawn. "Hattie, if you do that, Lucy and I will be your first customers. But only if you put on some romantic music and serve us spaghetti on one plate with no forks!" He grinned at Lucy, mischief playing in his eyes.

"Oh, that would be a bella notte!" she replied. "It means beautiful night." Sam and Hattie both looked confused, so she started to explain. "You know, it's in the song from that animated kid's movie where the two dogs meet. One is a high-class lady—"

Sam's face lit up. "Oh, that would make Mark the tramp!" He winked at Lucy.

Lucy tried to smother her giggles but couldn't. Hattie, finally catching the reference, joined in the laughter. Mark pretended to be annoyed with Sam.

Hattie stood up. "Tell you what. You and Mark come over and help me decorate, and you'll be on the VIP list for the first dinner!" She started to stack plates to carry inside. "Sam, you can be my date!"

Sam grinned sheepishly. "I'd be honored! I'll help you decorate too. It sounds like fun. I have some ideas for floral arrangements."

Lucy started to clean up the table on her end, but all three of her guests immediately objected.

"You just sit here and enjoy the peace, Lucy." Miss Hattie handed Sam the pile of dishes she'd been collecting and sent him off to the kitchen.

Mark insisted on carrying in the heavy tray in one hand and the wine glasses in the other. Hattie followed him, clucking at him like a mother hen to be careful and not break anything.

Lucy smiled and curled up in her chair. The night-blooming jasmine scented the air around her, and she could see several stars making an appearance overhead. Mark returned and made a couple more trips carrying things into the kitchen where Hattie and Sam were busy putting away the leftovers and washing the dishes.

When Mark returned, he came with her jacket and a light blanket. She was being spoiled. She would have to think about what she could do for each of her friends to thank them. Mark tucked the blanket around her curled-up toes and kissed her forehead. Tears welled up in her eyes. Her grandfather had often done the same thing. Lucy felt a warmth overtake her. She could trust Mark. She could trust him with everything.

Sam had driven himself home, and Hattie had gone straight to bed in Lucy's grandparents' room shortly after clearing up. Lucy was very tired, but she didn't want to go upstairs yet. She knew it would feel strange having Mark follow her up the stairs. It would be almost too intimate, and she knew they could easily take things too far, even with a sleeping Hattie just down the hall. Mark needed to return to his ship tomorrow evening, so this was also the last chance they might have to be alone and spend time together.

She fought back a yawn and stole a look at Mark. They had settled into a comfortable, plush sofa in the round room. Lucy loved this room, but she didn't spend as much time in it as she'd like. The Victorian architecture was lovely with warm wood built-ins and the row of windows that curved around the room. At the top of each window was a small panel of stained glass. Each panel was unique, all bearing the image of different flowers. The morning glory window was her favorite. The first rays of the morning sun lit it up, covering the room in spots of purple and blue, and pink and green. She'd been so fascinated by that window that her grandmother used to greet her with a cheery "Mornin', Glory!" when she woke up.

"Penny for your thoughts," Mark said, his voice quiet in the large room.

Lucy decided it was time to tell him everything. "Mark, bear with me. I feel like you deserve to know the whole story of what's been going on around here, at least as far as I know and understand it myself."

He listened quietly while Lucy laid out all the strange things that had happened over the summer. Some he knew—like finding her on an antique ship where her abductors barricaded her into a sailor's berth. Other things he didn't know—like the strange encounters with Fuchsia Butterfield, the poem in the book, the hidden compartment in her grandmother's desk, and even the odd double cellar below the house. He didn't interrupt her with any questions, for which Lucy was grateful. She wasn't sure she could remember everything as it was.

It was such a relief to unburden herself to Mark and to see that he didn't seem upset that she'd held some things back from him. She found herself resting her head on Mark's chest, with his arm wrapped around her. His chest provided the perfect place for her head, almost as if it belonged there. Exhausted, Lucy closed her eyes and snuggled into Mark's side.

*L*ucy woke up under a fuzzy sherpa-style blanket, her head on a couple of pillows from the sofa. Mark was nowhere around. Had he gone to bed upstairs and decided not to wake her? Perhaps he had been uncomfortable on the sofa with her propped on him. She felt both cared for and slightly annoyed—the blanket and pillows were nice, but why didn't he just wake her up so she could sleep in her own bed?

Lucy stood and stretched, then folded the blanket and put the pillows back in place. Her throat felt scratchy and dry, so she headed to the kitchen to get a glass of water. The clock on the microwave indicated that it was already after 3:00 a.m. Lucy yawned and drank nearly the entire glass of water in one go. She was about to refill her glass from the tap when she heard a noise under the kitchen floor. She froze, hoping it was only a tree branch rubbing the outside of the house. But then she heard it again. Lucy set her glass in the sink and raced up the back stairs. If someone was in the house, or rather, under it, she didn't want to take any chances.

She tapped on the door to Mark's room quietly, hoping not to disturb Hattie—at least not yet—and when he didn't answer, she gently turned the knob and crept into the room. There was enough light coming in from the window that she could tell Mark's bed was empty. The door to the en suite bathroom was open and the lights weren't on, but she called Mark's name anyway.

When there was no response, she figured maybe he was downstairs in another part of the house. Steeling her nerve, she crept back down the stairs, avoiding the squeaky spots the best she could. Her phone was on the charger in the kitchen, so she picked it up and turned on the flashlight. She made a quick pass through the bookstore and the dining room and peered into the round reading room but didn't see Mark anywhere. She peeked out the windows to see if his truck was still parked in the drive. It was.

Perhaps Mark had also heard the noise, and he went to investigate. What if something happened to him? If someone had broken in and caught him off guard? Her mind began to race as she thought of Mark in danger, or injured, or worse. The door to the basement was shut tight, but Lucy had to assume now that Mark was down there, and possibly not alone. She grabbed a heavy flashlight from the kitchen that would not only cast more light than her phone but would also double as a handy weapon if she needed one.

She stuffed her phone in her pocket and opened the basement door. She didn't hear anything, so she cupped her hand over the flashlight and directed its beam onto the stairs. She crept down as quietly as she could, but still, several stairs squeaked in protest. When she reached the basement floor, she stood silently, waiting to see if she had attracted any attention as she descended. After a minute or two of trying to quiet her breathing and slow her racing pulse, Lucy raised the light and swept it through the room.

Relieved that no one appeared to be nearby, she made her way farther in, avoiding boxes and dusty crates. The basement felt so much more ominous in the dark, but she didn't want to turn on a light just yet. She still needed to check the rooms beyond the main one and the pantry alcove where she'd hidden the trapdoor to the root cellar with a large cedar chest.

She crept forward, feeling her way now that she'd extinguished the flashlight. She paused to listen again when she was sure she'd reached the far side of the main room. Then she heard the same scraping noise she'd heard upstairs, but it was awfully close to her. She stifled her breath and stood perfectly still. *Of all the stupid things I could be doing right now—*

Suddenly a bright light blinded her.

"Hold it right there!" The male voice boomed and echoed through the basement. Lucy stumbled backward, flailing wildly in an attempt to catch herself. Thankfully a sturdy cloth-covered settee broke her fall before she tumbled off it and onto the floor.

She opened her mouth to scream, but panic had closed her throat, and only a squeak emerged.

"Lucy?" It was Mark. Relief flooded her body.

Mark grabbed her under the shoulders and helped her stand. She'd lost her grip on the flashlight as she fell. It had turned itself on when it hit the ground, so he bent over to pick it up. She felt very lightheaded, so she sat again on the settee.

"Mark, what are you doing down here?" Lucy looked up at him. Had he decided to explore the basement himself after what she'd shared with him earlier in the evening? Maybe he didn't believe her about not being involved in whatever smuggling operation he was investigating after all, and he was down in the basement searching for—she didn't know what.

"Lucy, I want you to go back upstairs immediately and lock the door to the cellar. Go find Hattie, and lock yourself in with her until I come to get you." Mark aimed the beam of his flashlight toward the basement stairs.

Lucy shook her head. She wasn't going anywhere until she got some answers!

"Please answer the question, Mark. What are you doing down here?" She lifted her chin, feeling the stubbornness solidify. "This is my grandparents' house—my house. I have a right to know what's going on."

"Do you trust me, Lucy? If you trust me, go upstairs. I heard something down here, and I don't want you here if someone's broken in. I'm trying to protect you!"

Lucy softened. She knew Mark cared deeply about her safety. He was here, wasn't he? In the middle of the night, in her basement, ready to take on anything that might be a threat to her.

"Of course, I trust you, Mark. I heard noises, and when I couldn't find you, I came down here. I was worried something happened to you." She stood. Mark was standing close to her and wrapped his arm around her waist.

"No one has worried about me in a long time, Lucy. That means more than you know. I don't think anyone is in these rooms, but I can't get into the doors over there. Someone may be inside one of them hiding. He aimed his beam at the second room of the basement, which had doors in each of the walls.

"I don't think anyone could be in those rooms. They've been locked for ages, and I'm not sure where the key is. I don't think anyone could enter them easily. I did check them recently." She shook her head. "What did you hear, exactly?"

"I must have dozed off not long after you did. I woke up from a dream where I heard footsteps and whispers. It startled me awake. I didn't move at first because you looked so comfortable there, and I didn't want to wake you, but then I heard something that sounded like it was underneath the floor. There was a thud, it sounded like something falling, then I heard a scraping noise. By the time I got down here, I think whoever it was, or whatever it was, had stopped."

Lucy had almost recovered from the fright and adrenaline rush. "Did you check the root cellar?"

"I haven't been able to find it yet. You didn't tell me where it was, so I've been trying to move some furniture around to look for it."

Before Lucy could tell him where it was, they heard a grinding noise coming from the pantry area. Lucy pointed. "It's over there. I think someone must be down there!" She clutched Mark's arm. "Do you think we should call the police?"

"Is there any other way out of there?" Mark asked.

Lucy hesitated. "I ... I don't think so. I couldn't find one when I was down there."

"Show me where the door is." Mark put a firm hand on her shoulder. "And then I want you to go upstairs. Be ready to call for backup if I need it. Just call Captain Harrison, not the station, okay?" Lucy agreed.

She led Mark over to where the trapdoor was. She was not surprised to see the cedar chest moved away from its spot. The door was closed, though, and no matter how hard Mark pulled on the handle, it wouldn't budge.

"Is there a trick to the door, Lucy?"

"No, it opened easily for me, almost like it popped open when I pulled. Lucy gave it a pull, but it didn't budge for her, either.

"Well, if there's no way out, we'll just keep them in!" Mark slid the heavy chest back into place, and for good measure, he added a couple of boxes of books from a shelf nearby. "That should hold them. It would be almost impossible to push that off from beneath."

Lucy pulled out her phone. It was time to bring Captain Harrison into this. She'd added the police captain's number earlier when he'd given her his card.

"I don't have a signal. I'll have to go upstairs." Lucy pulled the string connected to the overhead light, but it didn't turn on, so she raised her flashlight. The bulb was missing.

"I'll stay here and babysit the cellar," Mark said. "I'll hold my light up for you, and you can use yours. Just be careful."

Lucy was halfway across the room when someone turned on the lights from the top of the staircase, flooding the entire basement with light. Whoever it was drew back from the door, though, before Lucy got a glimpse.

"Who's down there?" a woman's voice called.

"I am. Who's up there?" Lucy answered.

"Lucy! I was worried sick! I think you better come up here." Hattie's pinched face appeared around the side of the door. She didn't look inclined to come down the basement stairs at all. "There's something you need to see."

Lucy decided to wait on calling Captain Harrison when she heard what Hattie had to say. She called down to Mark and told him to stay put and then followed Hattie up the stairs so she could see it with her own eyes.

"This is what woke me up," Hattie said. "Someone was in the bathroom here—I could hear the water running!" Hattie shivered. "It woke me up from a sound sleep." She pointed at the taps. "There was a message written on the mirror, Lucy!"

Lucy sighed, "Oh, that? It startled me the first time too. I saw it earlier this summer. It's nothing. My grandparents used to leave each other silly notes." Lucy thought perhaps Hattie had got up to use the bathroom, and in her groggy state, left the tap running, then woke up more fully after she'd laid back down. "The mind can play tricks on you, Hattie."

Hattie was adamant. "No, Lucy, someone was in here! I heard them turn off the taps. I thought maybe it was you, that maybe your bathroom was having a problem, so you came to use mine. But Lucy, when I called your name to see if you needed anything, no one answered. Then I started hearing weird noises, so I got out of bed and grabbed the lamp because I was afraid it was the man who's been following you." Hattie picked up the bedside lamp and demonstrated to Lucy how she'd crept up to the bathroom door. "I thought I would catch him by surprise and knock him over the head! When I flipped the lights on, no one was there. But the mirror still had the trace of a message in the steam."

Lucy didn't want to alarm Hattie, but she decided to tell her the truth.

"Mark has someone locked in the root cellar. He heard something under the floor and went down to check it out. We think we have whoever it is trapped down there." Lucy put an arm around the older lady's shoulders. "So, there's nothing to worry about. I was about to call Captain Harrison."

"Lucy, what did the message on the mirror say when you saw it?" Hattie asked.

Lucy tilted her head as she tried to recall. "I think it said, 'Meet me in the basement.'"

Hattie walked over to the vanity and turned the hot water on.

"That isn't what it says now."

Lucy's eyes grew wide. The words appearing in the mirror were "Get Lucy alone, and meet me in the center." Lucy could feel the hair stand up on her arms and legs. Someone had been here, after all. But how did they know about the messages on the mirror? Maybe the earlier message was not from her grandparents. Maybe someone—or more than one someone—had been coming and going through her house all summer. Lucy didn't like that idea at all.

For the second time in under twenty-four hours, Coast Guard Captain Mark Fellowes and Police Captain Andy Harrison found themselves in close proximity. This time, however, they were working together and using hushed voices. Neither of them could lift the door to the root cellar.

When Lucy called, Captain Harrison had answered the phone on the second ring even though it was the wee small hours of the morning. Lucy thought he sounded remarkably alert. He had promised to be right over, but Lucy was still surprised at how quickly he'd arrived. Hattie filled him in about the message on the mirror, and Lucy let Mark tell him about the strange noises and the person they believed they had trapped in the root cellar.

Captain Harrison had arrived alone and in his own car. Lucy assumed that he'd already called for backup, so she went to the kitchen and put on a pot of coffee. The sun would be up soon, and she knew that at least she and Mark and Hattie would need a pick-me-up. She sincerely hoped that all this would soon be over.

*M*ark sat at the kitchen table watching Lucy, twin creases between his eyes. Lucy knew he was concerned about having to go back to his ship. He'd already tried and failed to convince her to go stay at Hattie's until the person breaking into her house was caught. Andy Harrison had promised to keep watch personally and set a patrol at the house, and Hattie had volunteered to stay every night for as long as she was needed.

"Lucy, you and Hattie both mean a great deal to me. I can't stand the thought of anything happening to either of you." Mark shook his head. "I don't know what's going on here or why someone is playing games with you, but it worries me."

"I know, Mark. I'm just as frustrated as you are. And sleep-deprived! I think this is my third cup of coffee, and I'm not sure if the caffeine is making me jittery, or if I'm anxious. It's probably a bit of both." Lucy offered him a tentative smile. "Maybe it's good news that no one was in the root cellar?"

"I was sure someone was down there! Maybe I'm losing my mind." Mark put his face in his hands.

After a couple of hours of trying to get the root cellar door to open, it had suddenly clicked and opened easily. Mark and Captain Harrison had rushed down there but found no sign of anyone. Lucy showed them the shelves that swung out and the odd depressions in the wall, but neither man thought they were significant after pushing and pounding on them in turns. Captain Harrison decided that whatever they heard, the person must have slipped out and was long gone before Mark and Lucy made it to the basement. He'd gone home to catch some sleep but promised to set up more patrols and to be available himself in the evening.

The similarities between the men caught Lucy's attention again when Mark walked the captain to the door. She wondered if they saw it too or if they would think she was silly. Both were tall. Both had those light green eyes. Both men made her feel safe and protected, but Mark stirred a lot of other feelings in her too.

She put a hand on his arm and leaned toward him. He leaned forward too until their foreheads were resting against each other. She thought he might kiss her, but instead, he closed his eyes, so she closed hers too. Lucy sighed. Somehow this felt more intimate than a kiss and more sacred than a prayer. They would have to trust that things were going to be okay, even while they were apart.

Hattie, who'd left early to go open the cafe, called just then and broke the spell. The woman had terrible timing. Mark picked up Lucy's cell and handed it to her.

"Hello, Hattie"

"Hey, Lucy, hon, I had one of the guys pack up a lunch for you and Mark. You want me to have them deliver it?"

Lucy had put her on speakerphone and looked to Mark to see what he wanted to do.

"Hi, Hattie, it's Mark. All the excitement is over here. There was no one in the root cellar, so I'm thinking I should get Lucy out for some fresh air." He cocked an eyebrow in her direction, and she nodded her agreement.

"I have to go back to the ship around dinnertime. Could you pack up some of those cashew cookies for me to take back? I'm gonna miss your cooking!" Mark grinned at Lucy, who smiled in return. It wasn't her cooking he'd miss, not that he'd had much chance to try it!

Lucy decided to close the bookstore for the afternoon so she could spend every precious minute with Mark. He wasn't sure when he'd be back in town. It could be two days or two weeks, so Lucy didn't want to miss out on any time with him.

Just as they were about to walk out, a customer came in to pick up a special order that had recently arrived. Lucy sent Mark ahead, telling him she'd finish up and follow him in her car so he wouldn't have to worry about driving her home later.

A few minutes later, Lucy locked the front door and went to check the back. Satisfied, she picked up her purse and keys and headed back to the front of the store to make sure the security system was armed.

She gave Tor an ear and chin scratch as she passed through the dining room. He'd taken to napping in one of the chairs every day like clockwork. Lucy was already missing Mark and wondering what Hattie had packed up for them this time when she entered the bookstore area at the front of the house. Focused on hurrying to catch up with Mark, she didn't notice the elderly woman sitting in her grandmother's desk chair.

"Lucy! Slow down!"

Thinking she was alone, Lucy yelped and turned to face the unexpected visitor. Had someone been browsing when she locked up thinking the store was empty? Or was it someone else, someone dangerous?

"Lucy, I need to talk to you!" Fuchsia Butterfield pushed down on the arms of the desk chair and lifted herself out of it with a wince of pain.

Lucy was relieved and annoyed to see the woman. Whenever Fuchsia showed up, it usually meant a headache for Lucy.

"Fuchsia, what are you doing here? How did you get in? Do the police know where you are?" Lucy fired her questions in rapid succession. She pulled her phone out to call the station. She would show that awful Mooney. He had the nerve to believe she could not only attack someone but make them vanish too, but seeing Fuchsia in the flesh would remove her from suspicion.

"Lucy, I don't have time to explain. I've been waiting to get you alone, but someone is always here! Did you get the book I sent you?"

Lucy's stomach lurched when Fuchsia mentioned getting her alone. Maybe the older lady did mean to harm her!

"I did. I don't know why you left it for me, but one of the police officers took it at first and tried to use it as evidence that I somehow did away with you!" Lucy frowned at the woman. "What exactly did you mean by leaving that for me? Were the underlined words some kind of message?"

"Yes, Lucy, the words were a message. You're not very good at this, are you?" The older woman looked disappointed in Lucy.

"Very good at what?" asked Lucy.

The frail woman waved her hand around, gesturing at the ceiling and the floor and the stacks of books. "All of this. I expected you to understand." A look of panic crossed her face. "Do you still have it? Oh no. If the police have it . . ." The older woman looked distressed.

"Here, sit down," Lucy insisted. She helped ease the Fuchsia back into the desk chair. "I have the book put away for safekeeping. I don't think Officer Mooney hurt it with his sweaty, sticky hands, but he did find the underlined words and asked me what they meant. I had no idea, and I still don't. Why don't you explain it to me?"

"It isn't just about the words, Lucy! I hated to underline anything in a first edition of that quality, but I hoped it would mean something to you, and you'd figure it out! Where's the book? Give it to me!"

Lucy hesitated, but the book had come to her from the woman, so Lucy decided she had every right to ask for it back.

"It's here, in the desk. Scoot back a little, and I'll get it out for you. It's under some papers and mail. I meant to look it up to find its value, but I haven't had time, so I hid it back here in case it was worth something."

Lucy eased the book out from under the assorted papers and handed it to Fuchsia.

"'We dance round in a ring and suppose, but the secret sits in the middle and knows,'" Lucy quoted the underlined passage in the Robert Frost book. She knew it by heart—she'd pondered it enough and even had a strange dream of children dancing while chanting that song. "What does that mean?"

Fuchsia didn't answer. Instead, she grasped both covers of the book and pushed against the corners, causing the spine to pucker out a bit from the pages beneath. She then stuck her index finger into the tight space, wiggling it in as if fishing for something.

"What are you doing? You're going to ruin that book," Lucy said. The book was an antique, and now that she knew it was a first edition, valuable.

"No, it's okay. Look here." Fuchsia pulled her finger out, and sliding along under it was a square of folded paper. She carefully opened it to reveal a tarnished key that looked like brass to Lucy.

"You'll need this. It goes to the desk. Use the key to open the desk. There's a lot you don't know, and I don't have time to explain it to you now. You need to keep it a secret, Lucy, all of it. Can you do that?"

"All of *what*?" She was confused. She felt as if she were part of an early game show on television, waiting for the host to come out and make sense of the mysterious and bewildering events. Was Fuchsia Butterfield suffering from a mental health issue?

Did she have something to do with the people breaking into Lucy's house and skulking around on the grounds?

"Lucy, your grandparents weren't who you thought they were. You need to understand that. I mean, yes, they were your grandparents, but you have no idea what they were doing here. It's what caused them to . . ." Fuchsia bowed her head and shook it gently. She was struggling with the words. "It's why they disappeared."

"What do you know about it? You need to tell me what happened to them! Have you talked to the police?" Lucy was losing patience. Did this woman know something that could solve the mystery of her grandparents' disappearance? Was she suffering from some kind of delusion?

"Police! No, no police!" The elderly woman shot out of her chair. "Don't trust anybody, Lucy. Do you hear me? Use the key. I left the book for you because I think they knew I had it. I had to hide out to throw them off the scent. You see what's inside the desk, then you can make your own decisions. I don't want any part of it anymore. It leads to nothing but heartache."

The old woman shuffled quickly toward the front door. She unlocked it and turned to look at Lucy. "You're not safe here. Don't think you're safe. Same as what happened to them could happen to you."

With that, Fuchsia slipped out the door.

Lucy was furious. How dare she make all sorts of insinuations and threats like that. Lucy ran after her. If nothing else, she was going to take a picture of the woman looking alive and well to clear her name once and for all, but when she stepped outside, there was no trace of the elusive Fuchsia Butterfield.

Chapter
Twenty-Two

*L*ucy pulled into the parking area across the street from the Lace Curtain Cafe and parked next to Mark's truck. Mark was crossing the street to meet her, a concerned look on his face.

"There you are. I was starting to worry! I shouldn't have left you there by yourself." He scooped Lucy up into a hug, holding her close for a long moment before letting her go. "Was it just your customer taking her own sweet time?"

Lucy laughed and shook her head. "You're not going to believe this. Fuchsia Butterfield was in the store. Apparently, she'd been lurking around trying to get me alone."

Mark picked up Lucy's hand as they crossed the street. "She didn't hurt you or anything, did she? Did you tell her she's a missing person, and the police still suspect you might have had something to do with it?"

"I told her! I don't think she intends me any harm, but she said some strange things about my grandparents. I don't want to get into it right now. I just want to have a nice lunch with you. I know you need to go back to the ship tonight, and I want to focus on just enjoying the day. I closed the bookstore for the day. No more interruptions!" Lucy squeezed his hand and then let go as she climbed the steps to the cafe.

Hanging baskets of flowers and ivy decorated the four corners of the porch, and several beautiful Boston ferns dotted the spaces between outdoor tables. Lucy thought the cafe looked beautiful. "Do you want to eat out here? It's such a beautiful day!"

She inhaled the sea air. It was one of those perfect days, warm but with a mild breeze from the water—one with perfect, cottony clouds and a clear blue sky. The only thing that wasn't perfect was knowing Mark had to leave in just a few hours.

"I have a better idea." Mark winked at Lucy and stuck his head inside the door to the cafe, nodding to one of the servers. "How about we eat at the beach?"

Just then, two of the young men who had volunteered to help her during the fairy book faire came out of the cafe, each carrying several items. One had several bags of food and a frayed quilt, and the other carried a drinks cooler and had a canvas tote slung over his shoulder with chairs, an umbrella, and beach towels.

"Is this for us?" Lucy squealed with delight. "I've barely seen the beach this summer! Oh, thank you, thank you!" She reached up and kissed Mark on the cheek. He turned a bit red when the two high school boys whistled and winked at him.

"I would love to take credit for this, Lucy, but it was Hattie's idea. Something she said she's thinking of trying out—beach picnics to go. We're her guinea pigs, so to speak." Mark led Lucy down the steps as they followed the two young men. By the time they descended the stairs to the beach at the other end of the street and walked across the sand, everything had been set up for them. Lucy marveled that there was even a camping table that came in a bag but worked perfectly to hold their lunch. Mark thanked the young men and surreptitiously handed each of them a tip, and they each hugged Lucy.

"We'll be back in a couple of hours to carry everything back.

You don't need to worry about anything," one of them told Lucy.

Lucy offered him a wide smile. "You're Josh, right? And this is Kai? Thank you both! This is great!"

The boys nodded, obviously pleased that she'd remembered their names, and then took off. They both had a shift to finish at Hattie's cafe. She made a mental note to pick up something nice for Hattie as a thank you.

The meal was delicious and perfect for the beach. There were two sandwiches cut in half to share. One was a portobello mushroom, roasted red pepper, and grilled eggplant sandwich, the other a hot roast beef sandwich piled high with grilled peppers, onions, and provolone cheese, and topped with Hattie's secret sauce. There was a generous bag of freshly made sweet potato chips, pickle spears, and two giant chocolate and oatmeal cookies. Lucy and Mark polished off almost every bite, washing it down with honey mango iced tea from a couple of insulated thermoses. With the soft breeze blowing over her, a full stomach, and the sound of the waves lulling her, Lucy felt as if she could sleep for a week right there on the beach. She sighed and smiled with contentment at Mark. He looked sleepy himself.

The boys had laid out the quilt on the sand and put the two rolled-up beach towels on it so that it looked very inviting. Too inviting. She blushed at the thought that it resembled a bed and decided she'd better shake off the food coma. Besides, she didn't want to fall asleep and miss out on what time they had left to spend together.

Mark looked at Lucy with an amused smile. Could he read her mind? Lucy blushed even more furiously. He stood up and stretched and then bagged up the remains of their lunch containers. She pitched in and packed away the drinks into the cooler and cleaned up the crumbs. Lucy walked over to Mark and laid her head on his arm. She wanted to drink it all in—the beauty of their surroundings and the bliss of her companion.

Mark slipped his arm around her, and she wrapped hers around his waist. They walked together to the edge of the water, letting the foamy wavelets cover their naked toes. Lucy always marveled at how cold the Pacific water was, but she loved the refreshing tingle and fully alive feeling it gave her.

They didn't talk much as they strolled along the edge of the ocean, stopping now and then to pick up a shell or a pretty rock. Lucy spied a bit of sea glass nestled against some driftwood and quickly gathered a few pieces before the next set of waves came in and washed the rest away. She was thrilled—not only had she found the common greens, browns, and blues, but she'd also picked up a larger piece of pink and a smaller cobalt blue. Mark had scored a rare crimson red piece earlier as well as a couple of aquamarine ones. Lucy had spied a sealable plastic bag in their lunch provisions—probably for leftovers—and stuffed it in her pocket earlier. She carefully transferred all the shells and pieces of sea glass into the bag. It was a pretty collection, she thought, imagining it in a jar on her desk or perhaps glued into a picture for some craft project. But Mark spoke up first and asked if he could take them.

Surprised, Lucy agreed. Maybe he was thinking the same thing—that they would look nice in a jar on his desk, a memento of their delightful day. Seeing the sentimental part of Mark warmed Lucy's heart. *How did I get so lucky? Lucky Lucy, that's my name.* She tried hard to suppress a giggle. If Mark knew how corny she was, maybe he wouldn't find her as appealing. She couldn't quite keep the smile off her face though.

The time passed too quickly. The servers from Hattie's had packed up the picnic and carried it away before they returned. Only the quilt remained, with their shoes on the corners to hold it in place. Mark sat and pulled Lucy down to sit in front of him, allowing her to use him for a backrest. She turned her face up to him, and he responded with a sweet, lingering kiss.

Arms entwined, they watched the sun sink slowly toward the sea, staying as long as possible.

Hattie rocked in a chair on the front porch of The Cozy Cat Bookstore. It was nearly twilight, but the charming street-lights hadn't yet flickered on. Across from her, Lucy sat still and in silence in a matching rocking chair. The two women had become quite close. Lucy adored Hattie and was grateful for the older woman's presence in her life. Her willingness to pack a bag and stay with Lucy was remarkable all by itself, but when Lucy factored in all the practical and thoughtful ways Hattie had looked after her, she ran out of fingers on which to count her blessings several times over. Lucy had never eaten so well in her life, and having someone else in the house with her, besides Tor, had given her the peace of mind to sleep soundly again.

The only thing missing was Mark, who'd only been able to email her a few times from his current location. He'd sent her a message that morning, describing how they were inspecting the navigational buoys they were responsible for maintaining. Mark told her about a couple of new ensigns who'd just joined the ship. One was overconfident, and the other was nervous about driving the boat for the first time. In the end, the anxious young woman who felt unprepared did a better job than the one who was sure he knew what he was doing.

"Our motto is *Semper Paratus*, which means 'Always Ready,'" he'd written. Lucy smiled when she read that because sometimes Mark reminded her of a grown-up Boy Scout. He had a little bit of everything in his truck and was always prepared for pretty much any situation.

Lucy sighed. She loved this time of day. It was quiet except for crickets and treefrogs and the occasional bird calling its mate. It was still light enough to see, but the world slowly faded as the light dimmed. Lucy and her grandparents had enjoyed "the gloaming" many times as they sat in the same place and watched the lights come on in the houses down the street. Her grandmother even sang a little song about it with a haunting Irish melody, one that her own grandmother had sung to her when she was a girl. Lucy started to hum the song then began quietly singing it.

> In the gloaming
> oh my darling!
> When the lights are dim and low
> And the quiet shadows falling
> Softly come and softly go
> When the winds are sobbing faintly
> With a gentle, unknown woe,
> Will you think of me and love me
> As you did once long ago?

Hattie joined on the second verse, her rich, mature voice blending seamlessly with Lucy's.

> In the gloaming, oh my darling!
> Think not bitterly of me!
> Though I passed away in silence,
> Left you lonely, set you free.
> For my heart was crushed with longing
> What had been could never be.
> It was best to leave you thus, dear
> Best for you and best for me.

Lucy felt a sob catch in her throat. For just a moment, it was as if her grandmother were there with her again, singing along. Hattie was like an adopted grandmother, which added to the emotion threatening to well up and overflow. Lucy rose from her rocker and went over to sit on the porch next to Hattie, who stopped rocking and patted Lucy on the arm.

"Hattie, have you ever noticed the color of Mark's eyes? They're such an unusual shade of green. The color reminds me of some of the sea glass we found at the beach." Lucy wanted to take her mind off missing her grandparents, but missing Mark was also bringing tears to the surface. She wondered what he was doing and if he missed her as much as she was missing him. She felt a little wish of a prayer escape from her mind for his wellbeing.

"He does have beautiful eyes. I've always thought so. They look as if they're lit from the inside sometimes," Hattie mused.

"Did you ever notice that Captain Harrison has almost the same color of eyes? They have the same build too. How weird is that?" Lucy recalled how much the two of them seemed like bookends—one younger, one older—as they'd stood together earlier in the week.

"Yes . . . ," Hattie hesitated, "I have noticed. I don't think they've noticed, but I see it. Lucy, there's something you should know about Mark."

Lucy's stomach dropped. She couldn't bear any more bad news, any more secrets or unknowns or mysteries. She turned her face up to Hattie, who brushed a strand of hair out of Lucy's eyes as gently as a mother would. Her eyes pleaded with Hattie as her mind scrambled to imagine what Hattie was referring to.

"You know I took Mark in when he was younger, right?"

Lucy nodded. She also knew Mark was estranged from his mother and didn't know his father. He carried his mother's last name, and she had refused to talk about who his father was.

"Well, his mother used to live in town here. She was a nice young woman but came from a broken home and had some issues. Mark lived here with her when he was little, but then she left with him to live on her grandparents' farm in the Central Valley. Mark came back here on his own. He remembered the ocean and hearing his mother talk about growing up here.

"When she married a man who didn't want Mark around, he took off. At sixteen, runaways aren't a priority to the police, and I don't think she ever did report him missing. I never could understand how any mother could let a child leave that way and not even try to work things out.

"You see," she continued, "I found him behind the cafe one day not long after he'd arrived. He was dirty and sad—and far too thin. He offered to wash dishes for me for a meal. Well, I'd have fed him for free!"

Tears rolled unchecked down Lucy's face as the thought of Mark, her strong, proud, wonderful Mark, alone and hungry and unwanted as a teenager. He couldn't have found a softer place to land than Hattie's, she thought. She added it to her list of reasons she was grateful for the older woman.

"I know you would, Hattie. I know how much you love to feed people." Lucy beamed at her.

"I tried to give him food—no strings attached—but he wouldn't take it unless he earned it. Well, I couldn't let him wash dishes in the state he was in, so I sent him upstairs for a shower and found some things he could wear while his clothes were in the wash. I made him eat a Jammie Sammie before letting him do any work, though, because I didn't want him falling over in the dishwater!" Hattie smiled at the memory.

"I made him move into the spare bedroom. I told him I needed a man around the place and a security guard and handyman for the cafe. Lucy, he was the hardest-working child I've ever seen. It took a while for him to open up and let me in, but he eventually did. I made him go back to school, and he stayed with me right up until he went into the Coast Guard. I couldn't be prouder of him if he were my own child!"

Lucy reached up and squeezed Hattie's hand. "Thank you for taking care of him, Hattie. And thank you for telling me all that. But what is it you're not telling me?" Lucy could see that the dear older woman was holding something back.

"Well, I don't know this for sure, but I feel it in my bones. I think Captain Harrison is Mark's father. I haven't told Mark this, but they do look an awful lot alike. And whoever the father was, he was from here. I don't think Captain Harrison has any idea. I'm pretty sure Mark's mother broke up with the father of her child without ever telling him she was pregnant. I've wondered if I should say anything, but Mark never talks about who his father might be, and I've never wanted to intrude on that pain. But I've had half a mind to hunt his mother down and ask her!"

Lucy was speechless. Deep down, she already knew it was true. The two men had to be father and son. Lucy was unsure what to do about it. Mark hadn't opened up about his family to her yet, only that he'd left home young and hadn't been in contact with his mother for many years, and his father was a mystery. Should she ask him about it more and gently suggest the possibility? Should she let Hattie speak to him about it, as she'd known him for so much longer and knew his mother? Hattie hadn't brought it up with him so far, so maybe she never would. Lucy decided that she'd have time to think about it for a little while before making a decision. Right now, she was tired and emotional and a little overwhelmed.

She stood up and kissed Hattie on the cheek. "Thank you for telling me. I think you're right. I have no idea what we should do about that, so I'm going to bed. Do you remember the code to lock up? If you leave early tomorrow morning, can you reset the alarm?"

Hattie stood and hugged Lucy. "I'll just come in with you, and you can show it to me again. I'm ready to pass out for the night."

Chapter Twenty-Three

*L*ucy dreamed all night long, tossing and turning. Several times she woke herself up by talking in her sleep. In one dream, Lucy's grandmother was speaking to her, calling her name, but she was too far away, and Lucy could never find her. When she finally woke up for the day, Lucy could only remember feeling helpless to find her grandmother and the grief of never getting to say goodbye.

She checked her phone first thing, hoping to see a message from Mark, but there was nothing. She knew there was a possibility his ship would be in today or tomorrow for fuel and supplies, but she also knew he could be called away at any time and not be able to visit.

Lucy went downstairs to make a cup of tea before she had to open the bookstore. She was determined to have a normal day with regular business hours. Things had been haphazard in that area lately. Some of her regular customers had left voicemails expressing concern for her, so she'd sent out an email blast to let everyone know the store would be open all day and offered a 15 percent off coupon for anyone who came in and mentioned the email. She wondered equally whether anyone would take her up on the offer at all or if she'd be stampeded.

It turned out to be a slow morning. Only a couple of tourists dropped in for books to read on the beach. In the quiet, Lucy remembered the key Fuchsia had removed from the spine of the Robert Frost book. She'd stuck it in her jacket pocket on the way to meet Mark that day and hadn't remembered it until now. Her jacket hung on a coat tree just inside the dining room door—the space that separated her living quarters from the bookstore that occupied the former parlor and front rooms of the early Victorian home.

Lucy unwrapped the key and noticed a word written on it that she hadn't seen before. The italicized script, in a faded sepia tone, said only "Revelare." The paper itself felt homemade, thick, and slightly irregular. She pulled out her phone and looked up the meaning of the word. It was Latin for "reveal" or "revelation." Fuchsia said the key opened the desk, but Lucy didn't recall seeing a place to insert a key, and she'd looked over every square inch of her grandmother's gorgeous antique writing desk. Tor had somehow managed to open it—and had upset Lucy's lunch at the same time.

It was close to lunchtime now. Lucy usually closed for half an hour to make herself a sandwich and give Tor a treat. He was always hungry for a little bit of turkey or fish after his usual long morning nap. She pulled out his box of treats, which he sniffed but didn't seem interested in. He held out for something better, so she ran into the kitchen and chopped up a thick slice of turkey from the deli.

He was immediately at her ankles, purring as loudly as possible. She picked him up and kissed him on top of his head, then put him down with his favorite dish. She grabbed a banana for herself and made her way to the front of the store. She'd left the door unlocked and the sign set to open, so she didn't want to be in the back of the house for long.

It didn't appear anyone had come in to take her up on the discount yet, so Lucy settled in at the desk with her fruit and the key. She looked over everything again but still didn't see a keyhole. She thought about the piece of paper with the word Revelare on it. Perhaps it meant a hidden keyhole was waiting to be revealed? Or maybe the words underlined by Fuchsia Butterfield in the poem were the clue she needed? "We dance round in a ring and suppose, But the Secret sits in the middle and knows . . ."

She knew there were hidden drawers in the desk—she'd briefly seen inside one before she closed it instinctively when Fuchsia startled her. It had so completely disappeared into the grain of the wood that if she hadn't seen it herself, she might not believe it was there. Tor had been on top of the upper cabinet of the desk when he somehow opened the drawer, so she went to fetch him. He was licking the last of the turkey clean from his saucer and mewed at her for more.

"I think you've had enough for today, Tor." She scratched under his chin and his motor revved once again. "I do need something from you though." She scooped him up, and though he let out a little chirp of protest, he didn't try to wiggle out of her arms.

Lucy lifted Tor to the top of the secretary, where he jumped out of her hands and perched in the center, peering over the edge at her curiously.

"Now, last time you were up here, and you were trying to snatch my lunch and you sort of waved your arm over the side . . ." Lucy brushed the cabinet in the same circular motion that Tor had used while "fishing" for her tuna salad. She heard something make a small click above her. It sounded like it came from where Tor was sitting, so she grabbed a stool. She could see the top of the cabinet now, and sure enough, a tiny section of wood had slidden away. Tor was batting at the spot, so she picked him and put him on the desk below.

"Ah, there you are!" Lucy could see the narrow slit of a

keyhole, so she put the key into it and gave it a gentle turn to the left. Nothing happened. She turned it to the right. The drawer that had opened before popped out, startling the cat and pushing him off the surface of the desk.

Lucy whooped, causing Tor to give her his best annoyed growl before he disappeared back to the kitchen. Perhaps Tor had somehow unlocked it last time with one of his claws? She didn't know for sure, but that seemed likely. She hopped down from the stool and peered into the drawer. It was empty!

She was sure she'd seen a book and pen, and a velvet bag before. Lucy sank into her grandmother's chair, shoulders slumped in frustration. Were those items stolen during the break-in? Did Fuchsia Butterfield take them herself?

Lucy cradled her head in her hands for a minute. She'd wanted to have some answers by now, not more questions. After feeling around inside the drawer, she slammed it shut—a little too hard. When she did, another drawer popped open, one she hadn't seen before. The book and the pen were there, along with the little blue velvet bag.

Lucy's heart raced. She was sure those things had been in the other drawer last time. How had they moved into another secret drawer? She pulled the bag out first. It was heavy in her hand, so she opened it, carefully emptying the contents onto the desk.

Laid out in front of her was a small pile of treasure. There were four gold coins, three silver coins, and several plastic bags of gemstones in an assortment of colors. Two other bags held pearls—one cream, and the other looked to be Tahitian black pearl. She placed them all back into the bag and put the bag in a non-hidden drawer to examine later.

Next, she pulled out the book. It was fragile and showed signs of water damage at some point in its history. Lucy handled it gently, only opening it partway to avoid further damaging the already-weathered leather cover. It appeared to be a logbook of some sort, the script inside from a bygone era and difficult to read. She flipped pages to another section, stopping when she saw a hand-drawn map of a coastline. After trying to decipher the tiny words written around the map, she turned the book to the end. The last entry was short. "Hope is gone. It lies beneath."

Lucy closed the book, tears threatening to spill over the rim of her eyes. She picked up the gold pen and examined its ornate body—a curling pattern etched lightly into the metal around the barrel. She traced it with a finger and looked at the nib. The pen seemed old too, but maybe not as old as the book.

Lucy remembered that she'd also seen a folded sheet of paper the first time one of the secret drawers had opened. She checked the bottom of the drawer and then felt around the back and sides. Her fingers brushed against something on the roof of the space, wedged into a crack. She pulled it out slowly, not wanting to damage it. Did someone deliberately place it there, or had it gotten stuck on its own? Lucy had a lightbulb moment. She remembered reading about antique furniture with mechanisms inside that did several operations. It only made sense that something inside the desk moved the objects around.

Lucy put the pen and the book in the same drawer with the jewels—one she could lock but was just a normal drawer. It wouldn't pay to have these things disappear again into another secret compartment!

She unfolded the letter. It appeared to be a poem written in a shaky hand.

> O my Luve's like a red, red rose,
> That's newly sprung in June:
> O my Luve's like the melodie,
> That's sweetly play'd in tune.

As fair art thou, my bonie lass,
So deep in luve am I;
And I will luve thee still, my dear,
Till a' the seas gang dry.

Till a' the seas gang dry, my dear,
And the rocks melt wi' the sun;
And I will luve thee still, my dear,
While the sands o' life shall run.

And fare-thee-weel, my only Luve!
And fare-thee-weel, a while!
And I will come again, my Luve,
Tho' 'twere ten thousand mile!"

Lucy recognized the Robert Burns song right away. The sad ballad was both a farewell and a promise of return. Lucy folded it up again and held it against her heart. She wondered if it was a declaration of love or a heart-breaking goodbye for whoever had written it and put it in the drawer. Lucy was glad she'd finally found the hidden items in the desk, but they troubled her too. If only Mark were here, he'd know what to do. Maybe she should call Sam and have him go with her to the bank. Surely the things she'd found would be better off in a safety deposit box.

Lucy thought she heard someone starting up the stairs to the bookstore. Tor hissed and jumped from his seat by the window where he'd been sleeping in a patch of sunlight. Lucy looked but didn't see anyone outside. She shivered and hugged herself. She'd be glad when Mark was back. She put the note in the drawer with the other things and locked it. She would wait until she had time to discuss it with him.

She quickly forgot Tor's hissing, however, when a group of excited kids tumbled into the store. A woman who looked tired enough to be their mother followed them in. She waved a sheet of paper at Lucy and asked if the coupon was still good. Glad to have customers, Lucy grinned and gave her a thumbs up.

The bookstore was busy all afternoon. Lucy enjoyed catching up with some of her regular customers but was glad when she saw Mark's truck coming up the drive just as the last customer was leaving. *Perfect timing,* she thought. She grabbed her purse and carefully set the alarm before locking the door.

*M*ark led Lucy across the street from the parking area that overlooked the ocean. She had always loved the sight of the green cliffs jutting out into the water. It was a beautiful place to build a town. She could see a couple of surfers below paddling out to catch the next set of waves. *I wish I could do that.* Lucy loved being in the water but had never made it off what the locals called Baby Beach, where generations of the town's kids had learned to swim and surf. She enjoyed riding her bodyboard in the shallows but was still too afraid to swim further out.

It was nearly dinnertime, but Lucy wasn't hungry just yet, and Mark was in the mood to walk, so they ambled down the weathered wooden promenade to window shop. Lucy had wanted to explore a new art gallery that opened on the same street, so they stopped in for a few minutes and admired the various works on display. She loved the oil paintings of the rugged-but-beautiful coastline, but a collection of old photographs posed on a steamer trunk caught her eye.

"Mark, look at this! It's my house!" Lucy leaned in to look more closely. The grand Queen Anne Victorian looked much the same as it did now, but the landscaping was remarkably different. Several trees that Lucy loved in her yard weren't even saplings yet in the photo. At the bottom of the picture was a card that read, "Patterson House, 1881."

"Do you think that's right?" Mark raised an eyebrow. "Could it be that old?"

Lucy nodded. "I guess it could. I didn't know exactly how old it was, but that would fit the general timeline of when Victorian houses were first being built here." The picture was in a frame on top of the table next to the trunk. She walked around the table, looking at it from all sides.

Mark, meanwhile, had gone to find someone working at the gallery. He came back with a young woman who claimed not to know much about the photo or trunk. She told Lucy she was filling in for her uncle while he was at dinner with his wife. She took Lucy's number and promised to have him call her.

The wheels in Lucy's mind were turning. She wanted that photograph! There was nothing like it in the house itself, but she felt strongly that it belonged there. She felt a longing for it that surprised her. She hoped it was for sale and told Mark as much. He promised to bring her back again if she didn't hear from the gallery owner right away.

After checking out a few more stores, including an adorable green and gold storefront with a window full of everything Irish, Lucy's stomach growled. Mark must have heard it because he patted his own lean midsection.

"I'm getting hungry too," he said. "I did make a reservation for us. I hope you don't mind?"

Lucy had assumed they would be eating at Hattie's and hadn't dressed for a nice dinner. She looked down at the clean but plain shirt and knit black pants she was wearing. It would have to do.

Mark's eyes followed her appraisal. He put an arm around her and gave a little squeeze. "You look wonderful. But wait here for a minute. I'll be right back!" He ran back toward the Celtic store and disappeared inside.

Lucy sat on a bench at the edge of a beautiful little pocket garden sandwiched between buildings. A mass of blooms hung down beside the bench, wild miniature roses in a beautiful shade of pink. She turned her head and inhaled their fragrance. They smelled like roses *should* smell, she thought. She rubbed one of the velvet blossoms against her cheek.

She closed her eyes. The roses closest to her and the night-blooming jasmine at her feet, combined with the fresh sea air on a mild summer evening, put her into a state of bliss. Mark found her a few minutes later, eyes still closed, smiling contentedly.

"Lucy, I hate to break into your thoughts but . . ."

She opened her eyes. Seeing Mark, the smile grew until her lips parted. "I was just thinking how wonderful it is to sit here and just be still. I think I nearly fell asleep though."

"I got you this." Mark handed her a bag with the logo of the Celtic store. "I hope you like it." He looked almost bashful, which made Lucy adore him even more.

"What is it? You didn't have to get me anything!" Lucy was excited. This was one surprise she knew she'd love.

"Just something I thought would look wonderful on you!" Mark took the bag back and pulled out a package of fabric tied with a ribbon. "Here, let's see how this looks." He untied the ribbon and shook out a lovely green wrap. It was lightweight but warm enough for the cooler evening temperatures that always came in with the fog.

"Oh, it's perfect!" Lucy pulled her strawberry blonde hair to one side so Mark could drape it around her. Mark's face gave it away that he thought so too.

"Yes, you are," he said. He pulled her to her feet and kissed her gently. Lucy swayed, causing him to draw her closer and hold her more tightly.

Her stomach rumbled again, loudly, causing them both to laugh.

"Gee, I thought I'd swept you off your feet, but you were just hungry!" Mark pretended to pout, making Lucy laugh even more.

Lucy sighed and leaned back in her chair. Dinner had been just what she needed. The creamy stack of potato gratin, sauteed wild greens, and beef tenderloin with mushroom gravy was the perfect blend of upscale and comfort food. She couldn't quite finish it all, so she turned down dessert. Mark ordered a caramel apple custard tart and two spoons—just in case she found room.

It was Lucy's first time eating at the restaurant. The host seated them outside on a patio with glass walls overlooking the ocean, so they were able to watch the sunset during dinner. Lucy spent most of her time looking at Mark, though, marveling at this man who had come into her life so unexpectedly and in such a dramatic fashion. She couldn't believe her good fortune.

The fog had remained offshore until the sun was nearly down, but now it was rolling in quickly, turning the sky from bright pink to opaque blue gray. She shivered and pulled the wool wrap around her shoulders, grateful for the thoughtful gift. The only other couple seated outside were just leaving as Mark's dessert arrived. The server turned on an overhead gas heat lamp and surprised them with complimentary cups of rich French hot chocolate to sip. Lucy smiled at the server and thanked him. There was always room for chocolate!

Mark picked up the spoons and offered one to Lucy. "You can have the first bite if you want."

"No, you go ahead. I'm happy with the hot chocolate. It tastes as if they just melted expensive chocolate bars and poured them into a cup!" Lucy took another sip, savoring both the heat and the exquisite flavor.

"I need to tell you something," they both said in unison. "You first," they both responded.

Lucy laughed. "Mark, you go first. I want to drink this while it's hot!"

He smiled and gave her a look that made the warmth from the chocolate spread through her whole body, which made her blush and curled her toes.

"It's about the future, Lucy. I have some big decisions coming up. I want you to be a part of the decision-making."

Lucy took in the solemn look on Mark's face. She didn't want to ask him if he was sure about that—she could see that he was.

"Okay, Mark, I'm listening."

"I joined the Coast Guard just when I was eighteen, and I assumed it's what I would do my entire life. I've always been happy with my decision, and I've been given a lot of opportunities for advancement and training that I never would have had otherwise. But I'm at a point where I can reenlist, move to the reserves, or even just walk away. As things stand, I'm in line for a promotion in the next couple of years. Quite a few officers of a higher rank are set to retire soon. They're also offering delayed separation as an option, so I could tell them that I want to extend my current duty by a year. My concern is whether I should jump back in for another contract or not. If I do, I might be transferred somewhere else."

Lucy felt her stomach drop as she processed what he was saying. She did not want him to leave—that much was certain. But she wanted what was best for him too.

"Mark, the thought of you being transferred is not something I even want to consider! But I feel you need to make the decision based on what is best for you. I would never want to come between you and a career you love. I'm not going any-where. You don't need to worry about that." She reached across the table and put her hand in his. "What do *you* want to do?"

"I honestly don't know. I have the best crew. Being stationed here so close to you and Hattie is ideal. I've been exploring options for civilian jobs, and I've had a couple of offers already. Some of them sound amazing. I would have no trouble find-ing meaningful work that I enjoy. But other than an apartment on base, my only home to speak of is still a room at Hattie's. She's never let me pack up my things and move out completely. I would love to stay in this area, to put roots down here." He looked at Lucy intently. "Is that a possibility, Lucy? I know it's early days, but do you think you might also be willing to put down roots here with me?"

She looked up at him as he gently squeezed her hand. Power-ful waves of emotion washed over in time with the waves hitting the shore below. Her throat felt constricted, but she managed to answer. "I would love that, Mark."

He took her hand and pulled her up, engulfing her in the tightest hug she'd ever had. She hugged him in return until she needed to breathe again. Stepping back, she said, "Mark, I still need to tell you something too. But I don't want to do it here. Can we go back to the truck?"

"You haven't changed your mind, have you? Not already?" Mark teased.

"No, it isn't that. I just feel exposed out here even though we're alone. I'll tell you all about it when we go." The fog had continued to thicken to the point that Lucy wasn't sure she would know if they really were alone. She shivered again, but it wasn't from the cold this time. She followed Mark inside to find their server and pay the check.

The fog was so thick that they took their time driving home. Mark could just make out the road in front of him and knew the way, so Lucy wasn't worried about that. Still, she knew they wouldn't be able to see a stopped car or something in the road ahead of them until they were almost right on top of it. She wondered if she should tell Mark about the contents of the desk while he was driving or wait until they stopped.

Mark seemed to read her mind. "Do you want to tell me whatever it is now or wait? We're almost to the church parking lot. Why don't I pull over?"

Lucy agreed. She wanted to tell him everything, the sooner the better.

Mark stopped the truck and turned off the lights. He grinned at Lucy mischievously. "Are we too old to go parking?"

Lucy laughed, but secretly she loved the idea. She hadn't dated much in high school or even college.

"I don't know, Mark. Are we old enough to be parking? I've never been!" Lucy blushed furiously and was glad it was too dark for Mark to see.

"True confession time, I guess," he replied, sounding bashful. "I've never been parking either! Hattie kept me on a tight leash in high school, and the Coast Guard has kept me too busy since!"

Lucy's heart melted. She was sure he'd dated others in the past, but it seemed special to have a "first" opportunity like this. Mark must have thought so as well because he leaned over and kissed her. She was thrilled and decided to kiss him right back. After just a few minutes of this, however, Lucy started to giggle. Mark started laughing, and then they were both incapacitated with laughter.

"This isn't very comfortable, is it?" she asked.

"No! Not at all!" Mark rubbed his knee. "I don't think we missed as much as we thought we did as teenagers."

Lucy agreed. Still, it had been fun to try. She felt almost as giddy as a teenager, so she cleared her throat and shifted in her seat until she was sitting up properly. "I need to tell you what I found today. You're not going to believe it!"

Mark leaned in while Lucy told him all about the desk and the disappearing drawers and the treasures she'd discovered, along with the old book from the ship.

When she finished, he sat quietly for a minute before asking her, "Would you mind showing it to me? I wonder if someone knows about it, and that's why you've had so many intruders this summer."

The weight of the idea caused them to drive home in near silence. Mark texted Hattie to let her know he was going to stay over at Lucy's tonight and emphasized that he'd be sleeping downstairs, so she didn't need to come over. She texted back that she'd be over bright and early before the cafe opened to bring them some breakfast. Lucy and Mark knew that was her way of checking on them, but neither of them minded since breakfast was sure to be something scrumptious.

Lucy didn't wait for Mark to open her door. She was relieved to be home and off the road. The fog was thicker than she'd ever seen it. She yawned. Maybe an early bedtime was in order. She walked ahead of Mark and unlocked the door, stepping inside to disarm the alarm and turn on the lights.

As she turned around, she caught sight of something from the corner of her eye and managed to duck just as someone swung a crowbar straight at her head.

Her attacker stumbled off balance from the powerful swing not making contact. Before she could process what was happening, Mark was there.

He caught the man and flipped him hard onto the floor.

Chapter
Twenty-Five

It only took a few seconds of struggle before Mark had the man well and truly pinned down. Relief turned to anger. She momentarily considered delivering a swift kick to the ribs of her attacker, but it wasn't in her nature to do that.

Without looking up, Mark asked her to call the police.

She pulled out her phone, but before she could dial the number, she heard a knock on the doorframe and a cheerful voice calling her name.

"Lucy? Miss Patterson? Everything okay?"

She turned to see Officer Franklin standing in the doorway.

"Captain asked us to keep up the extra patrols by your place, and I saw your door was open, so I thought I'd just run up and see if everything was okay."

Lucy stepped aside so he could see Mark kneeling over the man on the floor. "I'm so glad you did. This man tried to attack me! He attempted to hit me in the head with a crowbar!" She picked up the metal rod to show him.

Officer Franklin jumped into action. He pulled his cuffs out and knelt over the intruder. He handcuffed the man and nodded to Mark. "Help me get him up. I'll take him to my car and call it in."

The man glared at Lucy as he was half-dragged out of the

bookstore entrance. Mark hesitated, not wanting to leave Lucy alone before he had a chance to check the rest of the house.

"Are you okay? I'll be right back. I promise."

She nodded. "I'll go put some water on to boil. I'm probably going to need some chamomile tea to help me get the adrenaline out of my system. I'm fine. Just a little shaken up. You go ahead."

Mark tried to reassure her with a smile before following Officer Franklin to his car. Lucy turned on the lights in the round room and the dining room as she passed through to the kitchen. Having all the lights on felt safer to Lucy, so she flipped the outside lights on as well. She carried the tea kettle over to the sink and glanced out the window.

The kettle fell from Lucy's fingers.

A person lay outside, unmoving, half on the grass and half on the patio. She could barely see the figure as the back porch light cut through the fog.

Lucy screamed, but nothing came out.

She ran back through the house, finally managing to loosen her vocal cords to yell for Mark and Officer Franklin. She ran out onto the front porch but couldn't see the men or the patrol car, so she continued her frantic yelling until Mark reappeared. He leaped up the stairs and grabbed Lucy, looking left and right for any sign of danger.

She told him what she'd seen, and then sobbing, added, "Mark, I think they're dead!"

Mark insisted that Lucy stay inside his truck with the doors locked and the keys with her. "You'll be safe in here. Just don't unlock the door for anyone but me, okay?"

Mark ran to try to catch Officer Franklin before he left.

Lucy watched him go. She was so glad he'd been with her tonight. She thought about what would have happened if he hadn't been. In all likelihood, it would have been the end for her.

Tears streamed down her face. Mark was like a guardian angel, she thought. She turned her face up to the cab of the truck and whispered a prayer. "God, if you're listening, thank you for sending Mark and watching out for me. Please keep him safe!"

She took the cape he'd given her and wrapped herself up in it. She lay down on the bench seat of the truck, thinking it might be best to lay low until Mark came back for her. Exhausted and overwhelmed, she fell asleep, using Mark's jacket for a pillow.

She wasn't sure how much time had passed when Mark tapped on the glass to wake her, but police cars and an ambulance filled the driveway. Hattie stood next to him, with arms outstretched for Lucy.

"Lucy, sweetheart, come with me. You're safe now. Come on inside." Hattie hugged Lucy and then took her hand, leading her up the porch stairs. Every light in the house blazed through the windows and cast shadows on the grass.

Lucy shuddered as she remembered what had happened. "Oh, Hattie, it was awful. First, someone attacked me, and then I saw someone lying out in the yard—I don't know how I fell asleep and slept through all of this," she gestured around the yard full of policemen, "but I feel as if I could sleep for a week now that they've caught the guy."

Mark and Hattie exchanged glances over Lucy's head. Mark's mouth was set in a grim line, and Hattie looked away, not wanting to make eye contact with Lucy.

Inside now, she turned to face them both. "What are you not telling me?"

Hattie, seeing the heat rising in Mark's face, said, "Don't worry. They'll catch him again. They even called for the State Police to come help in the search. It won't be long!"

Lucy couldn't believe what she was hearing. "Again? But he was in handcuffs. Mark caught him, and Officer Franklin was taking him to the patrol car. What happened?"

Mark answered. "When I heard you yelling for me, I left Officer Franklin alone with the attacker. He used the distraction to overpower him and take his keys before running off into the fog. Franklin has a little bit of road rash on his face and a bump on the side of his head. I found him on the ground in a daze. He's okay, but with this fog, they are going to wait until tomorrow to start the search.

"Do you think he'll come back here?" Lucy nodded toward the desk.

Mark, catching her meaning, said, "I really doubt it. It doesn't appear that he got what he came for, but I don't think he'll make another attempt anytime soon. Besides, I'm not going anywhere."

"Neither am I," Hattie said. "Mark, what did you mean by 'what he came for'?"

Lucy leaned in and whispered to Hattie. "I found some things that belonged to my grandparents in the desk. Some really valuable things."

Hattie's face went pale. "You didn't tell anyone what you found, did you?" Seeing Lucy's surprise, Hattie went on, "Yes, I knew. No, I couldn't tell you about it. You must tell *no one* what you found."

"I already told Mark," Lucy said. Lucy felt defiant. She was tired of secrets and tired of trouble.

Hattie beamed at her. "Well, Mark is okay, but no one else." She looked over at Mark and said, "You'll keep this secret, right? It's really important."

Mark nodded. "It isn't mine to tell. But I'm not sure it's much of a secret if people are breaking in to try to get to it. And Hattie, you need to tell us everything you know."

"I will, I promise. But right now, there are too many people here and too much going on. We'll discuss it in the morning." Hattie looked firm, so Lucy went to sit down on the sofa in the round room. She didn't know why, really, but it always felt like the most peaceful room in the house.

Mark went to open the front door for Captain Harrison, so Hattie sank into the sofa next to Lucy. "Tell you what, Lucy, we'll share a room tonight, so I can keep an eye on you. There are things you need to know. Things you will have to decide if you want Mark to know. I couldn't love him more if he were my own son, but you need to be the one to decide."

Lucy, still feeling upset and a little irritated at all the cloak and dagger stuff, replied, "I think Mark has had enough secrets kept from him, don't you?"

Hattie's face fell. She knew Lucy was referring to Hattie's theory on who his father was. Seeing that she'd wounded her friend, Lucy felt remorseful.

"I'm sorry, Hattie. I know you'll tell him when you think the time is right. I'm just in a mood right now. I haven't told you yet, but Fuchsia Butterfield was here saying the same things—not to trust anyone. She pulled a key out the spine of a book and gave it to me. But then she took off! The next time she shows up, I'm going to tie her to a chair and make her tell me what on earth is really going on!"

Hattie looked shocked for the second time that evening. "She did what? Do you have the key? Where is it?" She shook her head. "Lucy, she isn't coming back."

"What do you mean, she isn't coming back?" Lucy tilted her head and studied Hattie. "Yes, I have the key. It's somewhere safe. What makes you say she isn't coming back?"

Hattie sighed and picked up Lucy's hand. "Sweetheart, Fuchsia is who you saw in the grass outside. She's dead. I thought you knew."

Mark and Lucy gave their statements to Captain Harrison, and in turn, he told them the medical examiner had removed the body. He needed someone to officially identify her. Lucy didn't think she could handle seeing Fuchsia's body. Hattie offered to do it, as she'd known her for many years. She returned, looking grim.

"Lucy, I'm glad you didn't see her. Andy—Captain Harrison—told me he believed she was killed somewhere else and dropped where you saw her later. I overheard the M.E. telling Andy that it appeared to be blunt force trauma with a cylindrical metal object. Like a crowbar."

Lucy felt sick. The poor woman. Lucy regretted every uncharitable thought she'd had about her.

Andy returned to let Lucy know they were finished for the night. The "pea-soup" fog made it impossible for them to do much more until daylight.

"Don't worry, Lucy. I have men stationed in the front and back of the house, and they'll stay there. I understand Mark is staying here overnight?"

"Yes, I'll be sleeping on the sofa." Evidently, Mark wanted to make the arrangements clear to the older man once again.

"Lucy and I will be staying upstairs," Hattie added. "I'm not leaving our girl alone tonight. She squeezed Lucy's shoulder.

"Has anyone seen Tor?" Lucy asked. She hoped he was all right. She knew he probably hid with all the commotion, but with an attacker in the house and Fuchsia murdered and left on the lawn, Lucy was worried. That cat was her link to her grandparents, and she adored him.

"I'm sure he'll turn up," Mark said.

"We'll keep an eye out for him," Andy promised as he said goodnight.

Lucy walked toward the front door when it hit her. "Captain

Harrison! I set the alarm before I left, and I turned it off when I came in. How did he get in here without setting off the alarm?"

"Good question, Lucy. Are you sure it was set?"

Lucy nodded. "I'm sure! I remember setting it and hearing the tone for it being armed before I left."

The police captain reached out his hand and shook Lucy's. "I have no idea. We'll get the company out here to look at it. Maybe someone tampered with it. Thanks for pointing it out, Lucy. I just assumed you forgot to set it."

Lucy locked the door and set the alarm after Captain Harrison left. She also pulled down the shades of the big picture windows for maximum privacy, something she rarely felt the need to do.

"Let me show you two what I found, and then let's call it a night because I'm barely standing right now." She swayed as if to illustrate her point.

Lucy unlocked the desk and pulled out everything for them to examine. Hattie's eyes grew wide at the contents of the velvet bag, and Mark examined the coins closely. He seemed to find the ship's log especially interesting. He thumbed through the pages and stopped to read several entries. Abruptly he put everything back and locked the drawer, then handed Lucy her keys.

"I think tomorrow is soon enough to talk about this. Don't worry, Lucy. I'll keep watch."

"Mark, you don't have to do that. I'm more concerned about you than I am about this." She gestured to the desk. "Part of me wishes I'd never found them!"

Hattie still insisted on rooming in with Lucy but never had the chance to tell her what she wanted to say. By the time Hattie came out of the bathroom from getting ready for bed, Lucy was sound asleep.

The morning birds woke Lucy before the sun was up. She'd slept hard and hadn't dreamed at all. She felt a moment's peace with the cool air and cheerful song coming through the screen window, but then she remembered the events of the night before. She wished she could go back to sleep to forget for a little while, but there was no chance of that happening. Slipping out of bed, she visited the bathroom and washed her face, and combed her hair. She slid her feet into fluffy house shoes and put on a warm fleece robe before sneaking out of the room. Hattie, bless her, was curled up in a ball in Lucy's bed making the cutest little snoring noises she'd ever heard.

Lucy went gingerly down the back stairs. She thought she'd put on coffee and boil water for tea. She was worried about Tor. He could come and go as he liked, but he mostly liked to stay indoors and preferred a pampered life. His food dish was the same as she'd left it—half full—and his treats were all in the little silver dish next to his bowl, untouched. It was unusual for her to wake up and find anything in either dish. Usually, it would be empty, and Tor would be there mewing for more as if he were a starving stray.

Lucy started the coffee and then went to the sink to fill the kettle. She was being as quiet as she could, not wanting to wake Mark. She heard him moving in the other room and went to check on him. He was sitting up on the sofa, wrapped in a blanket, checking his phone, but he looked up and smiled at her when she approached.

"I didn't wake you, did I?" Lucy asked.

"No, I was already up. The policemen stationed outside woke me. One of them needed to use the bathroom so I let him in. I couldn't go back to sleep after that. Then I smelled coffee brewing and thought it was Hattie in the kitchen." He stood up and wrapped Lucy in a hug. "How are you doing? Did you sleep?"

"Yes, I slept like a rock! But then I heard the birds singing loudly outside my window. Why do they do that at four o'clock in the morning?" Lucy yawned.

"It's because they believe the sun is coming, and they have faith that the light will return." Mark smiled.

"Oh, and here I was thinking it was an evolutionary habit developed to establish territory and attract a mate!" Lucy winked at Mark, who kissed her forehead in response.

"This is what happens when you leave a girl in a bookstore too long," he teased.

"Girl? I'm not a girl—I think I found my first gray hair the other day." Lucy's shoulders slumped. "After the summer we've had, I'm surprised it was only one."

"It isn't going to be this way forever, Lucy. We'll get to the bottom of this. They'll catch the guy, and things will finally settle down." Mark stroked her back in an apparent attempt to reassure her, but Lucy wasn't having it.

"You can't say that. Every time I think things are settling down, something else happens. I feel as if it will never end." She leaned her head against his chest and sighed. "The one good thing, though, is you. If I hadn't been knocked out and left a mile out to sea, I wouldn't have met you."

Lucy sighed. There were still so many unanswered questions. "Mark, I want to show you something."

*L*ucy led Mark over to the antique piece of furniture and showed him how the desk worked. She popped the drawers out one by one, each of them now empty. Mark was impressed and let out a low whistle.

"There must be some kind of mechanism inside that moves the contents from one drawer to the next. I guess that's an extra layer of security, having the treasure move around inside the secret drawers," Lucy said.

"That's some kind of genius design!" he replied.

Lucy frowned. "It's so over-the-top though. I'm afraid if one person knows about this, maybe other people do, too, and eventually, they'll be coming after it."

Mark stuck his fingers in the drawer and tried to feel behind it, but the space was too small for his hand.

"I'm thinking that the secretary itself might be worth a small fortune, but I don't begin to know who to ask about appraising it. And since it was my grandmother's, I don't want to part with it." Lucy pointed at the still-open drawer. "I almost want to put something else in there and see if it disappears."

Scanning around the desk, she spied a button she'd found on the floor a couple of weeks ago and popped it into the drawer. She pushed it closed but it wouldn't quite shut, so Mark tried it.

He had to wiggle the drawer up and down a little, but it finally slid back into place. Lucy heard a brief whirring noise and a new hidden compartment opened near the top of the cabinet.

"How many of those are there?" Mark asked.

"Honestly, I have no idea." Lucy reached into the drawer and pulled out a set of keys.

They were modern and somewhat high-tech in their design. There were four of them, each with a tag. Mark read them out loud, "*Borealis, Meridionalis, Occidentalis, Orientalis.*"

"Oh, that's Latin," Lucy said.

"Yes, for the cardinal directions," Mark agreed. "*Borealis* is north. *Meridionalis* is south, *occidentalis* is west, and *orientalis* is east."

"Hidden talents? I'm impressed."

"No, just a question on one of my exams from my training days. History of navigation." Mark winked at Lucy. "That's about all the Latin I know. Unless it relates to ships or oceans, I'd be no good at trivia night."

Lucy laughed. "Most of the Latin I know came from the old books lying around here when I'd visit in the summer. I know my grandfather was interested in it, but I only learned a few things from him. I was a lot more interested in helping my grandmother in the kitchen or playing bookstore manager. My grandfather said I was a natural at selling books—I think he was happy to have time to study and work on his projects, so he recruited me pretty often."

Lucy shuffled the keys around in her hand. "Oh, I wonder if these unlock the doors downstairs? That must be it! There are four doors down there, all facing different directions. Oh, but the hardware on the doors looks like something from the turn of the century, and I don't mean the most recent one!"

"Still, that might be it. If you want, we can go down and

check it out, maybe after breakfast? I don't want you going down there alone." Mark drew Lucy into his arms.

"I love it that you want to take care of me, Mark. It's really sweet." Lucy brushed the back of her fingers against the early morning stubble on Mark's cheek.

Mark drew her even closer, wrapping her in the blanket he was still wearing, pressing her more closely to himself. "Lucy, you mean the world to me. It scares me every time I think about something happening to you. I know we haven't been together that long, but I care about you. I love you, Lucy."

Before she could reply, the tea kettle started to whistle. Mark gave Lucy a quick kiss and went to turn it off.

Lucy was dazed. She loved him too. She wished she'd said so right then! She could hear Mark pulling out dishes, so she nestled into the sofa. Hattie came down the front stairs and joined her.

Hattie patted her knee. "You're up early! I usually get up about this time to get ready for the day and open the cafe, but I talked to Hector last night, and he's going to open for me. Listen, Lucy, I know we didn't get a chance to talk last night. But you need to know that I have your best interests at heart. There are things I haven't told you. I didn't think they mattered anymore, so I wanted to let the past be the past and not have anyone else get hurt. It's about your family."

Lucy could see the tears welling up in Hattie's eyes, so she snuggled in next to her. The dear woman was like family, and she knew without question that Hattie cared about her.

"I don't want to keep any secrets from Mark," Lucy replied, "but tell me what you need to say."

Hattie stroked Lucy's hair back from her face. "I know Sam has told you about the trust and the various accounts. It's a lot of responsibility and a lot to absorb. But you're not alone in it. Your grandparents have been my friends since we were school children, and our parents were friends before that. There were several of us: me, your grandparents, Fuchsia, Sam—Senior, not young Sam—Doctor Wilson, and the minister. You remember him—he passed on a few years ago—Reverend del Campo? Well, we were all part of the circle ." Hattie paused for a moment and then continued.

"When your grandparents disappeared without a trace, those of us who were left decided to let it all come to an end. I don't know everything. I dropped out years ago to focus on the cafe and to take care of Mark. We were kind of a group of advisors. I guess you could say we helped your grandparents spend money. But the secret of where it came from belongs to you and your family. We only ever knew that it had something to do with the history of this house and the history of California. We also knew that they came by it honestly but there were reasons to keep it a secret—good reasons. Very *old* reasons, from what I've been told."

"So, you and the others helped my grandparents spend money?" Lucy asked. "What does that mean?"

"They did a lot of good things, your grandparents. They helped a lot of people. They relied on us to help them do it anonymously. Sometimes we would bring things to their attention and help them find ways to fund them or make donations to various charities for them. They helped so many people in this town get their start, either with business loans with very generous terms, or with scholarships, or by creating jobs for people. But it goes way beyond that.

"I don't know what all they were involved with, but I do know they felt the need to keep much of it a secret, even from us. Not because they didn't trust us, but because they'd never want to put us in harm's way. They were like that. I think that's why you knew nothing about any of it, even the trust. They wanted to protect you." The older woman rested her head on Lucy's head and said, "I want to protect you too. This house, and what lies beneath, it's full of secrets, Lucy."

Lucy sat up and looked her friend in the eyes. "I don't want any more secrets, Hattie. It sounds as if I'm stuck with a few, but I want life to be a lot simpler. Tell Mark about his mom and who his dad is. Please, for me. He deserves to know."

Hattie looked away and sighed. "Okay, I'll do it today." She stood up and said, "Why don't you run upstairs and get a shower, and I'll talk to him. He can help me make breakfast.

Lucy agreed and kissed Hattie on the cheek. "Thank you. I'm sure it's the right thing to do. We can figure out my mess later." Lucy turned to go but stopped and reversed. "Hattie, thank you for being such a good friend. To me and Mark and my grandparents. Carrying other people's secrets is never easy."

The sun was up and already beginning to burn off the morning fog by the time Lucy emerged from her shower. She'd spent more time than she meant to getting ready. Somehow, doing her hair and makeup helped her feel better about facing the day, especially since she'd only gotten a few hours of sleep.

She bounded down the stairs with three things on her mind: Mark, Tor, and bacon. What she found was sausages, but no sign of Tor or Mark. She also found Hattie in the kitchen, cracking eggs into a bowl mindlessly. Tears streaming down her face.

"Mark's gone out," she said. "It didn't go well." Hattie cracked another egg and dropped it into the mixing bowl. "I think he's feeling pretty hurt."

"Did he say where he was going?" Lucy asked. She didn't like the idea of Mark being upset.

"Somewhere to be alone for a while, someplace you showed him. He only left a couple of minutes ago."

Lucy blew the older lady a kiss and said, "I know where he'll be. If I go now, I can probably catch him. I'll be back as soon as I can!"

Lucy made her way back through the house, stopping to pick up a couple of stray cushions from the floor of the round room on her way out. As she threw them back onto the window seat, a piece of paneling slid open. Her heart jumped as Tor poked his nose out into the room and then made a beeline for Lucy. The poor darling was covered in dust and cobwebs.

So that's where he'd been, trapped somewhere in the wall? Lucy reached down to pet him as he mewed loudly and rubbed around her ankles. Her hand caught on something jutting out from his collar. It was a folded-up piece of paper addressed to her. She patted his head and rubbed off the dusty web from his fur. Tor caught wind of the smells coming from the kitchen and took off, his hunger being greater than his happiness in seeing Lucy.

Lucy unfolded the paper. It was written in large, sloppy letters, as if it had been written in haste. It said, "Lucy, I think your grandfather is alive. Tell NO ONE. F.B."

Stunned by the bizarre message seemingly from beyond the grave, Lucy crumpled the paper up and stuffed it in her pocket. She hurried to the front of the house, grabbed her phone and a jacket off a hook, then ran out the door.

She didn't catch Mark though. Officer Franklin and Officer Mooney stood squarely in her path. *I don't have time for this!*

Lucy smiled brightly at the two men. "Good morning, officers. I bet you're chilled to the bone! Do you think Captain Harrison would mind if you went in and had a little warm-up? Hattie's cooking breakfast!"

She hoped they'd be eager to eat and get coffee and let her go. Officer Mooney looked surprised but immediately headed toward the backdoor, but Officer Franklin didn't budge.

"Where are you off to? You realize that the intruder from last night is out there somewhere. And it's still pretty foggy. I think you should just head back inside." He pointed his head toward the door.

"I'll be fine. I'm meeting Mark just a block up the road. We're going for a walk. Don't worry. I know the way!" She pivoted and went around him, calling back over her shoulder, "Hattie made sausage! You really should get some before Mooney eats it all!"

She power-walked her way out of the yard and onto the road. Maybe it was a bad idea, but she knew she'd be perfectly safe when she caught up to Mark. Once she hit the road, she started to run.

*L*ucy didn't catch up to Mark as quickly as she'd hoped. He was tall, and he was upset, so he covered the ground more quickly than she could. By the time Lucy entered the gate to the trailhead, she was already slowing to a jog, and by the time she reached the tree where they'd stopped to look at the view, she had to stop and catch her breath. There was no view today. The fog, though beginning to burn off, was still thick enough to obscure everything more than a few yards away.

She did worry a little about the intruder who'd escaped Officer Franklin the night before. She thought of Fuchsia lying in the backyard and shuddered. Thankfully, she knew the trail like the back of her hand, and once she left the main trail for her secret spot, she felt sure she would find Mark. She picked up the pace again, but only to a fast walk. Making too much noise seemed like a bad idea, as did tripping and getting injured.

When she finally made it to the artesian well she'd shown Mark not long after meeting him, she stopped and looked around. She'd never seen the beauty spot in these conditions. The fog was clearing overhead, but thick patches and little wisps of it still clung to the ground, turning the ferns and bushes into something from a fairy tale. Drops of dew clung to a stand of wild grasses where a sunbeam turned them into a thousand shining jewels encrusting each stem. The sheer magical beauty of it overwhelmed her. She sank to her knees, where the damp immediately seeped through her pants, but she didn't care.

Lucy didn't see Mark anywhere. Her heart sank. Had she somehow passed him? Was she wrong in thinking he'd come here, to this spot? Lucy decided she should probably circle back to the house to see if Mark had returned, but she couldn't bear to drag herself away just yet. She was thirsty, and the artesian well water was pure and sweet, so she went over and cupped some water in her hands. It was cold, almost shockingly so, but it was so good that she drank a few more handfuls before turning around to sit on the ground next to the small pool of water.

Then she saw Mark. He came from behind some bushes holding a thick branch in a threatening manner. His eyes lit up when he saw her.

"Lucy, I heard you coming, but I thought you might be the fugitive. What on earth are you doing out here?" He settled down next to her on the ground.

Mark's eyes were red and a little puffy. She could tell that he'd been badly upset by what Hattie told him, and perhaps by how long she waited to do it.

"Hattie told me what happened. I knew you'd be upset, and I figured you might come here. I know it was a little risky coming after you, but I thought for sure that I'd catch up to you before you'd gone too far. I'm not in marathon-running shape, that's for sure."

"It just really shook me, Lucy. All this time, I could have at least found out whether it was true or not, and he's right here. I could have gotten to know him better . . ."

Mark looked off into the distance. "I just can't figure out why she would wait to tell me something like that."

"You know Hattie loves you. I'm sure she was just trying to protect you. Also, she doesn't know it. She just thinks it's likely.

Maybe she was afraid you wouldn't need her anymore, or maybe she wanted to spare you—both of you—from something that one of you might not want. Whatever her reason was, I know she had your best interest at heart." Lucy scooted a little closer to Mark and laid her head on his arm. "I'm glad she told you now, and whatever you decide—if you want to pursue it or not—I will support you."

Mark wrapped an arm around Lucy's shoulder and kissed the top of her head.

"I know you will, Lucy. I'm so thankful to have you in my life."

"I feel the same way, Mark. Thankful doesn't begin to cover it." Lucy offered him a small smile—her heart was breaking for him.

"You know I didn't have the easiest start. I've always felt like the rug could be pulled out from under me at any time. When I went to live with Hattie, I had the idea that she would eventually get tired of me and tell me to move on, but she never did. She gave me the first real taste of stability that I'd ever known. The Coast Guard did the same thing—it gave me a sense of stability, a home. But with the decision I'm facing now and with Hattie keeping something that important from me, it feels as if things are in danger of falling apart again. That's part of why I came out here. It's so peaceful, and it's the place I think I first fell in love with you." Mark stroked her hair gently and then lifted her chin with his finger until her eyes were even with his.

"Mark, I—" Lucy stammered.

"Lucy, wait. I want to tell you something." He kissed her cheek and rubbed it in with his thumb before continuing. "This last trip out, something happened. We were about eight miles off the coast. We were patrolling and taking samples for a couple of research projects. It was a still night, and except for the watch, everyone was in their rack asleep. I couldn't sleep, so I went out on the deck and found a quiet spot where I could sit and look out over the water. The stars were brilliant. So often it's just overcast and foggy out there with the marine layer overhead, but that night, the sky was black, and the stars were shining diamonds.

"I could see a faint trace of bioluminescence in our wake. It was like a glowing path behind us. It was unbelievably beautiful. I was sitting there, just looking up at the stars and down at the water, and this feeling of deep peace settled over me like a blanket. It seemed so clear to me—there must be more to this life, some kind of purpose behind it all. I've always been slow to trust people, to let them in. But being out there, I sensed something greater than myself, and all I could think about was sharing it with you. I found myself trusting whatever it was that made the stars and the sea and the redwood trees—and you."

He searched her face for understanding, and finding it there, he kissed her. She clung to him, kissing him back, feeling the rush of emotions overtake her.

"Stop! Mark, stop! I need to tell you something!" Lucy pushed him slightly away and said, "I love you too!" Then she kissed him again and again.

She wanted to keep his trust and show him that she trusted him too. To be open and honest with him. So she pulled the crumpled paper out of her pocket and held it up.

"I need to show you this!" Lucy said. *And I need to catch my breath!*

Mark took the paper and smoothed it out, scanning it rapidly. "Lucy, where did you get this?"

Lucy told him how she'd seen Tor come out from a panel in the wall in the round room with the note stuck under his collar.

"I think there might be something back there, like an old "priest hole" or something. He came out coated in cobwebs and dust though. It might just be a hiding spot? I wanted you to look at it with me."

211

Lucy thought of Fuchsia again. It seemed highly likely the note was from her. The last time Lucy had seen her, she'd left out the front door but was already out of sight when Lucy went outside.

"Do you think Fuchsia put the note under his collar? It reads just like she sounds. Or, sounded. Oh, Mark, what if trying to send me a message was the last thing she did? But why would she say that?" Lucy was careful not to say aloud what Fuchsia had written and warned her about.

Lucy couldn't imagine what purpose the elderly woman would have for giving her false hope, so maybe she was just mistaken about her grandfather being alive, or maybe she had poor eyesight. Perhaps she was just mentally unwell after all. Lucy shook her head, trying to stop her imagination from carrying her away.

"Whatever her reason, this is evidence. We need to get it back to where you found it and tell the authorities about it." Mark folded the note carefully and put it in his front pocket.

"It says not to tell anyone though."

"I think we have to, Lucy. Keeping secrets might be what got her killed in the first place."

The day was turning warm, and every trace of the fog had burned away. Mark took Lucy's hand and walked with her through the trees back to her home.

Lucy was quiet as they walked back through the gate from her favorite childhood hideaway. It hadn't lost its charm or beauty, but she felt like a different person leaving this time. She *was* a different person—a woman really in love for the first time. But more than that, she felt a new determination rising from within. Her experience with the police had been a very mixed bag. She trusted Captain Harrison, but Officer Franklin seemed inept, and Officer Mooney was a bully who apparently had it in for her.

If anyone was going to figure out everything and put a stop to it, it would be her, hopefully with Mark's help. Lucy realized that what she felt was an ending. She couldn't afford to be the wide-eyed child any longer—she was leaving behind the shelter of childhood.

When they arrived back at the house, there were no uniformed officers, and the backyard was empty except for some yellow police tape.

"I guess they've started the search for the man who escaped last night," Lucy said.

"Makes sense. Now that the fog is lifted, I'm sure they will have all hands on deck. Let's go in the front."

Mark steered Lucy away from the crime scene and toward the stairs that led up to the appealing front porch. There were baskets of overflowing ivy and planters filled with mint and lavender on each end, giving the porch a calm feel. Tor was asleep in one of the rocking chairs, and Lucy wished she could join him for a peaceful nap. Instead, she picked him up and he stretched and yawned before curling up comfortably in Lucy's arms. She nuzzled him with her cheek and felt the warm rumble of a purr begin. She was glad he was safe and sound and back to his usual job of lazing around the bookstore.

Mark opened the door for Lucy and Tor and followed them through into the foyer of The Cozy Cat Bookstore. Tor leaped out of Lucy's grasp and settled on his favorite chair where a ray of sunshine warmed the seat. Lucy liked seeing him there and gave him a scratch under the chin before hanging her jacket on the coat tree.

Hattie heard them come in and rushed into the room. She wore a pinched, worried look on her face.

"Mark, I'm so sorry. I should have told you what I suspected sooner. I really am sorry. Can you forgive me?" She held out her hands to Mark who crossed the room swiftly and took both of her hands in his, kissing each one in turn.

"Forgive you? Hattie, I love you! You've never done anything but help me and look out for me. I know you were only thinking of me and not wanting to give me false hope," Mark said.

"About that," Hattie said, "I talked to Andy. He called with an update on their search plans for the day and to check on Lucy. I didn't want to make the same mistake again, so I told him what I thought and asked him about your mother. He had no idea she'd had a child, but he thinks he may be your father. He was seeing your mother before she left and wanted to marry her. He's a bit stunned at the news, as you can imagine."

Mark nodded, his mouth grim. "I can imagine, yes."

Hattie went on. "He did say he would be proud if he's your father, Mark. He wants to talk to you later if that's okay. He's going to come by on his lunch break."

Tears threatened to spill over the rim of Lucy's eyes. She was so happy for Mark and Captain Harrison. They were alike in so many ways, and Lucy felt they both deserved all the happiness in the world.

"Of course, it's okay!" Mark laughed. "I'm glad you told him, Hattie. And I'm glad you put all the pieces together. You've given me a real gift." He squeezed the older woman tightly.

Lucy heard the door open and saw Tor jump out of his chair and bolt toward the back of the house—almost simultaneously.

"How touching," a man said, the sarcasm heavy in his voice.

Lucy turned around slowly. The intruder from the night before stood just inside the door, pointing a gun at her.

Chapter Twenty-Eight

*L*ucy glared at the man holding the weapon. She could feel the blood pounding in her ears and the heat rising from her neck as her whole body tensed.

"What do you WANT?" The words exploded from her mouth, defying him, even though her legs were starting to quake.

Mark put Hattie behind him and started to make his way over to Lucy. The man with the gun swung it Mark's way and gestured for him to move back. Hattie pulled on Mark's arm, but he stood firm.

"Who are you," Mark asked, "and what do you want? Just don't shoot. If you need a hostage or transportation, I'll go with you. Leave them alone."

"So noble. Ever the hero," the man jeered at Mark. "She knows what I want." He jerked his gun toward Lucy. "Open the desk, Lucy. Get it out and bring it to me."

"And then what?" Lucy demanded. "You just go on your merry way without harming any of us? You've already killed once!"

"Do as you're told," he growled, "or you'll be next."

"Fine. Take it. I don't care. Just leave us alone." Lucy's surge of adrenaline was beginning to wear off. She walked on shaking legs to open the desk but stopped when she heard the front door swing open again.

She was relieved to see Officer Franklin enter, followed by Captain Harrison. The man with the gun took a couple of steps back and swiveled the gun back and forth, aiming between the officers and Mark, Hattie, and Lucy.

"Move over there with them," he shouted at the new arrivals. "Not you." He gestured to Officer Franklin. "You take your gun out by the barrel and walk over to me. Hand it to me slowly."

Officer Franklin was quick to obey. He pulled open the snap on his holster and carefully drew the firearm out before turning it around in his hand and extending the handle to the intruder. Captain Harrison, who was unarmed, moved to join Mark, positioning himself as a barrier between the gunman and the women.

Once he had both guns, the man ordered Officer Franklin to use the zip ties on his belt to cuff the others.

"And make sure you put them on tightly. I'd hate to have to start shooting," he said. He raised and lowered one gun to mimic firing shots.

Officer Franklin nodded and obeyed without question. He started with his captain and then Mark, turning them around to show that the plastic ties were tight and in place. Then he cuffed Hattie with her hands in front.

He started toward Lucy, but the gunman called him back.

"Leave her. I need her to open the desk. Walk over here to me, slowly." The man then snarled at Lucy, "I told you to open the desk!"

"I will, I will! Just don't hurt him. He has his whole life in front of him." Lucy feared the gunman was going to shoot the young officer.

The man with two guns laughed. "Hurt him? Why would I do that?" He smirked at the young officer standing near him now and pointed one of the guns at him. "I'd never hurt a hair on his head. His mother would kill me!"

Officer Franklin laughed and took the gun from the intruder's hand. "Thanks, Dad." Now he pointed the weapon at the group. His father handed him the other gun as well, which he tucked inside his waistband.

Franklin's father was the intruder? Lucy's mind raced. That explains how he got away—his son just let him go! Lucy sensed the rage building up in Captain Harrison. His face turned purple, and his hands balled into fists. Mark was white-hot beside him. Lucy was afraid one, or both, might try to play hero, and she didn't want either to get hurt.

"I'll give you whatever you want. Just promise me you'll take it and leave," Lucy begged.

"Oh, I'm not making any promises. I'm going to get what I came here for. What happens after that will depend on you. I've waited a long time for this." He pointed at Mark, Hattie, and Captain Harrison. "You three, over there. Sit down on the floor and do not move."

After they settled on the ground, he walked over to Lucy and gathered up a handful of her hair close to her scalp. "Such a pretty color." He yanked her hair hard, causing her to gasp. Mark started to stand up, but Officer Franklin warned him off.

"I'm okay, Mark, don't. Just stay there." Lucy tried to reassure Mark. "My keys are right here. I'll open the desk." Her hands shook as she tried to pull out the correct key.

Lucy found the right key and fumbled with opening the drawer. She handed it to her captor because she could see his agitation rising. He took it and started to unlock the drawer. She turned her head, trying to think of a way she could save Mark and the others. She caught sight of Officer Mooney creeping through the bushes next to the house, obviously snooping. She took a gamble and shouted, "You'll never get away with it!

Just hurry up and take the stuff and leave us alone!" She hoped Officer Mooney, bully that he was, had heard it and would call for backup. She prayed he wasn't involved with Officer Franklin and his father.

The older gunman responded by shoving Lucy hard, knocking her to the floor. He pulled the drawer open and rifled through it, looking for the items she'd hidden under other documents and envelopes. He pulled out the velvet bag and poured the jewels and coins onto the desk. He searched again and this time, pulled out the logbook and pen. His eyes lit up as he leafed through it. He held it up and turned to his son, who still had a gun trained on Mark and Andy.

"I've got it. Let's move." He stuffed the book into his shirt.

From her vantage point on the floor where he'd pushed her down, Lucy could see Officer Mooney creeping around the corner of the dining room at a crouch. His hand was on his holster, but he hadn't yet drawn his weapon. She needed to buy him some time.

"I thought you were after the jewels. Don't you want them?"

"Trinkets. They mean little. I got what I came for. Now, what to do with you." He grinned at Lucy. "Maybe I'll take you upstairs and tie you up—"

Officer Mooney had heard enough. He stepped around the corner, drawing his weapon on the intruder.

"Police! Put your hands in the air!" Mooney shouted.

"No, you put your hands in the air." The man smirked. He gestured toward his son.

Mooney, taking in the scene, realized that Officer Franklin was pointing his gun at Captain Harrison, the Coast Guard captain, and Miss Hattie. He quickly swung his weapon around and pointed it at Officer Franklin.

Lucy knew Mooney was vulnerable with the standoff. He couldn't cover both men, and they knew it. She had to even the odds a little bit. No one was looking at her. They were all focused on the guns and each other.

Lucy's hands were still free, so she reached behind her, feeling along the bookshelf for something she could use as a weapon. Her fingers encountered a thick spine, so she slid the book out carefully, moving as little as possible. Drawing it closer to her body, she picked it up and stood up in one fluid motion.

As the men all turned to look at her, she shifted her weight and spun, then slammed the heavy book into the side of her captor's head. He crumpled unconscious to the floor. Lucy took the opportunity to plant herself directly on top of him. She smacked him in the head once more, half because she wanted to make sure he was completely out and half because she was still furious.

Officer Mooney grunted in approval and took a few steps toward Officer Franklin.

"Drop it, Franklin. I won't hesitate to shoot you. There's no way out of this." Mooney's hands were steady as he held the gun.

"Do what he says, Franklin! That's an order!" Captain Harrison spoke up.

"I don't take orders from you, in case you haven't noticed," Franklin snapped. "As a matter of fact, you're going to take orders from me. You're going to pick him up and put him in my patrol car, and then you're all going to the basement. Do as I say, or the first person I shoot will be Lucy."

Mark started to object, but when Franklin pivoted the gun to point at Lucy's head he stopped.

"Get off him right now, Lucy. Don't make me tell you twice." Officer Franklin's eyes narrowed, and his jawbones were bulging.

Lucy started to stand but lost her footing, falling back even harder onto the still unconscious man. This infuriated Franklin even more, who fired off a round into the bookcase behind Lucy. Lucy screamed, and Captain Harrison let out a string of expletives.

Franklin pointed the gun at her head again and said, "You're coming with me. Get up."

Lucy was terrified. Her ears rang, and her whole body shook, but she managed to get her feet under her. As she arose, a panicked yowl jerked her attention away from the intruder. *What in the–?* A frightened Tor streaked by and dashed around the room, jumping on and off furniture. Lucy felt sick. She knew he was scared, and she couldn't comfort him. And worse, she worried that Franklin might shoot him.

Lucy started to call out to Tor, who was tearing wildly from wall to wall, but before she could, the terrified cat climbed up Franklin's leg, across his chest, and dug his claws in, hanging on for dear life to Franklin's face.

Franklin screamed, dropping his gun to try to pry the cat from his head.

Everyone sprang into action at once. Mooney raced to retrieve the gun. Mark hurried to Lucy. Hattie ran over and sat down hard on Franklin's dad, who was starting to stir.

Tor let go, jumped away from the flailing officer, and ran up the stairs. Lucy was relieved to see him out of harm's way.

Captain Harrison, hands still tied, slammed into Franklin, knocking him onto his face on the floor. "Stay down, Franklin. Mooney, if he so much as wiggles, shoot him." He backed up to Lucy and asked her to cut him free. Lucy grabbed the scissors from her desk and sawed off the zip ties–first the police captain's, then Mark's, and finally Hattie's.

Mark helped Hattie up from her seat on the man's back and made sure she was okay. Captain Harrison and Mooney cuffed the two men on the floor, and Mark helped them stand the men up. Lucy walked over to the man who'd caused her so much trouble and who had killed Fuchsia and left the harmless old woman on Lucy's back patio. She desperately wanted to punch him, but instead, she reached inside his shirt and pulled out the book.

Captain Harrison looked the other way as Lucy took it—a gracious choice on his part, she thought, to avoid having to put the valuable book into an evidence locker. The captain pulled the man's ID from his jacket pocket. Lucy could see it was a passport book from the European Union. It read Union Europea—España. It was odd, she thought, that he hadn't had even a trace of an accent.

Mooney and Mark took Franklin outside and locked him in the back of his own patrol car. Mooney sent Mark back with a handful of evidence bags for the captain.

The captain bagged up the guns and the book Lucy had used to hit the man, telling her that because it was a cloth cover, it would be hard to get a fingerprint from it, but the man's DNA would be all over it. He winked at her, clearly proud of her quick thinking.

"We're going to have to put up crime scene tape, Lucy. Investigators will want to comb through everything." He looked pointedly at Lucy's desk where the jewels lay spilled out. "Mark and I are going to take this fella outside and put him in a patrol car until medical gets here and clears us to take him to lock up. It'll probably take us a few minutes."

Lucy nodded, "Okay, I understand."

Hattie, also catching on, said, "I think I'll go make some tea, something calming with lavender and chamomile. It will take me at least ten minutes." She turned and walked toward the kitchen, giving Lucy a private wink.

The man she'd knocked out with the book was slowly shaking off the fog of what had happened. More alert now, he appeared ready to kill Lucy with his bare hands. She wanted to quiz him—to find out who he was and why he wanted her book so badly—but Mark and Captain Harrison were in a hurry to get him away from her and booked into custody.

Once the men left, Lucy scrambled to gather up the small treasure and the book. She pulled the old pen and letter out of the drawer too. She wanted to hide the things upstairs because whatever the secrets were, they were hers and not something she wanted to be taken in as evidence or broadcast in the news. Lucy hesitated. If her whole house were searched, there wasn't a better hiding place than where she found them herself.

She pulled out the small key Fuchsia had given her from the spine of the book and adeptly opened the desk's secret drawer. Sure enough, the button she'd put in it with Mark was gone, safely hidden inside the next drawer in the succession of hiding spots within the clever piece of furniture. Lucy quickly stashed everything into place and carefully closed the drawer. She hadn't quite figured out all the quirks of the mechanism yet—what factors caused a series of drawers to open and what allowed just one drawer to open without triggering others—but she felt that the safest place for these things was to leave them where her grandparents put them. Anyone who searched the desk would come up empty unless they knew the secret.

As an afterthought, she grabbed the book Fuchsia had given her. It was a valuable first edition with the poem the acerbic woman had underlined for her in pencil. She examined the book quickly for any other potential hiding places. Satisfied, she stuffed it in the top drawer where the ship's log had lain previously. She hoped it was enough of a decoy to convince investigators that it was what the intruder had been after all along. She had a strong feeling the man wouldn't reveal the truth himself, and neither would Franklin.

ired of waiting for the others to return, Lucy thought she'd better see what was going on. She peeked out the front door and called for Hattie to come to have a look.

The older woman appeared with a large tray filled with cups and saucers, sugar and cream, a coffee pot, and hot water for tea. There were several small glass jars of tea and reusable tea bags. Lucy marveled that even after having been tied up and held hostage by a gunman, Hattie was still always thinking of everyone else.

Lucy helped her set the tray down on a pedestal table and motioned for her to come see. Several more police cars had arrived as well as a task force van Lucy remembered seeing before when they'd come to explore the hidden tunnel in the woods behind her house. The van's side door was open, and Lucy could see surveillance equipment inside.

On one side of the porch, Mark and Captain Harrison had their heads close together, talking as if they didn't want anyone to overhear. The two men shook hands, and Captain Harrison clapped Mark on the back affectionately. Captain Harrison hurried over to speak to the task force while Mark went around the side of the house toward the back. Lucy ran to let him in.

"Okay. Yes, Hattie too. I'll see you in a few minutes." Mark ended a call and turned to Lucy and Hattie, who had followed her into the kitchen. "That was Sam. I called him to come over. Listen, I want you both to let Sam talk for you. He's going to tell the agents outside that both of you will be happy to give your statements but only after you've been seen by your doctors."

Lucy nodded. "Okay, whatever you think is best."

"The task force hasn't cleared you as a suspect involved with the smuggling ring yet, so I want you both to delay giving statements until Andy and I can convince them to focus on Officer Franklin and his father. His name is Juan Carlos Jimenez, by the way. Does that ring a bell?"

Mark had been speaking rapidly, so it took Lucy a minute to process it all. "Sam's coming, and we're stalling. I've got that, and no, the name doesn't ring a bell."

"Sam's not my lawyer though," Hattie replied.

Mark pulled out a five-dollar bill and handed it to Hattie. "Give that back to me," he said, "and tell me to hire Sam for you."

Hattie handed Mark the five dollars and said, "Mark, would you be so kind as to give this to Sam for me and ask him to be my counsel?"

"Perfect." He winked. "I'll do that now. He should be coming up the drive any minute. He'll come to get you. Stay in the kitchen till then. I take it there's nothing interesting to find in the bookstore?"

Lucy shook her head, feigning innocence. "I didn't see anything at all, but I'll leave the key to my desk with you in case anyone wants to have a look inside." She handed him the key to her regular desk drawers. "Nothing in there but an old book."

He raised his eyebrows at her and said, "Thank you for your cooperation. I'm sure that will go over well with the task force. Do you have, ah, all your house keys with you?"

"They're in my purse. I'll grab it when we go out with Sam."

Mark patted his shirt pocket, which reminded Lucy that the odd note from Fuchsia was still in it.

"What about . . ." Lucy started.

"I have a lot on my mind, Lucy. I will probably forget things and remember them later." His phone buzzed, and after looking at the message, he said, "Sam's here. Stay in the kitchen, I'll bring him through to you in a minute. The investigators are coming into the bookstore any minute now."

Lucy didn't fully understand, but she trusted Mark and Captain Harrison to look out for her best interests. "Thanks, Mark." Feeling weary, she sank into a kitchen chair.

As Mark went back out the way he came, Hattie called after him, "Be sure to offer everyone tea and coffee! It's by the front door!"

Lucy laughed at the idea of the stern agents drinking tea from her grandmother's good china, but she decided she was glad Hattie hadn't made them cookies too.

Sam came through the kitchen door just as the agents were coming in the front.

His face was serious as he asked Hattie to confirm she wished to hire him to represent her.

"Yes, please," Hattie said. "And do you think you could drive us to see Dr. Wilson? I'm concerned about Lucy. She was handled pretty roughly."

"I think that's best," Sam said. "Dr. Wilson will want to have a look at you, too, Hattie. I heard you were physically involved in restraining the attacker, so it's best to get you looked at. Also, it's been quite a shock to you both, I'm sure."

The women nodded their assent, so Sam went through to the front of the house to speak to the agent in charge. He came back a few minutes later and told Lucy he'd agreed to have them give their statements as soon as Dr. Wilson cleared them. He'd withdrawn any consent for anything other than pictures and evidence material to the hostage-taking to be removed from the house. Lucy's eyes widened at that—she'd never considered they might take the whole desk!

Sam led them through to the front, showing one of the agents that the purse Lucy was taking contained only her wallet, keys, and a small bag of personal items. Then he shuffled them straight to his car, putting Hattie in the front while Lucy took the backseat. He backed out of the driveway quickly.

When they were a couple of blocks away, Sam pulled over and parked the car under a large shade tree.

"I don't know exactly what happened, and I'm going to need you both to tell me everything you can recall before you give any statements. But first, Lucy, I wanted to tell you that I finally got in touch with my grandfather. I told him what had been happening here, and he passed on some interesting information. We're going to need to speak about it later." He avoided looking at Hattie. "There are things you need to know."

Hattie reached an arm across to Sam and said, "It's okay, Sam. I already told her what I know. Your grandfather probably knows more than I did, but we're all on the same team here."

"Yes, it's okay, Sam. Anything you need to say, you can say in front of Hattie, or Mark for that matter," Lucy added.

"Okay, got it. But first, we need to talk about the last twenty-four hours. Tell me everything." Sam pulled out a notebook and pen so he could take notes, and then he took a small recorder from his pocket. "I'm going to tape this if you don't mind? It's privileged information, so feel free to be completely honest—not that I'd expect otherwise. Hattie, you first."

By the time both women had given Sam a rundown of events in the last twenty-four hours, Lucy realized she was starving. She'd missed out on Hattie's breakfast, and now it was late afternoon, and she hadn't yet eaten a bite. So Hattie called the cafe and asked them to deliver three late lunches to Dr. Wilson's office. She had them throw in a slice of peach pie for the doctor too.

The women took turns eating and telling the doctor what happened, and he was quick to give them both a thorough going-over. Lucy had some bruises developing on her hip, and her scalp was sore from the hair pulling, but she was otherwise fine. Hattie's blood pressure was high, so Dr. Wilson gave her a pillow and turned the lights down, telling her to rest for a few minutes before he did a second reading. He left Lucy in the darkened room in case Hattie needed anything, telling her to try to relax and take deep, slow breaths as well. In the meantime, he took Sam to his office to have his pie and a conversation.

Lucy looked over at the woman who'd become so dear to her these last few months. She'd always adored Hattie, but now she felt even closer to her. Hattie was family, and Lucy didn't want anything to happen to her. The older woman seemed frail as she lay there with her eyes closed.

A surge of protective feelings flooded Lucy's body—all she wanted was to keep safe the people she loved. She closed her own eyes and lifted that thought, that request, to whoever was listening. No secret, no amount of money, was worth letting harm come to any of those she held dear. *I'll get to the bottom of this, and then they'll be safe. Please keep them safe.*

Hattie's next blood pressure reading was close to normal, much to Lucy's relief. Dr. Wilson invited both Hattie and Lucy into his office, where Sam was waiting.

"I could release both of you right now, but I think I should keep you here for observation a little longer. Sam thinks it's best if you lay low for a while. I don't have any more appointments today, so unless we get a walk-in, I get the privilege of spending some time with you two lovely ladies." Dr. Wilson winked at Hattie, who started to blush. "I've had a very interesting conversation with young Sam here."

The elderly doctor leaned forward and reached for Lucy's hand. She rested her hand in his, and he gave it a reassuring squeeze. "Lucy, there are things you need to know."

Lucy started to laugh. How many people were going to say that to her? Did the entire geriatric population of Seaview know something she didn't?

"I suspect none of us knew the full extent of it, Lucy. Your grandparents probably did that to protect us. But we were all involved, in one way or another," Dr. Wilson admitted.

"Involved in *what*, exactly? I know about the trust and some of the charitable work that's gone on, but that doesn't really equal some big secret that got Fuchsia killed. Why would someone kidnap me, break into my house, hold us hostage—over a trust fund? It doesn't make sense. All he seemed to be after was an old book. He overlooked other, more valuable things."

"Dr. Wilson knows about the jewels," Hattie told her. "We all knew. They were kept safe in the desk for a rainy day. There is a history behind them, but I don't know what it is. Your grandparents never told me, only that they've been in the family, untouched, for generations. The gems don't exist on paper or in any account, at least not in this country. As for the book, I don't know what it is, or why they want it."

"I wish I could tell you more, but you know most of what I know. I can tell you that your house is not what it seems," Dr. Wilson added.

"I saw Tor come out of the wall. He pushed a piece of paneling out and emerged covered in cobwebs. Is that what you mean? That it has hiding spaces in the walls?" Lucy asked.

Dr. Wilson and Hattie both looked surprised. "No, I didn't know about that, actually," Doctor Wilson said. "But there are tunnels and not just the one you were locked in."

"There are tunnels that lead from your house, Lucy, a whole network of them. Some of them run under the town. Some go to other places. I don't know how old they are, but they're old. Very few people know, and we only know because our grandparents did. Only a few families have ever known about them, and it needs to stay that way," Hattie said.

"And now Sam and I know because of our grandparents," Lucy said. "What about your children and grandchildren? Do they know?" Lucy asked Dr. Wilson.

"No, they don't know. I didn't tell them at first because both my boys were a bit reckless and too willing to take chances, and then they were both eager to go to college and move away. Maybe if one of them ever moved back to make Seaview his home, I'd consider it. But for now, it seems safest to leave them out of it."

"I think that's what my grandfather was doing," Sam added. "He never told my dad, that's for sure, and I don't think he would have told me even after I moved back to take over his practice. I think he only told me what I needed to know to help Lucy with the trust, but he's filled me in now because of the danger she's in. I guess he figured at this point, I needed to know. However, he didn't tell me any more than what we've already talked about."

"Mark is like a son to you, Hattie. Why did you never tell him about it?" Lucy asked. "I know he's trustworthy."

"Of course, he is. There's no one I'd trust more. After he joined the Coast Guard, I figured he'd probably go all over the world while he served and that he'd end up somewhere else. I thought he'd find someplace more exciting than here to settle down and raise a family. I didn't want to burden him with secrets that weren't his to bear."

Lucy scoffed. "There is nowhere more exciting than here." She rubbed her sore scalp, wincing at the little sparks of pain that shot into her head.

Dr. Wilson reached into a drawer and pulled out a chemical ice pack, shook it, and handed it to Lucy, who gratefully balanced it on her head.

"So, what was Fuchsia's role in all of this?" Lucy asked. "And why would she write a note saying she thought my grandfather was alive?"

"What note?" Hattie asked. "When did you get a note?" Hattie's face had paled. She looked down at her hands folded in her lap as tears began to fall freely onto her shirt.

Dr. Wilson looked shocked and then confused. He started to speak, but his mouth opened and closed several times without any sound coming out. Sam shrugged in consternation, but she hadn't really expected him to know anything. Lucy wondered if she should have kept the note to herself. It had felt like a cruel trick when she first read it, but she hadn't considered that it might have the same effect on her grandfather's friends. The last thing she wanted to do was to cause them pain.

Lucy sighed. "It was tucked in Tor's collar when he came out of the wall. It said to tell no one, but now that Fuchsia is dead, it's evidence. Mark has it. He thinks we should turn it over to the police later."

Sam, Hattie, and Dr. Wilson all exclaimed "No!" at the same time, startling Lucy right out of her chair. For a long minute, no one added anything, each one looking at the others to elaborate, but before anyone explained, the silence was broken by three cell phones all buzzing and pinging at once. It was Mark, texting Lucy, Sam, and Hattie. The message said, "All clear. Franklin confessed. You can come back now."

Sam showed the message to Dr. Wilson. He walked them out, closed the office, and followed Sam and the women back to Lucy's home.

Chapter Thirty

*L*ucy and Hattie gave their statements about the events of the day to two agents who seemed eager to wrap things up. Lucy was a little nervous giving her statement, but the agent either didn't notice or ascribed it to the ordeal she'd just been through.

Dr. Wilson sat on the front porch to be close at hand if needed but not underfoot. Mark stayed outside with one of the other task force members until they were done and then chatted with the three agents for a few minutes. The two men waited until they were gone to rejoin the group inside.

Lucy was exhausted. Sam and Dr. Wilson pitched in and gathered up the coffee cups and tea things. Hattie looked pleased that the agents had helped themselves.

"A little hospitality can go a long way in making people look innocent!" she mused.

Lucy snorted. "I *am* innocent! But yes, I'm sure it helped."

Mark sat on the chair arm next to Lucy and smiled when she leaned in for a hug.

"No one can resist Hattie when she puts on the charm," Mark said. "But what helped most is that Officer Franklin—sorry, former Officer Franklin—is not the hardened criminal his father is. When Mooney suggested that his father was in the other interrogation room laying the blame on his son, Franklin rolled over pretty quick. Seems like his dad sent him to live with his mother years ago in the States to be educated here. He directed Franklin to join the academy and apply to the force in Seaview. At first, he just had the kid spying and running errands and doing small jobs for him. But eventually, he pulled him into his smuggling operation."

"But why here," Lucy asked, "and why was he targeting me? How did he know about the house and the tunnel and the book? Even I had no idea about any of it. It makes no sense."

"I don't have those answers yet, Lucy, but what I do know is that Interpol is on the way to pick him up. Juan Carlos Jimenez is a prime suspect in their investigation of a multinational smuggling operation. He has a Red Notice out on him, so our government will most likely hand him over. Either way, he isn't going to bother you again."

"What about Franklin? Are they taking him too?"

"He has dual citizenship—his mother lives in Oregon—so the process is a little bit trickier. With turning on his father the way he has, he will probably make some sort of deal, but we have enough charges even without the international factors to put him away for many years." Mark paused, considering his next words carefully. "There may be a trial here, and we may be called as witnesses, but that's still a long way off. For now, just know that he isn't going anywhere except to prison. He's a flight risk, so I don't think he'll be offered bail at any amount."

Lucy curled her knees and feet up into her chair, hugging her legs. "That's a relief. I will probably sleep like a baby tonight."

Hattie agreed and added, "And I'll make you some sandman tea just to make sure you do!"

Sam and the doctor returned with a tray of lemonade and some cookies from Lucy's pantry on a plate.

"Hope you don't mind, Lucy," Dr. Wilson said, "but I felt like everyone needed a little pick-me-up. Just this once, I'm going against medical advice and giving you permission to eat your dessert first. Oh, and I ordered some pizzas. They'll be here in about forty-five minutes."

Lucy popped up from her chair and kissed him on the cheek. "You always were my favorite doctor," she said, "and you always will be!" She grabbed two cookies from the plate and offered one to Mark, who ate it in one bite.

"Pizza sounds perfect. Thanks, Doc," Hattie said. "I'm too tired to even call in an order to the cafe!"

Lucy washed down the cookie with a long drink of lemonade. It was a lot of sugar, but she was running on fumes. "Mark, I told everyone about Fuchsia's note. Do you still have it?"

Mark looked surprised. "I did forget all about it! No kidding!" He pulled the paper from his pocket and handed it to Hattie, who looked it over and handed it to Dr. Wilson.

"That's her scrawl, all right," Hattie said. "I'd know it anywhere!"

Lucy motioned for the others to follow her as she led them into the round room.

She pointed to the panel she saw Tor come out of, but no amount of pushing or pulling caused it to move at all. Frustrated, Lucy began pushing on all the panels in the room. Mark started to help her, knocking on various panels to see if he could hear a hollow sound.

Dr. Wilson cleared his throat and said, "Lucy, I don't know where the cat came out or what else the house might be hiding, but there is one thing I do know. One day about forty years ago, I saw something I don't think I was meant to see. Your grandad told me that there was a "priest hole" in the house with a staircase that led upstairs and downstairs into the basement. Do you have the keys? It comes out in the Occidentalis room, but you have to move some things around in there to get to it."

"You know about the keys?" Lucy asked. "I guessed they might go to the doors downstairs, but I haven't had a chance to try them. Do you know where in the house the staircase comes out?"

"I know one place for sure—it opens up in the bookstore in one of those built-in niches in the wall. But I suspect it also opens up into a smaller bedroom upstairs too. I don't know. But it comes out in the room below and opens into what lies beneath." Dr. Wilson hesitated and then went on. "I've never seen it myself. That's one tunnel none of us has ever been invited into. I am curious about it though—always have been."

Something sparked in Lucy's memory. "You said 'what lies beneath.' I've heard Hattie say that too. Fuchsia wrote something like that in her first note to me. It said, 'The truth lies beneath.' It came with that book she left me, the one with the poem underlined in it. What does that mean, what lies beneath?"

Hattie lifted her shoulders in a gentle shrug. "It's just what your grandparents always said when they talked about it, which wasn't often. I'd love to know myself."

"Lucy, what did the poem say?" asked Dr. Wilson.

"We dance round in a ring and suppose, but the secret sits in the middle and knows," Lucy answered.

"Ah! That makes sense," he replied.

"Does it?" Lucy looked skeptical. "It doesn't make any sense to me at all."

"It will be easier to show you. Grab your keys, Mark. Do you have a flashlight?"

"I'll stay here and wait for the pizza guy," Sam offered.

"I can do that," Hattie said. "Don't you want to see what the fuss is about?"

Sam said, "Maybe later. As Lucy's lawyer—and yours—it's better if I stay here until we know what we're dealing with. This feels like something you might need to decide on exactly who you want to know about it."

Hattie nodded, "I think he's right. Sam and I will both stay here and wait for the pizza."

"Mark, I want you to come. I'm not sure what we'll find. I know you have a duty as a member of the service, but I don't think I want to keep any secrets from you, ever." Lucy was earnest. She couldn't imagine a situation where she'd want to hide anything from him ever again.

"I'm coming. We'll figure it out together," he said.

Sam and Hattie went to sit outside and wait for the pizza. Lucy felt better about that. Otherwise, the delivery boy might come into the bookstore and overhear or see something he shouldn't.

Dr. Wilson led Lucy and Mark over to one of the niches set into the wall. It was housed in a very short connecting space between the bookstore and the dining room and faced an identical space directly across from it. Both niches had shelves built into them, which were currently full of books and a few odd knickknacks for sale.

It was a lovely space with carved woodwork decorating the alcove and shelves. The top of the built-in shelves came together in a sharp archway, with decorative wooden trim all the way around. After feeling around for a minute, Doctor Wilson pushed two places on the left side of the trim at once and pushed against the shelves with his shoulder.

Lucy didn't know what to expect, but the entire alcove swung inward, revealing a dark space behind it. With the light from both of their phones shining into the darkness behind the alcove, all Lucy could see was part of a spiral staircase in front of her.

"This secret staircase is hidden in the middle of the house, Lucy. I think it's the reason Fuchsia underlined those verses," Dr. Wilson said. "She must have known about it."

Lucy thought it was possible. "I recall seeing her fiddling around over here the first day she came into the shop. I thought she was just browsing, but she did spend a lot of time over here looking at things. I bet she was trying to figure out how to open it!"

It was a tight fit, so Mark had the others wait while he took the stairs going up to check it out. When he returned, he told them that he'd found a peephole that looked into the room where Hattie had stayed, and he could make out the outline of a door but couldn't figure out how to open it. Lucy shuddered to think that someone could have been spying on her when she slept in her grandparents' room.

Mark insisted on leading the way down the stairs, too, with Lucy squeezing in after him and Dr. Wilson bringing up the rear. When no one was holding the alcove door open, it swung firmly shut, leaving them with only the light from the two phones. Lucy felt a touch of claustrophobia at being closed in the dark passage and sandwiched between the two men. She had to push the thought that they might not be able to get out again firmly away from her mind.

The trio wound their way down to the basement level of the house where the stairs opened onto a landing. But another stairwell was situated on the other side that led further downward. Mark walked over to examine the wall and called Lucy and the doctor to come to see. There was another peephole, but Lucy couldn't see anything through it.

"It's probably the basement. Makes sense that it would be dark. Want to keep going?" Mark asked.

Lucy did want to keep going, but she also wanted to make sure she could leave in a hurry if she had to.

"Let's see if we can find a door first," she said.

Mark pointed at a faint line in the wall. "I think it's this, but I couldn't figure out how to open the one like it upstairs," he said.

Lucy thought about it. Where would she hide something that would open the doors to where she wanted to go? She imagined that she would put it somewhere out of sight but easily accessible if you knew what to look for. She shone her light over the staircase. It would have to be somewhere that you wouldn't accidentally trigger it, she thought.

She ran her hand along the handrail. Everyone would use that, she determined. But what about the support bars attached to the railing? She bent over, peering at each one closely with her flashlight. They were all wrought iron, attached to the staircase top and bottom, except for the last one. That one attached to the floor, or so it seemed.

Lucy couldn't see a button or any kind of mechanism on it, but when she wrapped her hand around it, she could feel it give a bit. She tried pulling it, but nothing changed. Then she tried rotating it in a circle and heard a quiet click.

She looked up to see the entire wall moving silently, swinging inward from the center as if on an axis in the middle. Mark held up his light in the room. Lucy stuck her head out to see where they were, shining her light lower than Mark's.

Her breath caught in her throat. This wasn't the basement. This was the root cellar hidden beneath.

"Mark, this is how the man escaped when we thought we had him trapped down here! I knew something was not right in here, but the wall never opened for me no matter what I did," Lucy said.

"That's because you didn't have the key." A weak voice came from behind some nineteenth century milk cans across the room.

Lucy suppressed a scream and buried her face in Mark's side. Mark wrapped a protective arm around her.

Dr. Wilson shouted, "Ulyss!" He pushed past Mark to rush across the room. Lucy stiffened when she heard the name. It couldn't be, could it? She felt as if the ground beneath her feet was falling away, and Mark was the only thing holding her upright.

"Larry Wilson, is that you? Get over here and untie me, you old goat," the voice said.

Dr. Wilson let out a whoop and yelled for Mark to come help. Mark looked down at Lucy, who could only get a whisper past the lump in her throat.

"Grandpa."

Chapter Thirty-One

$\mathcal{M}$ark half-carried Lucy over to a crate and sat her down. He used his phone's light to check the room for any other surprises that might be waiting to pop up. Seeing the room was otherwise empty, Mark sprinted up the stairs and hit the light switch. He took them two at a time on the way down to help Dr. Wilson untie the man and stand him up.

The single bulb seemed excessively bright to Lucy's eyes, so she shielded them with her hand. Her mind raced, and her heart kept pace. If this was her grandfather, where had he been all this time? She concentrated on slowing her breathing so she didn't pass out—or worse. If only her legs would hold her up!

Mark and Dr. Wilson steadied the older man and helped him over to sit on a crate next to Lucy.

There was no doubt about it. Lucy slid off the crate onto her knees in front of her grandfather and wrapped her arms around his neck, sobbing.

Sam settled Lucy's grandfather on the sofa in the round room. The elderly man had insisted that Mark go up and close every window and pull every shade before he'd allow the men to help him upstairs. Mark had raced off to find Hattie and Sam to help him. He hadn't told them what was happening but had warned Hattie to brace herself. Sam had gone down with him, and the two young men brought Lucy's grandfather upstairs. Doctor Wilson followed with Lucy, who held his arm for support.

Hattie was gathering blankets and water and putting the kettle on while Mark had scrambled out to the doctor's car to get his bag. After the initial shock and tears, Lucy settled on the arm of the sofa, holding her grandfather's hand. She alternately beamed at him and frowned with worry. Deep down, she was afraid that if she let go, she'd wake up and find it was all a dream.

Doctor Wilson was moving faster than Lucy had any idea he could. He started at her grandfather's feet and worked his way up, checking for injuries. He delicately probed a large bruise on the side of his face and winced as he saw the goose egg raised on the scalp above his ear. He gently removed Lucy's hand from her grandfather's and asked him to squeeze his fingers. Then he shone a light from his bag into each eye and listened to his breathing and chest sounds. Satisfied that his patient wasn't in immediate danger, he helped him sit up on the sofa and gave him a few sips of water.

"Not too much. You can have some more in a minute. Let's just take it slow," Dr. Wilson said. He pinched the skin on the back of Ulysses' hand and asked Lucy if she had any sports drinks in the house.

"Yes, I have a couple. They're in the pantry." She started to rise, but Hattie pushed her down into a chair next to her grandfather.

"You stay here. I'll get them," Hattie said.

Lucy was grateful. She still felt numb. How was it possible that her grandfather was here? Alive? And what about her grandmother? Now that her mind was coming back online, she had so many questions.

Dr. Wilson sensed Lucy's agitation and turned to look at her. "Lucy, you're pretty pale. You look as if you've seen a ghost, and I guess you have. You're going to have to wait a few minutes to start asking questions. Your grandad's dehydrated, and I'm not sure he doesn't have a concussion."

Lucy slumped back in her chair. Of course, he was right. She looked her grandfather over carefully. He was thin—much thinner than she was used to seeing him, even if it had been a long time. He'd always been fairly robust and tall, with Irish good looks. He seemed so frail. Lucy couldn't imagine what kind of trauma he'd been through.

Doctor Wilson tucked a blanket around Lucy and took Mark aside for a quiet word. Mark looked at Lucy. She could read his alarm. But he relaxed when she gave him a reassuring smile. She knew Dr. Wilson was probably warning Mark to keep an eye on her. She'd been through an ordeal, it was true, but she didn't feel she was in any danger of going into shock.

Hattie returned with two bottles of electrolyte drinks and a couple of glasses filled with ice. "Here you go, Doc. I brought an extra in case you wanted one for Lucy," she said.

"You read my mind, Hattie, as usual."

"It isn't hard, Larry. There isn't much up there," Ulysses joked.

This unexpected quip caused Sam and Lucy to crack up. Hattie was trying hard to keep a straight face.

"Now I know you're gonna be fine, you old mule," Dr. Wilson responded. "Here, have another sip."

Lucy's grandfather took another sip and said, "Quit fussing over me, you old nanny goat!"

The two old friends were smiling at each other, and Hattie was smiling at them both.

Tears slipped down Lucy's face, first just one or two, but then the floods came, and several pairs of arms tried to wrap her up in a hug all at once.

Dr. Wilson insisted on giving both Lucy and her grandfather something to help them sleep. Lucy consented, but only because he and Mark agreed to stand watch over her grandfather. Hattie made up a bed on the sofa and pulled out extra blankets for Mark and Dr. Wilson. Hattie promised to stay with Lucy until she fell asleep, and then she'd sleep in the room next door that she'd used before.

Lucy resisted going to bed until she asked one question. Doctor Wilson finally relented but added that it would be best to keep it short.

"I know what you're going to ask, Lucy-bug," her grandfather said. "And the answer is I don't know. They separated us right away, and I haven't seen or heard anything about her since. But I live in hope, Lucy. While I breathe, I hope."

Lucy nodded, tears pricking her eyes again. "I love you, Grandpa. Please be here in the morning."

Lucy let Hattie take her upstairs and get her settled. She asked Hattie to leave her alone with her thoughts. Already drowsy from the sedative Dr. Wilson gave her, she curled up on her side, hugging her pillows. She felt herself drifting but wasn't quite asleep. For a moment it seemed as if she were floating in the ocean, being rocked by the waves. She panicked with the fear of drowning and sent up an SOS prayer for help. A wave of peace washed over her, and it seemed someone was holding her in the water, cradling her like a child. In her dream state, the last thing she saw before the darkness of sleep overtook her was a rose floating by as it washed ashore.

Lucy woke up feeling clear-headed and well-rested the next morning. She was in a hurry to see if her grandfather was awake and if he needed anything. So she took a quick shower and combed her hair into a ponytail. She put on a pair of comfortable yoga pants and a baby pink summer sweater, feeling that comfort was more important than style at the moment.

Dr. Wilson was helping Hattie set the table when she came down the back stairs into the kitchen. Lucy smelled bacon and saw sausage gravy next to a platter of fresh biscuits. There was also a steaming bowl of scrambled eggs and a pile of pancakes on a tray.

Hattie bustled into the kitchen, ready to make a fuss over Lucy, but Lucy held up a hand and declared she was ready to help.

"What can I carry? I'm starving," Lucy said.

"Start with the eggs and bacon, and then just keep it coming," Hattie said.

Lucy grabbed a large serving spoon, stuck it in the eggs, and put a fork on the bacon plate before carrying them both into the dining room. Lucy's eyes popped. There was already a coffee and tea station set up on the sideboard next to a pile of muffins and sweet rolls.

Lucy made a couple more trips to the kitchen and then asked Hattie if her grandfather was awake. She peeked through the dining room into the round room beyond and saw the couch back to normal. All the blankets and pillows were put away, but there was no sign of her grandfather. Lucy's stomach lurched. She turned around to question Hattie again.

"Relax, Lucy. He's okay," Dr. Wilson said. "He's upstairs. Mark and I helped him up there to get a bath. Mark's staying in the bedroom in case he needs anything, but he shooed me out. He's going to be just fine. I promise. He just needs a little time to recover." Dr. Wilson winked at Lucy and asked, "And you, my young patient, how did you sleep?"

"Like a baby," Lucy replied. "But I never got to eat dinner last night, and I'm starving!"

Lucy heard Mark call from upstairs, asking Dr. Wilson to come up. Lucy started to go along, but he stopped her and told her that it would be best to stay and help Hattie. Lucy stayed put, but she wasn't happy about it.

"He's *my* grandfather," she muttered to Hattie.

"That he is, but we've known him much longer," Hattie said, "and one thing you don't know is that your grandfather hasn't been treated gently. He has some scarring and bruises he doesn't want you to know about. I'm telling you because I think you do deserve to know, but let him keep his pride, Lucy."

Lucy's heart broke over the thought of his mistreatment, so she nodded her head and tried to keep the tears at bay. No more crying. What she wanted now were answers. And her grandmother. She missed her family. It dawned on her that she needed to call her parents! Her dad would be stunned, but he'd be over the moon that his father was alive and home safe.

She grabbed a sweet roll and kissed Hattie. She knew it might take a while to get them on the satellite phone, so she wanted to try right away. Lucy hurried over to the desk to find the number. Then she heard her grandfather's voice from the stairs.

"Lucilla Phoebe Patterson, what are you doing playing on your grandmother's desk?"

Lucy knew from his teasing tone that he wasn't serious. She rushed over to him and hugged him gently, then gave him her arm for the last few stairs. Lucy couldn't stop grinning at him. He looked dapper in a short-sleeved button-down shirt and a pair of khaki pants that were too big now, held up by a tightly cinched belt. She was glad she hadn't donated his old things and made a mental note to order him some new clothes that would fit him now.

"I was just about to call Dad," Lucy told him. "He's going to be beside himself!"

"Hold up, there, Lucy. You can't do that. You can't tell anyone I'm here. We have to keep it a secret for now."

Lucy was confused. It seemed like the best news ever, and she wanted to shout it from the rooftops that her grandfather was alive.

Mark came around and put a hand under Lucy's elbow. "I know it seems strange, Lucy, but your grandad and I have had a long talk, and I think he's right. Let's all go sit down and eat, and we can talk about it."

"Okay," she said, going along to the table where Mark steered her. She was a little annoyed, though, and pulled her arm free from his hand before she sat down. "Where's Sam?"

Her grandfather answered, "He's running some errands for me. Foundation business."

Dr. Wilson passed Lucy the bowl of eggs, and she took an absent-minded scoop. She started to pass the bowl to her grandfather but thought better of it and scooped out some eggs for him. He smiled his thanks, and Mark stretched across the table to take it from her.

They all ate in silence for a few minutes. Lucy felt as if she were going to implode before her grandfather finally pushed his plate away. He'd only eaten about a third of what Lucy had given him, but she didn't push him to eat more. He probably needed to eat slowly and work his way up to something normal. She knew she needed to wait for him and go at his pace. She was just so happy to have him back that she could barely believe it. It felt like a miracle.

Chapter Thirty-Two

*U*lysses Patterson reached over and picked up his grand-daughter's hand.

"Lucy-bug, I know you have a lot of questions. Doc's been filling me in a little bit here and there, and Mark has been too. I'm so proud of you, I can't even begin to tell you. You've done so well here, and you've managed everything like a pro. I'm sorry you got dragged into all this."

Lucy started to speak, but just then Tor burst into the room, jumped on the table, and stalked over to her grandfather. He let out one long, loud meow and started rubbing himself all over the man, demanding attention as only a cat can do.

Ulysses picked the cat up and scratched his ears and under his chin, which started the cat's motor purring.

"That cat slept next to you all night, Ulyss. I thought he had better taste than that!" Dr. Wilson couldn't seem to help poking a little fun at his friend.

"He has perfect taste, Larry. That's why he slept with me and not you!" Her grandfather laughed at his own joke.

Lucy smiled to see that her grandfather cracked himself up in much the same way she always cracked herself up, but right now she was determined not to get sidetracked.

"Dragged into all *what*, exactly? I know about the foundation and the charity work and bits and pieces, but I need an explanation. Are there going to be more people crawling out of the woodwork, breaking into the house, looking for old books, and who knows what all else?" Lucy felt her eyebrows drawing together and knew she looked cross, so she smoothed her face back into a smile and lowered her voice a little bit. She didn't want to put added stress on her grandfather.

Dr. Wilson stood up, thanked Hattie for breakfast, and told her to call right away if anyone needed him. He also handed her a list of instructions and told her he'd be by in the evening.

Lucy thanked Dr. Wilson. She knew he needed to get to his office.

Then Mark stood up as well. "Lucy, I'm gonna run down to the police station. Andy needs to see me, and I have to fill out some paperwork for the task force. I also need to call and extend my leave. Otherwise, I'd have to be back on the ship tonight. I'll call you."

"Mark, don't you want to know what was going on?" Lucy asked.

"I've heard enough for now. Your grandfather hit some of the highlights when we were upstairs. But I feel like the rest of it belongs to you and your family, and if I need to know, you'll tell me later." He bent down to kiss her but then caught her grandfather's eye. "May I?"

Her grandfather laughed and said, "Go right ahead. I'm sure it isn't the first time!"

Lucy blushed furiously and then offered Mark her cheek, which he duly kissed and took his leave. She could hear him whistling on his way out the door.

Hattie then pushed back from the table. "Lucy, I already know as much as I want to know for now, before you ask. I'm going to start the dishes and put away the food. And then after that, I need to run over to the cafe. Hector is threatening to go on strike. I think he just misses me though."

"Hattie, you've been more than generous with your time, more than any friend should ever ask. Please do what you need to do. We'll be fine."

"I know you will, but I'll be back. I need to spread the right rumors around town that the bookstore is simply closed for a couple of days because you were roughed up by the intruders and need to rest. I want people to know that you were an innocent victim in all of this. Andy says he's going to leave the crime scene tape up for another day or two, just to make sure no one bothers you." Hattie stood up and started gathering plates. "Why don't you two go sit in the other room. It'll be a lot quieter there."

"Thanks, Hattie. I love you," Lucy said.

"Ditto, old friend," her grandfather echoed.

"Aww, don't you two make me start crying! I love you both. Now get!" Hattie playfully waved a napkin at them.

Lucy stood and helped her grandfather up. He put his hand on her shoulder and leaned on her just a little for support and sank gratefully into one of his wingback chairs in the bookstore.

Lucy sat in the chair next to his and looked at him expectantly. She would tolerate no further interruptions!

"Lucy, there are things you need to know—" began her grandfather.

"Oh dear, not you too," she said with a giggle. "Everyone says that to me. Just start at the beginning."

"How well do you remember your state history, Lucy? This house, or rather, this place, has a history that goes back to the earliest days of European exploration. This house was built with gold rush money, but it was built to replace a house that was already here. It was a *rancho* house that had been part of an even earlier small Spanish mission. Even before that, it was an important place for Native Americans. So, it changed hands many times, but our family has been living here since just after the time of the Spanish missions."

Lucy whistled. That was a lot of history, well over three hundred years. She nodded to show she understood.

"Long before the Spanish missions were started in 1769, the Manilla galleons sailed up and down the coast of California carrying treasure from Mexico to the Philippines to send back to the Spanish Crown. They took advantage of the trade winds by sailing across the Pacific from near Japan to the Russian river in Mendocino County. The first one was way back in 1565. The ships sometimes needed a place to take shelter, a harbor where they could wait out storms and repair damage to the ships. We think some of them found our harbor to be perfect for that.

"The natives were known for being welcoming, and there was plenty of fresh water and game to find here," he continued. "But it is a small harbor, and it doesn't show up on maps until much later, so it wasn't heavily used. However, we do have reason to believe both Spanish galleons and the pirates who dogged them took shelter here."

Lucy frowned. "When I said to start at the beginning, I didn't mean you should go back to Adam and Eve!"

Ulysses chuckled. "Now, the rest of this is what we've been able to figure out. At some point, a ship was too heavily damaged to complete her journey. She was heavy with a treasure that the Spanish looted from the indigenous peoples in South America and Mexico. They left the ship here with a small crew to work on repairs or wait for help to come. Only it never came.

"Most of the crew died, and fearing the treasure would be stolen, those remaining hid all they could. They buried some of it in various places, and they moved it through the lava tunnels into a cave system that terminates under this house. Before they could move all of it, however, another storm swept in and pulled the derelict ship with some remaining amount of treasure out to sea, where it sank somewhere just offshore north of here. Pieces of silver were found in one of the tunnels that flood when the king tides come in.

"Occasionally, every decade or so, a few silver ingots or coins or even jewels will wash into the tunnel, so we know it's still down there. It's too dangerous to try to retrieve—a suicide mission. The currents and tides make it almost impossible." He looked troubled and added for emphasis, "It isn't worth it, not worth losing a single life trying to get it."

"So, these sailors, they buried it, and it was forgotten?" Lucy asked.

"Well, no, not exactly. Much of this is oral history handed down, so you have to take it with a grain of salt. It seems that some of the crew integrated into the local tribes, marrying and having children. The land was already a sacred spot for the tribes, who believed great beasts with burning breath had carved out the tunnels. So the sailors used that to keep the curious away, spreading the rumor that something like a dragon lived below. The surviving two built a shelter and lived here with their families, passing down the knowledge of a hidden treasure but great danger. The tribe absorbed those families in a few generations, though, and nothing but the story was handed down.

"So that's where the little bag of treasure hidden in the desk came from? From a sunken ship carrying treasure to Spain?" Lucy wondered if the story was more myth than truth.

"That's my belief," he said. "When the Spanish built the Presidio in 1769, one of the native laborers told the story of the dragon cave to a priest, who journeyed on horseback with the man from Monterey. He claimed the ground for the Catholic Church and the Spanish Crown. He built a small mission here and claimed the boundaries of it to include the harbor and inland for many miles. He used the awe and fear the native tribes held for the place to coerce them into being unpaid labor. It was a widespread practice in the day, but I find it repugnant."

Lucy couldn't agree more. She hated to see anyone exploited. "Didn't the Mexican government overthrow the Spanish and take over this whole part of California though?" she asked. "Did it become a rancho then?"

"It did," he replied, "but let me back it up a little bit. You see, this Spanish priest wasn't an ordinary priest. He was born into a cadet branch of Spanish royalty and was a member of the Order of Montesa. His family was part of the Kingdom of Aragon—remember I used to tell you stories about Aragon when you were little?" he asked.

Lucy's eyes lit up. "Oh, I do remember! I remember the stories about a good king who protected the brave knights—the Knights Templar—is that right? And how the church went against them and accused them of terrible things. Oh, but the knights from Aragon were found innocent, and their king protected them, and he changed their name to protect them even more. So, this priest who built the mission here—he was one of those?" Lucy rubbed her forehead. She wanted answers, but she was getting a history lesson. "I thought those were just stories you made up to entertain me."

"Well, yes, he was a descendant of one of those. When the Spanish started exploring the West and expanding their territories, they also wanted to convert the native tribes they'd encountered to the Catholic faith. Since he was both a priest and an heir to the Order of Montesa, he had private wealth and political power. He carried with him certain items from the treasuries of the Kingdom of Aragon left in the care of his order for hundreds of years. Long enough, that they were likely completely forgotten as the various monarchies consolidated and changed hands."

Lucy gave her grandfather a skeptical look. "How do you know all this? It sounds like more than oral history to me." Lucy shook her head. "And what does this have to do with what happened to you?"

"Patience, Lucy. I'm getting there. He left a record. He expanded on the tunnels, using natives to do the work. He built a vault that would last and then sent the natives who worked for him away to as laborers for the soldiers in San Diego. He planned to start a chapter of his order in the new world, but he died here. Other priests came but found the natives unwilling to come near the place, so they gave up, never knowing what lies beneath."

"So, then it became a rancho?" Lucy asked. This part of California history she knew well. Every fourth grader had to study it.

"Yes. After the Mexican government expelled the Spanish, they gave the land to one of their decorated soldiers. He turned the modest mission house into a large home for his wife and their daughter."

"I still don't understand what all this history has to do with now, as fascinating as it is." Lucy could feel her impatience growing.

"There is a lot more I want to tell you, Lucy, and it's important. But it will have to wait for another day. It's enough for you to know that the Pattersons came into the story after the Mexican soldier's daughter grew up. She married one of our ancestors who came here after the gold rush.

Chapter
Thirty-Three

*A*ll this family history, and I've never really heard any of it." She loved history and couldn't imagine why they'd kept this from her.

"Our ancestors came out early in the gold rush and hit it big. It was a father and son working together, but the whole region was lawless and dangerous. They barely escaped with their lives and their gold by giving away their equipment and pretending to give up in frustration." He stopped and took a sip of water. Lucy could see that it was costing him a lot of energy to tell this story.

"They ended up here where the son fell in love with the soldier's daughter." He continued, "It was just her and her mother running one of the largest ranchos in California at that time, but that's a story—and a dark one at that—for another day. I will just say that they knew what lies beneath and guarded it well. They raised a large family as the coast was gradually being settled. In the 1880s, they built the house that we're in now, and soon a whole town sprang up around them. This was one of the first Victorian houses built on the west coast, and I'm sure it's the only one that has its distinctive features." He beamed at Lucy, obviously proud of the house their ancestors had built.

Lucy had become so wrapped up in the story.

"Ever since, a Patterson has lived in this house and has only shared the knowledge of what lies beneath with those they truly trust. Each generation has built on the work of the last and invested in good things that help other people. But I'm afraid somehow the secret has gotten out."

Lucy felt the familiar dread rising in the pit of her stomach.

"But how? Is that what happened to you and Grandma?" Lucy was worried. She knew Interpol had the man in custody, but what if he were just the first of many?

"A few years ago, we found some things hidden in the vault that we'd never seen before—that there was never any kind of record for. They were incredibly old and historically significant. Your grandmother and I decided one of the pieces should be in a museum somewhere. It belonged to the people. That's the work we chose to do with some of the treasure." He gave Lucy an appraising look, as if hesitant to say more.

"We have contacts all over the world who engage in humanitarian work. From time to time, they help us move something along to people who can return it to its rightful home. We do it this way so it can't be traced back to us," he said. "The way we see it, the house is ours and the land is ours, and much of what lies beneath is ours via inheritance. But since it predates the United States—all of it was deposited when this land belonged to the Native Americans and there were only a handful of European settlements on the East Coast—we see ourselves more as the stewards of it. All our regular businesses and accounts are all on the level, no worry there. And all the inheritance taxes were paid for each generation, too, so don't fret. Uncle Sam has been well-compensated and given more than his fair share."

Lucy could only trust him about that. "But what happened? You said you found something important?"

"Yes, right. Well, we tried to return it, and somehow it came back on us. A museum in Spain was meant to retrieve it from an associate with a cover story of finding it while doing a renovation in an old chateau in the region. It was completely plausible, and it should have worked, but somewhere along the chain, someone slipped, and it was traced back to us." He shook his head sadly at the memory of what came next.

We got a call to meet our friends for a dinner cruise on a ship just up the coast, which we've done many times in the past. But the assailants were waiting for us. They led us onto a boat and separated us. I think they may have transferred your grandmother to another boat. But they kept me locked up, using her as leverage, demanding I tell them where the object had come from. I never gave up. If they were going to kill her, they'd already done it. If not, they were probably asking her the same questions." He paused to wipe the tears from his eyes.

"It's been so long, and I have no idea where she is, Lucy, or even if she's still alive. I don't know where they took me, but they kept me locked up for many months, trying to force me to give them the information they wanted. They brought me back here a few months ago and kept me locked up on a boat offshore. I guess then they finally figured out how to get into tunnels under the house. Before that, they'd only managed to find some of the dead-end tunnels." His hands shook, so he folded them under his arms.

"They locked me in one of the tunnels behind the house in the woods!" Lucy told him.

Her grandfather leaned over and kissed her forehead. "When I think about them coming after you, my blood just boils. I'm so thankful you're okay. And that you have Mark to look out for you. I really like him."

Lucy felt the heat creeping up her cheeks. "I really like him too!"

"A couple of nights ago they dumped me in the root cellar, and I think they planned to lock all of you up in there with me.

They killed Fuchsia and took her key. That's how they got in." A small sob escaped his lips, and Lucy thought maybe it would be better to let him rest for a while.

Hattie must have heard it, too, because she came in carrying a drink with a straw and handed it to Ulysses. "Doctor's orders. You need to finish this whole thing before I leave. So, drink it down, and then rest for a while." Hattie turned to Lucy and said, "I finished up the dishes, and the fridge is stocked for lunch. Sam will be back in a few minutes to help you. He's taking the whole afternoon off. I left you another bottle of that stuff and a note in the kitchen with instructions. You see that he drinks it down and don't let him give you any trouble!"

"You ol' mother hen! You're not the boss of me," he mock-growled at Hattie, causing Lucy to giggle.

"I'm not," Hattie said, pointing at Lucy," but she is. She's a tough cookie. I wouldn't go against her!"

Lucy's grandfather laughed and said, "I wouldn't dream of it." He sipped the drink. "That's actually not bad. I was prepared for the worst!"

Hattie left, going out the back and locking the kitchen door behind her.

Lucy was about to suggest her grandfather lie down for a nap when Tor came in mewling loudly again. He jumped on the desk and sent several things flying. Lucy went to pick them up and saw the letter with the roses painted on it. She carried it over to her grandfather and took the letter out of the envelope.

"Do you have any idea who this woman is?" Lucy asked and handed him the letter. "She does such beautiful work. Look at the little rose on the letter and it came in this." She held up the envelope.

Her grandfather nearly choked on the drink he was sipping and struggled for a couple of minutes to catch his breath. Lucy was concerned. She took the drink from him and asked if he wanted her to call Dr. Wilson.

He clutched her arm and gasped, "Where did this come from? When did you get it?"

"It came in the mail earlier this summer. There was no return address, or I would have written her back to tell her my grandmother had passed away. I guess it's a good thing I couldn't do that. The poor lady might not have taken it well!" Lucy said.

"I should say not—this letter isn't *to* your grandmother, it's from her! That little rose, that's her signature. Read me the letter, Lucy, hurry!"

"Okay, okay, calm down," Lucy said. "It says, 'My Dearest, How I long to visit with you once again. I thought of inviting you over for Easter dinner, but I was too tired to cook. My daughter Carolina and her husband Gilbert came to visit and brought their new baby, Kiri. I'm just batty over her! You should see her. She's a doll, just don't wake her! I do hope we can connect. I'm in a new relationship. I can't wait for you to meet him. He's super and keeps me financially afloat. Hopefully, I'll see you soon! All my love, Mariana Marshall.'"

Her grandfather looked shaken. She picked up the phone to call Dr. Wilson.

"Lucy, you clever girl! Let me see that letter. Quick, bring me an atlas! She left us a map!" Her grandfather groaned.

"What? Atlas? Why? Just tell me what you want me to look up." Lucy was confused. The letter hardly made sense, let alone looked like a map.

"Those are islands, Lucy. She's giving us coordinates! Here, let me see that. Search these—the Marshall Islands, Mariana Islands, Easter Island, Cook Islands, Gilbert Island, Carolina Island, oh and look at this . . . Kiri, batty. How smart! Add Kiribati to the list! Oh, and Wake Island, add that too. If I'm right, and I think I am, all those islands are in the same area of the world. That must be where she is!"

Lucy decided her laptop might be a better choice to look up all those names, so she went to get it off the charger and turned it on. She pulled up a mapping program and asked for the list again. They went through each of the names, and her grandfather was right. They were all islands and all in the same part of the world. Lucy's heart began to fill with hope.

"What about the rest of this letter? It says she's in a new relationship, and he's super and keeping her financially afloat. What do you think that means?" Lucy asked.

"I think it means we're going to go get your grandmother, Lucy. She's on a ship, a superyacht from the sound of it, and probably owned by a banker. They're traveling from one remote island to the next. Call Sam. Call everybody. We have to go!" Her grandfather stood up, swayed, and sat right back down in his chair.

"No, Grandpa. These people are dangerous. We need to have a plan. I'm going to call Mark. Don't worry, we'll get her. We're going to bring her home." Lucy closed her eyes, and when she did, she remembered the feeling of floating and being carried that she'd had the night before. She remembered the vision of the rose floating by her in the ocean and the deep sense of peace that had overtaken her. Her grandmother was the rose. She was sure of it now. They were going to find her, and they were going to bring her home.

*G*loria Patterson leaned as far as she dared over the polished chrome rail of the ship. The water below was a tantalizing shade of blue, but what held her fascination was the sunlight dancing across the wavelets in dazzling, graceful lines. The crystal-bright light looked like fancy handwriting across the surface of the water. Mesmerized, she tried to read the lines, but they were gone as quickly as they formed. The wind picked up a tuft of her creamy white hair and ruffled it into her eyes, breaking her reverie.

She'd lost track of how long she'd been on the ship. It had been long enough that the men holding her captive no longer thought of her as a threat. She'd played the helpless grandmother role to perfection. Most of them felt sorry for her, but they were under strict orders to have no contact with her. Three times a day, they brought her food and kept her supplied with anything she needed. The captain was a ruthless man—she'd seen it in his eyes when they first brought her aboard. But the man he worked for was far worse.

She'd only been bold enough to slip outside now because she knew neither of the men was on board. The owner of the vessel—the man who kidnapped her and her husband—had left on another ship a couple of months ago. And two days ago, she'd seen the captain and his engineer pull away on the ship's tender before the sun was fully up. Usually, only one of the two men would leave to pick up supplies or arrange for fuel. The other crew members were all hired hands, but the captain and engineer were the full-time staff attached to the ship. It was unusual for both to go, but it was also unusual for them to be gone more than a few hours.

Gloria—Glo as she was known by those who loved her—knew something was up. She hadn't felt this much tension on the ship since Naseem was fired. He'd come to pity her and had begun to sneak little tidbits from the crew's table to her. She'd rewarded him with smiles and pats on the arm and compliments about his mother who must have been a good woman to raise such a kind son. The ship's cook—who looked more like a weasel than a man—had informed on Naseem to the captain.

When Naseem snuck into her room that evening to say goodbye, Glo had been ready. She'd slipped an envelope into his pocket along with some money from a hidden compartment in her purse. They'd provided her with art supplies and paper, so she'd made the best of it and written a convoluted letter addressed to herself, hoping somehow to get word to her family that she was alive and roughly where in the world they held her captive. If Naseem made it off the boat alive, she hoped he'd find a way to mail the letter for her. He told her he was being put off the ship the next morning. She knew that if he tried to help her, his own family would suffer the consequences, so she just thanked him for his kindness and urged him to go before they caught him. She hadn't seen a friendly face since.

Sticking to the ship's wall that was under the overhanging deck above, Glo inched her way toward the front of the boat. They'd been at this same anchorage for three days—also unusual—so she hoped to overhear the crew talking and learn what was going on. She could hear raised voices above her, and as she got closer, she could make out what they were saying.

". . . not going to do that. I say we take the ship. Move it to another island. Anchor it someplace. I can get my cousin to pick us up. He's a commercial fisherman."

"But the note says to stay here and wait for orders."

"There aren't going to be any orders. The captain's quarters are cleaned out. The engineer took everything. They're not coming back. They left us out here with no tender, not a lot of fuel, and *her*. My guess is the captain has already reported the boat stolen and is dumping this whole mess in our laps!"

"That's why we gotta get rid of her now."

"I told you, I'm not going to do that. She's an old lady. What is she gonna do? Call your cousin and have him pick us up. Then he can radio it in later that he found a ghost ship and we'll be scot-free."

"She's seen our faces. She might have heard our names. We gotta get rid of her somehow."

Glo had heard enough. She knew the cook was in the galley, and the other two men were on the bridge deck, so she crept into the interior and made her way up a set of stairs used by the crew to carry things from the kitchen to the main salon. She picked up a knife sitting on the bar next to a bowl of limes and hid it in her sleeve before she tiptoed across the midship interior. She knew there was another set of stairs near the front of the boat that led to the captain's quarters and beyond that, to the bridge. She'd come down that way on her first night on the ship.

Just before the captain's closet was an unmarked door. It had been ajar the last time she passed it, giving her a glimpse of gunmetal gray stored behind the door. If she could jimmy that open and not get caught, she'd have at least a fighting chance.

It turned out that she didn't need to do anything. The door once again stood open. The room was bigger than she'd thought it would be, so she slipped inside and pulled the door almost closed behind her. The collection of weapons was impressive, filling two walls and several sets of shelves. There was some serious firepower on this boat! She grabbed a gun she was familiar with—a GLOCK 19 with a 15-round magazine. She tucked it in the back of her waistband and stuck an extra magazine in her front pocket. She spotted a marine knife and inserted it in her other pocket. She was turning to go when she heard a thump from above.

Glo hid behind the door. She watched through the crack. The larger of the two crew members dragged the smaller one down the stairs by his heels, letting his head thump against each carpeted stair without remorse.

She ran up to the bridge and locked herself inside. *Now what?* She heard a splash off the port side and craned her head around to see the inflatable dinghy launched in the water. It was tied to the ship by a rope, which the crewman pulled in until the dinghy was flush alongside. Glo gasped when she saw what came next. The man hoisted the smaller crewman up and over the side of the boat, tossing him neatly into the dinghy.

Just then, the cook ran out onto the deck, waving his arms wildly and obviously yelling, even though Glo couldn't hear the words from her position on the bridge. The larger crewman, annoyed, took a swing at the weasel-like chef and knocked him out in one blow. He followed up by tossing him over the side of the ship and into the dinghy as well.

Glo couldn't believe it. Two down, one to go. She looked for the ship's radio, hoping to get off a message before the big man returned. She found it, but the wires were clipped. She peered out again but didn't see the taller crewman.

She'd have to hurry if she didn't want him to catch her. He was a force to be reckoned with even though she was armed! She spotted a familiar green case under a shelf. *Oh, if only . . .*

She hauled the case up to the console and popped it open. Her wish was granted. The SAT phone she and her husband had been carrying with them when the abductors took them was right here in front of her and fully charged. She closed the case and started to look for a place to hide where she could make a call.

When she peered out the side window again, Glo couldn't believe her eyes. The larger man tossed down a case of water into the boat. Then he attached a rope ladder to the railing and went over after it. She realized he must be planning to send the dinghy off but had to turn on the small motor manually.

She didn't hesitate. Glo dropped the SAT phone and ran for the deck.

She got there just in time. The dinghy was puttering away with the two unconscious men in it, and the larger man was starting to climb the ladder from water level. He hadn't seen her yet, so she hurried to detach the ladder from the rail. As hard as she pulled, though, she couldn't unclamp it.

The man shouted up at her. He'd seen her and was climbing as fast as he could now. Glo took a deep breath and pulled out the GLOCK, pointing it down the ladder.

The man froze. With his eyes zeroed in on the gun, he didn't notice at first that she had pulled the knife from its case in her pocket and was using it to saw one side of the rope ladder.

The keen blade made short work of the first rope. The man below bellowed as the ladder went swinging and he lost his grip on one side.

She quickly sawed on the other rope, not wanting to give him time to regain any momentum. He looked as if he was going to climb up despite the loaded gun she held. The ladder began to shift even more, and she could see the fear in his eyes.

"You can't do this!" he shouted.

Glo just hacked at the rope even harder.

"You can't leave me out here to die!" he screamed.

The remaining rope snapped under his weight. Gloria watched as he fell back into the water. She felt the thrill of an adrenaline rush! She was safe, at least for the moment. She looked around and spotted a life preserver, which she threw like a flying disc overboard. She leaned over the rail and said, "If you swim fast, you might still be able to catch the dinghy!"

She ran up the stairs double time—the adrenaline propelling her body to move—and picked up the SAT phone. Then she decided that first she should power up the boat and move away from the man she'd just sent overboard with only a life preserver. She couldn't have him swimming back to the boat and finding another way on board. She started the engine, pulled the anchor, and eased forward. Only then did she dial the phone.

It took a few minutes for her call to go through, but when it did, she said, "Hello, Coast Guard? My name is Gloria Patterson. I was abducted off the coast of California about eighteen months ago. I'm on a ship—a luxury superyacht—in the Marshall Islands. I'm not sure exactly where I am but I'll read you the coordinates. The ship is The Queen of Aragon. Yes, I'm alone. I managed to escape and got the crew off the boat. They're in a dinghy somewhere nearby. Oh, and please hurry! I've been away from home a long time!"

Thank you

To my readers: Thank you for reading first of The Cozy Cat Mysteries, *The Secret Circle*! I hope you enjoyed reading it as much as I enjoyed writing it. Book two, *The Rose and Crown*, is already well underway. Look for it in early 2022.

Some of you may be wondering where the town of Seaview is located, especially those familiar with California history. Seaview is a fictional town inspired by places I love such as Mendocino and Santa Cruz and Carmel. The fictional town of Seaview would be located on the central coast, near Monterey County or slightly south of there. There is one real, living icon who must be mentioned. The inspiration for this series may have been slow-blinked into my mind by "The Great Catsby"—a noble and popular feline who lives in a wonderful bookstore in the town of Mendocino. You can find him online.

For notification on new releases and to see other works by Lisa-Anne, visit her website at **lisa-anne.net** or sign up for her newsletter at lisa-anne.netlify.app/newsletter for the inside scoop on upcoming events, sales, and the occasional secret recipe!

To my people: Thank you for all your help, support, encouragement, handholding, pre-reading, and chocolate-bringing. Special thanks to the entire Wooldridge and Birdwell families, to my amazing husband, Andrew, to my dear friend (and first audience, always) Jessica, to my coach and mentor Kathy Carlton Willis, to my crackerjack editor and cover designer Michelle Rayburn, and to my gifted cover artist Ivy Wooldridge, who somehow manages to paint my dreams. Thanks also go out to the wonderful and supportive online community of women who write books and encourage others to do the same. I am grateful for each of you.

For a free printable version of the
vanilla pudding cookies recipe, go to
lisa-anne.net

Vanilla Pudding Cookies
Servings: 18 | Cook Time: 9–11 minutes

Ingredients
1 cup sugar
¾ cup butter
2 large eggs
1 tsp vanilla extract
3.4-ounce package instant vanilla pudding
¾ tsp baking powder
1 tsp baking soda
1 ¾ cups all-purpose flour

Add ins:
(Choose 1 or any combination up to 1 ½ cups)
1 ½ cups white or chocolate chips
½ to ¾ cup of pastel rainbow sprinkles
1 cup chopped nuts
1 cup mini candy-coated chocolate candies

Directions
350-degree oven

Parchment paper-lined cookie sheet

Using a mixer, cream butter and sugar, then add eggs and vanilla. Mix until combined.

Add in box of pudding and mix until incorporated. Add dry ingredients until just combined. Stir in add-in ingredient if you wish. Chill dough for 20 minutes.

Using a cookie scoop, drop balls of dough onto prepared pan, leaving 2 inches of room.

Bake for 9 minutes. Cool for 5 minutes, then transfer to a cooling rack.

Made in the USA
Monee, IL
28 August 2021